PRIZEWINNER

To my fellow warrior Alex, my companion on this scleroderma journey.

Much love as always

Lynn.

Copyright © Lynn Steblecki

This book is sold subject to the condition that it shall not, by way of trade or otherwise, be lent, resold, hired out, or otherwise circulated without the publisher's prior consent in any form of binding or cover other than that in which it is published and without a similar condition including this condition being imposed on the subsequent publisher.

The moral right of Lynn Steblecki has been asserted.

ISBN: 9781521502259

Contents

FOREWORD 5
ACKNOWLEDGEMENTS 9
DEDICATION 10
ABOUT THE AUTHOR 11
Chapter One 3
Chapter Two 10
Chapter Three 16
Chapter Four 22
Chapter Five 29
Chapter Six 35
Chapter Seven 42
Chapter Eight 49
Chapter Nine 55
Chapter Ten 61
Chapter Eleven 72
Chapter Twelve 80
Chapter Thirteen 88
Chapter Fourteen 98
Chapter Fifteen 109
Chapter Sixteen 116
Chapter Seventeen 122

Chapter Eighteen 130

Chapter Twenty-One 152

Chapter Twenty-Two 160

Chapter Twenty-Three 166

Chapter Twenty–Four 172

GLOSSARY 175

FOREWORD

by Simon Callow, CBE Actor-Director-Writer.

The book you have in your hands needs no introduction from me: start reading it and you won't stop until the last page. It's a romantic, highly-charged story which sweeps you up into the drama of its hero and heroine; it's touching and funny and sexy and exotic – and paints a very alarming picture of South Africa today. All of that you will see for yourself. So why am I writing these words? Simple: because Lynn asked me to. If you ever meet Lynn, you'll discover pretty quickly that 'No' is not a word that means a lot to her.

In fact, I met her in a hospital, in the famous Charles Wolfson Centre for Reconstructive Surgery at the Royal Free Hospital in North London, of which I am a patron. Everyone said to me: "Oh, you must meet Lynn. What a character." When I finally did, I was baffled as to why she was there: a very attractive 30-something. What could have brought her here? And then I noticed that, yes, perhaps the skin on her face was a little tight, and then I noticed that her hands were a little rigid. Nothing very obvious. Little did I know what lay behind these mild symptoms.

It transpired that for the last fifteen years she had been suffering from one of the most alarming and unpleasant medical conditions in existence: scleroderma, an auto-immune, rheumatic, and chronic disease that affects the body by hardening connective tissue. The surface of the body becomes increasingly rigid – your fingers can't move (which is how Lynn first knew that something was wrong), your lips begin to seize up, opening your eyes becomes increasingly difficult. You are, in effect, trapped inside a body which is closing down, being buried alive with frightening speed and efficiency by your own system. No one really knows what causes it – it might be genetic, but it might not – and only recently has it been possible to arrest the symptoms. Not to cure them: to arrest them. It's a long, slow and exhausting process, both mentally and emotionally – a recipe for despair.

But scleroderma reckoned without Lynn 'Never-say-no' Steblecki. Once she was told what was going on – once she got a name for her condition – she set out to beat it. I realised from the moment we started speaking that this was one feisty dame, fiercely determined. But the miraculous thing was that she saw the funny side of it all. How?

Had even a tenth of what has happened to Lynn happened to me, I would have curled up into a ball and crept away into a corner to die. Not her. She took it on, without hesitation. And laughed at it, spooky old scleroderma. And because of that – because of her refusal to give in, and perhaps even more because of her determination to laugh in its face – she has made astonishing progress. It wasn't so long ago that, because of the hardening of the tissue in her mouth, she actually couldn't laugh. But she was having none of that. Her profound optimism, wherever it comes from, has kept her going. And she laughs like a drain.

She even managed to use her thumbs to type again, despite the inflexibility of her fingers. At that first meeting, she told me that she was planning to write a novel. I asked her to send it to me when she finished it, and now she has. I lazily assumed that it would be a story about what had happened to her. Not a bit of it. It's about the search for love, the strength to believe that one is entitled to love and to be loved. I think that, in the end, is Lynn's secret.

She believes in love, you see: its power and its healing potential. And nothing that has happened to her has dented that belief. It's very inspiring, and a little bit humbling.

by Simon Callow, CBE Actor-Director-Writer –
London, 2017

FOREWORD by Professor Dame Carol Black

It gives me great pleasure, as Lynn's previous Scleroderma specialist, to endorse the courageous path she has taken since the diagnosis of what was for her a devastating condition. Scleroderma changed Lynn's appearance and functional abilities, and made her adapt to a situation which considerably limited her activities although thankfully not immediately life-threatening. She has faced her condition and changed life with courage and resilience, and with determination to help other patients by being a spokesperson for them and their relatives. I salute her and her most recent venture, the novel *Prizewinner*.

Professor Dame Carol Black.

Lynn Steblecki author of "Prize Winner"

This book is written by a remarkable woman, one of the most remarkable women I have ever met.

    Meeting Lynn for the first time, over ten years ago because she had a condition called scleroderma, has had an impact on my life. As a young surgeon I was trying to develop a new solution to an insoluble problem.

    Lynn's condition was one where surgeons traditionally steered clear, as patients were usually on an enormous number of drugs which significantly increased chances that surgery would fail, and that historically not only healed badly but sometimes disastrously.

    Through her, I was given encouragement and support to perform more extensive surgery, both on her and others as well as develop new treatments.

    Lynn acted so willingly as my guinea pig that without her I wouldn't have ventured so far; because of her I was able to develop a new stem cell treatment that benefitted not only her, but so many others with extensive internal scarring caused by other illnesses.

    Through adversity that would quell a mere mortal, this amazing woman emerges. A true essential spirit visible from the very first time you meet her.

    Through all this she has written a wonderful novel based on her roots in South Africa, while also supporting research and innovation that will help many patients as an ambassador, educator and inspiration.

Professor Peter Butler May 2017

ACKNOWLEDGEMENTS

I couldn't have written this novel without the support I've had from my husband Karol and daughters Nikki and Roxana.

In particular I'd like to thank Brendan McCusker, journalist, tutor and friend. My writing colleagues in the Lymington autobiography and creative writing classes have also helped me enormously; especially Russell (for his forensic analysis and perceptive assistance.) Denyse, Suki and Lesley and all my many friends.

Of course none of this could have happened without the endless specialist care from the surgeons, doctors, nurses and staff at the Royal Free Hospital, London.

I can't thank the dear supportive friends who have been taken from us too soon by Scleroderma, but they will always be in my thoughts.

DEDICATION

For my husband Karol, and my daughters Nikki and Roxana for their love, encouragement and unfailing patience.

ABOUT THE AUTHOR

Lynn Steblecki is a first time author.
Born in England but brought up in Zimbabwe and South Africa. Disabled by Scleroderma for fifteen years she was determined to show her gratitude and fortitude to her wonderful family, friends, and medical staff at the Royal Free Hospital London; who all encouraged her to write *PrizeWinner*.

What's Lynn been doing since writing this book?
For latest news and where she'll be speaking next visit lynn-steblecki.co.uk. You can also subscribe to her regular updates.

Contact
lynn@lynn-steblecki.co.uk

 @LynnSteblecki

 lynn_steblecki

 Lynn Steblecki

#prizewinner

PRIZEWINNER
by Lynn Steblecki.

Chapter One

"Ladies, welcome to the one and only South African male dance troupe...*Saints and Sinners*!" a deep male voice announced. My jaw tensed as it twisted into a knot. The chair scraped back as I stood up, I grabbed my handbag off the table and marched out the auditorium.

"Chantelle! Where are you going? Come back!" Kirsty yelled after me.

"I shouldn't be here—"

"What are you talking about?"

I stopped, yanked my cellphone out my bag and shoved it in her face.

"Look! See this? Franco dumped me."

Her eyes darkened. "That text's been on your phone for three months. Get rid of it!"

"I can't."

The tears pricked at the back of my eyes. Her slender hand gripped my arm.

"Chantelle! Your cheating boyfriend left you three months ago. Get over it! You're coming back in with me."

I pulled back.

"You want to go back in? Then you go on your own."

"We came together and agreed to go home together."

"But I feel uncomfortable in there."

"Fine. Go home then, but you're on your own. Remember, it's not safe out there at this time of night," she huffed.

I could not go back in. I ignored her and continued marching down the road.

"Remember there're hijackers with guns out there," she yelled, but her voice became quieter as the distance between us widened.

After walking for a further five minutes, I could no longer see as the street lights came to an end. It felt eerie and quiet...too quiet.

"Shit! What am I doing out here alone?" I gasped. I spun round, marched to the next street lamp where I managed to balance myself against it, as I pulled off my shoes and sprinted back to join Kirsty.

"See you changed your mind," Kirsty smiled then pulled out a chair for me. Feeling breathless, I sat down and crouched forward to slip my tight shoes back on.

"You missed some brilliant dancing. Here, I bought you a raffle ticket. We can go home after the *Saints and Sinners* come back onto the stage for the draw."

She waved a slip of paper at me. I deliberately avoided looking at it but continued looking down while fiddling with my shoes. The haunting opera tune *O Fortuna* from Carmina Burano mixed with an exuberant African beat, blasted through the auditorium, immediately silencing the chatter and laughter from the audience of excited ladies. The stage curtain opened slowly revealing four handsome, athletic twenty-something-year-old men.

For the next thirty minutes, the audience sat in awe, hypnotized by these young men, teasing them with their provocative dance moves. One by one they ripped off their T-shirts flirtatiously. In their tight-fitting jeans and cowboy hats, they moved in sync with each other, to the upbeat sexual music.

"Oh no!" the audience sighed when the music stopped.

The short, stocky compere came back on stage introducing them one by one.

"Chris!" (tanned and blond), "Stephan!" (tall and toned), "Marcus!" (mysterious and moody) and "Max!" (black and powerful).

"Ladies, I hope you remember their names as I have a surprise for you. Take out your raffle tickets and one lucky lady will have the pleasure of choosing one of the *Saints or Sinners* for a champagne breakfast date," he announced smiling lasciviously at the expectant audience. There was a short silence. The compere continued.

"Ticket number...142...Kindly come up and choose your date!"

The only audible sound was that of rustling paper as the excited audience scrambled to retrieve their tickets.

"Come on ladies —"

I shuffled in my chair and muttered, "That's so embarrassing ...I'd die if that was me."

Kirsty elbowed me, "Don't be such a prude. These guys are hunks."

Heads turned to look around for the winner after no one claimed to have number 142. The compere stiffened and said authoritatively, "The ticket holder must be here. For a second time, would the holder of ticket number 142 please come onto the stage?"

Kirsty glanced over at me. "Where's your ticket?"

"I don't know where you put it. It must be in your pocket."

She fumbled in her pocket. Kirsty pulled out the ticket and squinted at the number and shrieked, "Chantelle, it's your ticket! Number 142!"

I gulped down my glass of red wine.

"I can't do this. You go up, Kirsty," I hissed.

She stood up, grabbed by hand and pulled me along with her. We weaved our way through throngs of coiffed ladies, catching whiffs of their perfume, until we finally reached the stage to the sound of thunderous handclapping. I awkwardly stood on the stage glancing at these handsome men.

The heat from my flushed face intensified as I felt all eyes fixed on me. The compere seemed to size me up and down before he asked, "What's your name darling?"

I cleared my throat before replying, "Chantelle."

"So who are you going to choose?"

Who could I be myself with? Which one could I trust? None of these guys would want to be seen with me. The most average looking guy was the tall, toned and athletic dancer. The others were just too preened, perfect and polished. I had to decide on my own.

My hand shook slightly as I was handed the microphone. My mouth suddenly went dry. I needed another swig of wine. Once again I cleared my throat.

"Stephan?" I mumbled shrugging my shoulders.

The compere frowned and asked, "You have to speak up. Did I hear you say, Stephan?"

Suddenly this felt too much for me to handle. All I could do was nod in response to his question. When Stephan smiled back at me, I started to flounder. Was this really happening? Was he secretly wishing I was someone prettier and younger? Was he hoping it would soon be all done and dusted?

Stephan came forward and held out his hand. His hand was masculine with long artistic fingers; his nails were clipped short and his skin tanned to gold. I took his hand and felt the strength of it. His hazel eyes seemed to penetrate mine. I felt awkward, nervous and speechless. Everything was a whirl. It felt like a dream.

"Chantelle, nice to meet you," his friendly voice greeted me.

The background dance music grew louder making it difficult for us to hear each other. This prompted Stephan to move a step closer to me.

"Let's go outside," he gestured to the backstage door. I hesitated. But he led the way leaving the thumping beat behind.

The fresh cool breeze was welcoming. I was aware it was a full moon, as I could quite clearly see Stephan's exquisitely chiselled cheekbones. Wearing only his fitted jeans, he leaned against the wall. His athletic body glistened in the moonlight. A fuzzy warm feeling flooded over me. I felt awkward in his presence. There wasn't a cloud in the African sky only a myriad of twinkling stars. Stephan took a deep breath inhaling the perfume from the frangipani blossoms.

"Chantelle! Did you enjoy the show?" he asked in his Cape Town accent.

"I wasn't here to see all of it," I shrugged as I could not tell him that I did not want to come to the show.

His voice deepened, "How come?"

"I was late as a close pal of mine, Kirsty, surprised me with a ticket at the last minute!"

"So what do you do Chantelle?"

"I'm a photographer."

"A photographer! Interesting. What do you photograph?"

"Well, I'm freelancing with a fashion company at the moment, but I much prefer wildlife."

"Wildlife!" His eyes lit up. "Anything, in particular, birds, animals, reptiles?"

"I've longed to photograph a white lion. I know they're rare, so I don't expect it to happen. It's just a dream."

Stephan mischievously smiled.

"Dreams can sometimes come true."

"So do you have a day job?"

I swallowed hard, feeling my mouth drying up.

"Now, that would be telling," his lips curved.

"Your face looks familiar—"

Stephan changed the subject. "So which fashion house do you photograph for?"

"*Afrika Fashion*...I'm based at the head office in Rosebank."

"Don't they advertise in *SA Vogue*?"

His taut arm accidentally brushed against my shoulders. I nodded.

"You still haven't told me your day job—" I brushed invisible lint from my dress.

"What's a good time to meet up for breakfast tomorrow?" his voice lowered as he deliberately ignored my question.

Why doesn't he want to tell me what his day job is? What is he hiding behind that mysterious smile? Was he put off because I ignored his question?

I hesitated before replying, "I'm not sure I can make tomorrow."

"Oh! Let's swap numbers and you can let me know later," he said pulling his slim black cellphone from his fitted jeans pocket.

"What's your number?"

Even in my uncertain state, I could not help noticing his dark eyelashes and his olive-shaped eyes when he smiled at me. Feeling vulnerable, I crossed my arms.

"First give me your number!"

"74 9129440," he said slowly as I punched his number into my phone.

When he leaned in closer, I was engulfed by the scent of his sporty aftershave as he bent down to whisper, "Chantelle, thanks for choosing me."

My body tingled.

Just then the backstage door flew open. Kirsty called, "Chantelle I'm waiting for you."

I spun round and called out to her. "Come and meet Stephan."

Kirsten wasted no time making her way down the steps towards us.

"Hi," Stephan put out his hand to greet her.

"*Howzit*? I'm Kirsty...*Phwoar*! I can see why Chantelle chose you," she flicked her straight dark hair.

"Pleased to meet you," he smiled.

The backstage opened again. This time it was the compere.

"Stephan, you still down there?" he shouted.

"*Ja*."

A pulse beat in Stephan's neck as he faced the compere.

"You've missed three numbers!" he reprimanded.

"Coming," he sighed as his eyes became shadowed by his brow.

Stephan followed behind me, with his warm hand placed on the small of my back, as he guided me up the steps and back into the auditorium.

I sat in the darkness, watching this stranger dancing and wondered what had I let myself in for. Should I even go on this date? At the end of the show, Stephan casually made his way over to Kirsty and me.

"We're going to make our way home now," I said.

"Let me walk you out."

He led the way creating gasps of admiration from colourful patrons, who were still chatting and laughing loudly in the foyer. Stephan stopped at the entrance door then turned round to face me.

"Remember to text me your cell number. Hoping to see you tomorrow Chantelle." Then he bent down to peck me on my cheek.

I shrugged, "Maybe!"

Kirsty elbowed, nodded and frowned at me mouthing, "Go!"

I glared back at her. She faced Stephan, "Chantelle's shy... I'll give you her number."

I moved behind Stephan and shaking my head at Kirsty, I mouthed, "No!"

Stephan had his cell phone ready, "Thanks, Kirsty —"

"0 7 8 7 5 6 1 2 5 1," she slowly called out my phone number."

"Drive safely. Watch out for carjackers," he called after us in a serious tone.

Once we were out of the building, Kirsty hugged me.

"I can't believe you've won the prize."

"I don't really want to go. You go on my behalf. I'm still hurting after Franco walked out on me."

"Don't be a wet fish. Learn to have some fun." Kirsty suggested not listening.

"Did you check the look on those women's faces when Stephan walked out with us?" Kirsty gloated.

"*Ja,* I did! I bet they're gossiping about us right now."

On reaching Kirsty's white *Mazda*, we clambered in, locked the doors and sped off. She turned on the radio. Adele's sobering lyrics *Someone Like You* was playing, which reminded me of Franco.

"What the hell am I doing? I'm not ready to go on a date yet," I shook my head.

"Chantelle, your cheating boyfriend dumped you three months ago. Get over it. Franco has already moved on and so should you," she elbowed me.

"He sure had moved on...before he even dumped me," I lowered my head.

"Besides this is just a fun date with a hunk that happens to be a hundred times better looking than that two-timing ex of yours," her tone escalated.

"*Ja* and he knows it."

I rolled my eyes.

"*Hun,* that's what attracted Franco to you —-your sensitive and naive personality."

"You sound like my mom." But Kirsty was right, Franco had already moved in with the young nurse whom he had left me for and I was the one, returning to an empty house.

* * *

Although it was a hot, dry night, the cool crisp white Egyptian sheets cooled my half- naked body. The room was quiet apart from the gentle whirr of the ceiling fan and the annoying buzz of a mosquito. I tossed and turned, constantly checking the time. Finally I drifted off to sleep.

Every cell of my body tingled as he held me tightly, kissing me passionately. His soft lips moved down my neck and he gently tugged on my tangled hair. His moist mouth glided over…

I reached over for Franco. The bed was empty. This was all just a dream. I hate you Franco. I hate being alone. I hate myself for being such a failure. Hot tears trickled onto my pillow and in this piteous state I once again fell asleep.

"Don't stop!" I hungrily moaned. As I unbuttoned his shirt, I could feel his heart pounding as he pressed his smooth firm naked chest against mine.

The car windows steamed up. Everything moved faster. His hand slid down the side of the car seat laying it flat. Neither of us could hold back any longer. Our hormones raged. My legs were trembling as —

Abruptly I woke to the raucous sound of Hadedas in the early morning. Equally as abruptly I realised I was alone. It was 5 am. Who had I been dreaming of? Franco? Stephan?

"Stop this Chantelle," I cautioned myself as comparisons between Franco's unfaltering surgeon hands on my body and Stephan's youthful strong ones, ran amok with my mind and my emotions.

I was so confused. Should I even go on this date? Surely I was putting myself in a position to be hurt all over again. The optimistic and more trusting side of me argued back: You'd be a fool not to take the chance.

I must have drifted back to sleep as I woke up at 6 am to the bleep of my cellphone, alerting me I had a text message. After rubbing the sleep from my half-open eyes, I fumbled over to pick up my phone and read: *Morning Chantelle. Hope you're able to make our breakfast date. If so, does 8 am suit you? BTW I have a surprise for you. Stephan.*

I was nervous but curious to find out what the surprise was. An adrenalin rush of possibly seeing Stephan, jump-started me into action. After an extra brushing of my teeth and a quick shower, I came to a halt. I had to make a decision whether to go or not, and let Stephan know. I answered his text: *I should be able to make 8, but won't be able to stay long.*

He immediately texted back. *Great! Pity you're unable to stay for long…any chance of twisting your arm? BTW, bring your camera…Meet you at the Michelangelo Hotel.*

Chapter Two

I stood staring at the rail of dresses and skirts in my wardrobe, unsure what to wear. My mind began to wander.

What did I wear on my first date with Franco? My eyes scoured the top rail jammed with dresses all varying in size. A turquoise blue chiffon dress jumped out at me. Aha! That was the one. I can't believe I've still got it. I'd never fit into that dress now. My eyes glimpsed a sea-green dress. That was always my lucky dress. We'd made such a good couple, my dress complimenting his navy suit. Franco and I were all dressed up for Freya's wedding. He was a real gentleman that day.

"Meet Dr Franco de Preez!" Freya's excited voice had introduced us. I recall how elated I felt when my Uni buddy made this formal introduction.

Our first date went well. I admired his immaculate manners, his taste for good food and wine and his devotion. I should have seen the early signs. On one such occasion, Franco took it upon himself to tell me how to use the layered cutlery, saying for everyone to hear, "Start using the cutlery furthest from your plate first." This was just the beginning of his controlling power over me.

It was my fault. I had allowed him to manipulate me. In retrospect, he was moulding me into the trophy wife he could be proud of. It was nothing to do with how I felt but he fooled me into believing that he was proud to have me on his arm. He derived pleasure from showing me off with all the niceties in front of his buddies.

My smile became like a light bulb, switched on and off, to please Franco and his cronies. I pretended to fit in, but quite honestly I always felt so uncomfortable at those snobby dinner parties. I'll never forget the way one of his colleagues treated me, questioning my knowledge on work politics. They boasted about politicians and esteemed people they rubbed shoulders with. This eventually rubbed off on Franco and he emulated their ways. Was this when the distance between he and I began to widen?

I snapped out of my reverie and realised how much time I had wasted having a pity party. Without further ado, I ended up wearing my trusty soft peach summer dress. I had just turned twenty-nine and already had crow's feet round my eyes from living in the scorching African sun. Unlike Kirsty, I eschewed Botox accepting the fine lines. I rolled my eyes at myself gazing back in the mirror. What am I going to do with this hair of mine?

It looked dull from overuse of hair straighteners. I kicked myself for missing my hairdresser's appointment. In frustration I caught my fine mousey brown hair back into a pony tail, leaving a few tendrils falling onto my face and clipped on my silver hoop earrings. I settled for a slick of peach lip-gloss and coat of mascara. With the last spritz of my favourite *Gucci Guilty* perfume that Franco had given me, I grabbed my camera bag and made my way to the kitchen.

Mavis, my maid, was like a substitute mother and confidante to me. She had a fresh cup of *rooibos* tea waiting for me. My mother had employed Mavis as a nanny for me and so over the years she had become an integral part of our family. I was overjoyed when Mavis asked if she could work for me once I had moved into my own home.

Mavis was black, soft and well rounded. She always looked smart dressed in her checked uniform with a white apron. Her matching blue-checked scarf wrapped stylishly around her head covering her short tight curls.

"Mavis, does my tummy and bum look too big in this dress?"

"Chantelle! *Ag,* of course not!" she replied with a disapproving shake of her head.

"I might look slimmer if I wear these?" I lifted out my new pair of snakeskin high heels from a shoebox. I managed to balance near the doorway as I pushed my feet into the tight stilettos.

"You never wear such high shoes. Can you even walk in those?" her nose wrinkled. Mavis was too polite to ask where I was going all dressed up, at this time of the morning.

"Does my bum look smaller?" I spun round patting my chunky bottom.

"Your big backside looks very good in that dress. You know in our culture the bigger the bottom, the more beautiful!"

Mavis chuckled as her buttocks bounced beneath her tight uniform as she strode over to the sink, bringing a smile to Chantelle's face.

It was only 7am when I drove off in my silver *VW Golf.* The scent from the rich lilac-flowered Jacaranda trees wafted through the open car window. At this time of the year they were in full bloom and lined the street, creating a magical sight with the reflective blueish purple petals carpeting both sides of the road.

As I approached the industrial suburbs, I glimpsed pedestrians in western attire hurrying alongside the main road and thumbing lifts from passing taxis. Hawkers lined the roadside with their wares.

This always made me more alert being a woman driving on my own during the day. My car doors and windows were always locked and my handbag stashed out of sight in the boot. I knew full well the risks of muggings, carjackings and rape was the highest in Joburg. I was particularly cautious at *robots,* where criminals targeted motorists when the lights turned red.

Today my mood changed. I pursed my lips in thought. What would Stephan and I talk about? I started to get butterflies in my stomach as I drove into the car park of the high-class hotel.

* * *

My snakeskin high heels clattered on the polished white marble floor as I nervously hobbled into the trendy ornate entrance of the plush Michelangelo Hotel.

"Chantelle! Good to see you again," Stephan greeted me with a warm, friendly smile exposing his even teeth, brimming with self-confidence. Damn! He looked so sexy and athletic. His shoulders, broad without being too bulky, emphasised his lean waist. Stephan wore dark sunglasses, jeans and a fitted white cotton short-sleeved shirt which offset his golden skin. I could smell his intoxicating aftershave as he walked up to me.

"Stephan. How are you?" I smiled nervously.

"*Howzit* Chantelle. You look good."

"You think?" I frowned, not expecting this response.

"You must know you're lovely," he added, making me more confused.
I didn't think I was lovely. I saw myself as heavy hipped mousy-haired and boring.

His long fingers gestured to the African themed restaurant.

"I don't know about you, but I'm starving. Let's go and eat."

We were greeted by the delicious smell of freshly-brewed filter coffee and pastries. I felt like a VIP as heads turned and all eyes were on us whilst we were being led by the waiter to our table. Women were ogling him but were glaring at me with envious daggers. Stephan sure had a presence about him. Golden sunlight streamed through a large sliding door where we were seated. The local African drumming music throbbed through ceiling speakers. It was the beginning of a hot day so we both ordered *Buck's Fizz*. I felt a tangy sizzle in my mouth as I took a gulp. The champagne mixed with fresh orange cooled me instantly. We both became giggly as the alcohol kicked in on empty stomachs. Stephan was clearly at ease with himself.

"Chantelle, tell me about yourself. Are you in a relationship?"

"No, I've just come out of one."

His eyes lit up. He changed the subject going on to say, "I've something to tell you."

"Go on," I urged leaning forward as he now had my full attention. I felt my confidence sapping as I waited nervously hoping not to hear the worst. Please don't tell me you are gay or married I inwardly cursed myself for being so gullible.

"Last night's show was a one-off! I was dared by friends to stand in for our mutual mate, who went off sick. It was just for fun, so now I can get back to focusing on swimming. My training's definitely stepping up because the Olympics are coming up soon," he revealed.

"Olympics!" I said stunned as I felt my jaw drop.

"*Ja*, I'm a professional swimmer and I'm hoping to represent South Africa for the 2016 Olympics!"

He lifted his head to empty his glass just as our fresh fruits, cheese and croissants arrived.

"I moved here from Cape Town six months ago," his mouth curved into a smile.

"Coffee ma'am?" the waiter asked.

"Please."

I could have done with something stronger like a double espresso to sober me up. The waiter placed a jug of hot filter coffee on our table. An *Omega Seamaster* watch moved slightly round Stephan's wrist as he poured me a cup. I felt his fingers brush against mine as he passed me my coffee, sending electric charges through my body. There was a short silent pause between us.

"What made you move here?"

"It made sense. My swimming coach is based here."

His voice softened.

"What made you become a professional swimmer?" I continued firing the questions which was very unlike me.

"My father had a big influence on me. He inspired me to achieve my dream of becoming an Olympic swimmer."

Taking a bite of his croissant, he continued, "I'm a sucker for perfection!"

"*Eish*, you must've a regimented training routine—"

"Early nights and crack of dawn training sessions. To become an Olympic swimmer is my entire focus. There's no room for anything else."

I was enjoying his company and felt I already knew him after such a short time. He was friendly, polite and confident. His self-belief had allowed him to become a self-motivated, determined and devoted swimmer. I wanted to know more about this man.

"Do you miss Cape Town?"

He pursed his lips in thought then replied, "*Ja*, I do. For starters, it's so dry here. But for now, I have to live here to fulfil my dream and…"

He stopped abruptly.

"And?" I prompted him.

"Never mind. So could you ever live in Cape Town?" he cocked his head.

What was he hiding? You're just asking too many questions; I reminded myself.

"Maybe, but do people ever work there? They seem to spend their days in and out of coffee shops."

"That's cos life is so fast here. Folks just don't know how to relax. But the money is here."

He was definitely a Capetonian.

"So what've you got planned for the rest of the day?" he asked, not taking his mesmerizing eyes off me.

"Not sure," I said while crossing my legs under the table.

"What would entice you to spend the rest of the day with me?"

Startled, I blinked. I could feel his entire focus was still on me.

"Are you able to?" he added making his cultured voice vibrate through me.

As I flicked a piece of hair off my face I teased, "Maybe!" not wanting to sound too keen. His thumb brushed over my cheek.

"I have a surprise I'd like to share with you. We'll be driving out of Joburg."

Stephan gently tucked a stray tendril of hair behind my ear. I picked up my glass with a not-so-steady hand and asked, "Where to?"

"If I tell you it'll ruin the surprise. Chantelle, please trust me."

He ran his fingers through his thick brown hair, waiting for me to reply.

"Okay, but I have to be home early evening."

What was I thinking with this impulsive answer? Fortunately, it was Friday and I had no other commitments. But I hardly knew Stephan and where was he taking me? Could I trust someone I had only just met? This was South Africa with a rape and murder record of 45 people per day.

"I was hoping you'd say that," he replied with a cheeky twinkle in his eyes.

Stephan pulled out a charcoal wallet from his pocket, removed a platinum credit card and settled our bill.

I needed a minute on my own. I slipped into the scented Ladies bathroom and rummaged for my cellphone in my bag. I called Kirsty. It went to voicemail, so I left a message: *Hi darl, my date's going well. He's even more handsome in daylight. We're going out of town. He's got a surprise for me. A bit impulsive, I know, but after all I've been through, I'm up for a bit of fun and adventure. Besides I've got a good vibe about him. Hugs. C*

I washed my hands, brushed my hair letting it hang freely over my shoulders and left my worries in the bathroom.

Stephan was patiently waiting outside, leaning against the wall with his hands shoved casually in his pockets.

"Everything okay?"

I nodded and he placed his hand on the small of my back, steering me gently outside. His touch rippled through me in a way that made me wild. His hand then fell away as the valet drove up with his immaculate polished black *Land Rover*.

I squinted as we were greeted by the glare and heat of the intense African sun. I slipped on my *Aviator* sunglasses. He opened the passenger door for me. I was struggling to climb in my stilettos when Stephan's strong arms scooped me up into the vehicle. I adjusted my dress and relaxed into the black leather seat. When Stephan closed the door, the *cubby hole* dropped open, revealing a black 9mm pistol!

Chapter Three

The knots in my stomach tightened. I swiftly closed the cubby hole. But what was he doing with a pistol? Was I being paranoid? It must be for self-protection, but then why leave it in an empty car? Or was he an undercover cop? My mind swirled with possibilities, but I decided it must be there as a precaution because this had become a common practice nowadays with crime rates and hijackings on the increase.

He climbed briskly into the driver's seat then turned round to place my camera bag on the back seat. There was a swift click as he pressed the central locking switch.

"Rather safe than sorry," he muttered.

"Come on! Tell me where we're driving to." I probed.

"Now that'll ruin my surprise," he laughed.

As he started the engine Sam Smith's lyrics *Stay With Me* blasted out of the speakers; he leaned over to turn the volume down chuckling.

"Shit! I forgot this CD was on. I'm prepared to lose man points here, but Sam Smith's new album is epic." His cheeks turned bright red. He was blushing! This soft romantic side to him was very attractive, but I was also drawn to his mysterious side.

"Actually I like that track," I reassured him, but he switched on the radio instead.

A confident and cultured female newsreader's voice announced, *"Good morning! This is the South African Radio Corporation, I'm Yolanda Van den Berg. Today's top stories at this hour are..."*

She went on, *"Superintendent Bogani Mahwebo from the Anti-Carjacking Unit claims that last year, 14602 carjacking incidents occurred in the entire country and fifty percent happened in Gauteng. Some of these motorists were shot dead by carjackers, mostly while the victims were waiting at robots or pulling into the driveways of their homes. Carjackers usually work in gangs of three: one is familiar with the mechanics of the target vehicle, whilst one keeps watch and another carries the gun, Not only luxury cars but also four-wheel-drive pick-ups are targeted, and the stolen vehicles wind up being smuggled across the borders.*

She paused then continued, *"Let's see what the weather has in store for us. Mostly sunny conditions with a high of 31 Celsius, with no expected rain."*

Stephan turned down the volume commenting, "Shit! This place is dangerous; Cape Town's more chilled than here."

"*Ja,* violence and crime's getting out of hand in Joburg. More and more people protect themselves with guns," I replied, giving him a chance to explain that black pistol.   But he didn't, he just went on.

"I feel like a bloody caged animal in this city forced to survive behind electric fences and to live in gated communities. It'll be a relief to get out of here today."

We stopped as the *robots* had turned red. I felt him skim over my profile before his soft long fingers brushed lightly but firmly though my hair, "Chantelle...your hair feels so silky soft," he murmured.

His touch sent goose pimples erupting through me. Why did Stephan have that effect on me? I wanted his fingers to stay there longer but he abruptly removed them as he turned to open his window. A scruffy toothless hawker wearing a cap, checked shirt and jeans, stood blurting, "*Airtime* for your cellphone, newspapers, sunglasses?"

"No thanks!" Stephan shook his head closing all the windows.

The hawker moved closer, aggressively selling his merchandise, "Come on guys! Buy some *airtime.*"

As the lights turned green his grip on the steering wheel tightened and he pulled away quickly, cursing the pushy hawker. We turned onto the very busy highway; all vehicles were exceeding the speed limit. Mini-bus taxi drivers doubled the legal nine-passenger capacity limit, to swell their coffers, honking at every opportunity. We sped past billboards which were advertising cellphones and various electronic devices which track carjacked vehicles.

"Why don't you take off your high heels?   You'll feel more comfortable," he suggested in his raspy South African accent.

My feet felt relaxed, cooler and soothed soon after I kicked off my sweaty, tight stilettos. Thank goodness I remembered to spray them with shoe deodorant. I noticed him smile as he glanced down at my toenails, painted pale pink.

    We left behind the smog and dust that had already smothered the city as we drove along the Malibongwe Drive off-ramp and headed north towards Lanseria International Airport privately owned since 2012.

"This is the way to Sun City. Are we taking a light chartered aircraft there?" I hinted, hoping this was the case as I was starting to feel a bit uneasy.

"Nope!" he continued smiling as we drove past the turnoff to the airport.

My breathing and heart rate increased when, without warning, we slowed down in the middle of nowhere. Before long he turned left onto a narrow road, with scraggy bushes that littered the landscape of the deep red earth. A rusty, mud-splattered bus, with cages of flapping and squawking chickens tied on the roof, drove past us. The midday sun was beating hard and relentlessly now. I was sweating, was agitated and kept shuffling around because my bottom was numb from sitting in one place for so long.

"Where are the mountains like we have in the mother city?" his eyes drifted to the monotonous dry and dead bush.

"Where the hell are we?" I shook my head, wiping beads of sweat from my forehead as I kept remembering the dreaded black pistol in the *cubby hole.*

When Stephan did not reply immediately, fear consumed me. I've made a bad decision. Kirsty's the only person who knows I'm on a date with a total stranger. However, she's not aware that I've driven off into the wilderness with this man. I wish I'd reached her on my cellphone earlier on. Surely he wouldn't pull the trigger on me, dump my body in the bushes and drive off.

"We're between Joburg and the Hartebeespoort Dam. We'll be there in half an hour or so."

"I'm not happy not knowing where I'm going," I pursed my lips.

"Chantelle! Relax, I promise you'll be chuffed when we get there. But if it makes you happier, I'll tell you," he said in a soothing voice.

"Give me a hint," I swallowed hard as my mouth was dry.

"A hint's too obvious. It'll give the surprise away," he answered.

"Try me."

"Something for you to photograph, hence bringing your camera," he glanced across at me with a sparkle of mischief in his eyes.

"Huh? What photograph the bush?"

I was puzzled, irritated and afraid. If I screamed for help, nobody would hear me. If I could not run barefoot on the scorching dirt road, where would I go? I was trapped and longed to be back with Mavis in the safety of my own home.

"You okay?"

Stephan looked concerned.

"I can't guess. I'm too thirsty, too hot and sweaty to think straight," I glared back at him.

"Shall I tell you?"

"I'll give you the benefit of the doubt, but if we're not there within half an hour, then take me back to Joburg."

"There's a market coming up, so I'll stop and get us some cold drinks," he gently patted my knee.

My cellphone bleeped with a new text message. I fumbled for my phone in my bag and checked who the message was from. It was Kirsty.

WTF! Are you crazy girl going out of town with Stephan? You only met him last night. Keep me updated and look after yourself. K xx

I could see Kirsty's disapproving face. Her words, '*you only met him last night'*, sounded a warning to me. I must tell her where I am. I tried to reply, but lost the network connection.

"You won't get a signal from here on," Stephan said.

"Shit! The aircon has stopped working."

My tongue was swollen, sticky and dry. I desperately needed to quench my thirst. Eventually we arrived at a local market selling fresh produce. Stephan parked under a tall wide umbrella tree grabbing any bit of shade he could find. He asked me what I wanted to drink.

"Anything cold and fizzy," I replied through my parched lips.

He climbed out making his way to the outdoor stalls where catchy African tunes were blasting from a small portable radio. I stayed in the vehicle with the door open wide. This heat was unbearable and added to my dilemma.

I checked my cellphone for a network connection. Damn! Still nothing, so I chucked it back into my handbag in frustration. I stared at the activity nearby.

In contrast to the modern glamorous ladies of Johannesburg, these humble local black women swathed themselves in long bright, colourful cloths of material wrapped round their waists and teamed it with short-sleeved T-shirts and *tackies.* Many of them carried babies strapped to their backs. Friendly smiles exposed their white, gappy teeth. On their turbaned heads which hid their black peppercorn curls, they balanced bowls or baskets containing their purchases.

Stephan returned with cans of cold drinks, fresh ripe mangoes and bananas. Pushing his *Oakley* sunglasses up on his head, he popped open an ice-cold tin of ginger-beer before handing it to me. I immediately felt rehydrated, cooler and uplifted after downing my drink.

I decided to stop being paranoid and to allow myself to enjoy the adventure. We continued our journey with the windows wound down, allowing the hot air to blow in, tangling my hair.

"*Jislaaik,* your temperature gauge's showing 38∘C," I read out.

"And my AC decides not to work on this damn hot day. It's even hotter than when I lived in Arizona," he added, removing a white cotton handkerchief from his trouser pocket to wipe the beads of sweat from his forehead.

I looked over at Stephan, "You lived in the States?"

"Only for a few years. Won a swimming scholarship to Arizona Uni. It was tough, hey, but it was worth it."

He puffed his chest out.

"I'd love to visit America. They say Joburg's a mini New York."

"You should. It's a different world. Those years were some of the best years of my life even though I had to be in the pool for 5am to train. Come early evening I'd be ready to hit the sack. Sundays were our only chance to lie in."

"Phew! Training to be a swimming champion must take serious dedication and will-power," I encouraged.

When I realised we were heading deeper into the *veld*, my emotions continued their roller-coaster ride rushing high with excitement then plunging into the depths of despair. There were fewer cars on the road, which had narrowed and become more potholed. I still had no idea where we were heading. My eyes darted around. My jaw clenched. My grip tightened on the seat. My heart raced.

"You're very quiet, Chantelle," Stephan prompted.

I squinted at him, "I can't relax as I don't know where the hell we're going!"

After fifteen minutes, we slowed down, before turning onto a red-earthed rutted, dirt road, bordered by Savannah grassland and bush. Stephan battled to avoid potholes, swerving all over the road. Then suddenly we came to a halt. What's he doing? Why's he stopped here in the bush? The black pistol? I shuffled around nervously with my eyes fixed on his hands and that *cubby hole*. My breathing became harder, matching my uncontrollable thumping heartbeat. He stared at me. His penetrating eyes seemed to have changed colour from hazel to steel grey. I froze.

His lips curved into a smile when he distracted me by saying, "Chill! We've more in common than you realise. Apart from swimming, my other passion is rescuing wildlife from those heartless poachers. I hate the greedy bastards. If I were given half a chance, I'd shoot the devils. Sorry about my outburst. Last night you told me you're a photographer and your dream is to photograph a white lion. Right?"

I nervously nodded, biting my lip. Was he trying to distract me?

"Nkuti Wildlife Rehabilitation Sanctuary. *Heard of it?*" he grinned. All I could do was nod my head.

Chapter Four

"The Sanctuary's about five minutes from here and that's where we're heading."

His eyes beamed with excitement as he started the *Land Rover*.

"It's run by Carl, a family friend. Now that I'm back in Joburg, I'm trying to spend more time with the animals, when I'm not training of course," he explained as he continued driving.

"You serious?" I relaxed and I stretched out to arch my stiff back.

"That's the surprise. You'll meet Shumba, the white lion cub."

"You're such a tease. You had me worried," I playfully poked him on his shoulder.

"My dream's about to become a reality." I giggled and slapped my thighs with excitement. I was warming to this enigma of a man more and more.

"Did you know white lions are the rarest animals in the world, coming over from the Timbavati region here in SA?"

He clenched his jaw before adding, "And they're now extinct in the wild, being sought after by those bloody greedy trophy hunters."

He slipped out a piece of white A4 paper from under his seat and handed it to me.

"This is just the beginning of a draft of an ad I wrote, to put on the website," he said proudly throwing back his head. I read: *Deep in the African bushveld lies Nkuti Wildlife Rehabilitation Sanctuary, a vast wilderness that is the true quality of Africa. The spacious enclosures and the open grounds provide the visitor with a feeling of peace and tranquillity. The Sanctuary is home and rehabilitation to many indigenous species of South African animals including white lion, cheetah, leopard, rhino, elephant, giraffe and bushbuck.*

I looked out the window and noticed the dust spewing up behind the vehicle like a vapour trail. My eyes focused on the road ahead.

Stephan! Watch out! There's a snake!" I shrieked.

Dam! That's a black mamba. We can't get close to the bastard. They're notorious for getting into car engines," he shouted as he swerved to avoid the six-foot grey snake slithering in the middle of the road. But he didn't and we ended up in a ditch.

I clasped my hands tightly over my face, whimpering, "I hate snakes!"

Stephan slammed his fingers onto the automatic window switch closing all the windows. He put the *Land Rover* into reverse and revved the engine hard in his attempt to get the vehicle out the ditch. Dust flew everywhere as the wheels spun round and round, sinking us deeper and deeper into the soil. Churning stones struck the bodywork sounding like bullets.

"I thought this was a four-wheel drive," I said as I gripped my seat.

"It started life that way!"

He tried reverse gear, but the vehicle wouldn't budge. The only sound was the straining of the engine.

"I can't believe this is happening."

I felt the hairs rise on the back of my neck. Stephan instructed me authoritatively, "Just keep the windows closed. I'm getting out to push. You take over the driving."

He patted his seat as he jumped out saying, "Keep the engine running gently and when I give you the go-ahead, release the clutch and put your foot on the accelerator."

"Don't let that bloody poisonous snake get in," I pleaded, annoyed with myself for behaving like a sissy. Why did I allow him to see my vulnerable side?

"Chantelle, just keep the windows closed. If you see that snake, don't move."

Feeling nervous I slid across to the driver's seat. I turned to watch Stephan, waiting for his next instruction. Taking a shovel from the boot, he began digging around the wheels. He gathered broken branches and small stones to put under the tyres. I jumped when he startled me by opening the door.

"The ditch's actually quite shallow. I'll try to push. Are you ready?" he asked brushing the dust from his hands on the sides of his jeans. Sweat was dripping off his forehead.

"What happened to the snake?"

"Probably disappeared. I'll beat the living daylights out of it with this shovel if it comes anywhere near us," his fearless voice was reassuring.

He closed the door and then moved round to the front of the vehicle. I admired his athletic body poised in starting position with his strong arms leaning onto the *Land Rover*.

"Ready, Go!" he shouted and slammed the bonnet to give me the go ahead.

Obeying his instructions the vehicle roared to life backing us out of the ditch. My breathing returned to normal after I let out a sigh of relief.

With the handbrake firmly up, I slid over to the passenger seat to allow Stephan to take over. Gently rubbing my shaking hands on my legs.

"Eish! My legs feel like jelly."

"It's your adrenaline levels coming down...you'll be back to normal just now," he said wiping his sweaty face.

"Thanks for getting us out of there," I praised him with a pat on his thigh.

"I won't lie. It was a close shave. Now let's get to the sanctuary."

He revved the engine, released the handbrake and drove back onto the road.

I eased back into my seat exhaling. I saw a large sign in bold black print, NKUTI WILDLIFE REHABILITATION SANCTUARY, set on an olive-green and gold background. In smaller print underneath, was written: Drive Slowly.

The security guard dressed in camouflage uniform recognised Stephan.

"Hello Mr Stephan!" he greeted and opened the high steel gates. He waved us through.

I bent over to squeeze my swollen feet back into my tight stilettos and then eased back into my seat exhaling. Another bold sign, DO NOT FEED THE ANIMALS, came into view. Stephan drove up and parked besides a thatched-roof building marked; Reception. He climbed out and strode over to my side to open the door. He held me by my elbow in a gentle manner, as I slid onto my feet. It felt good to stretch my legs. Stephan reached for my camera bag and swung it over his shoulder.

We were greeted by an attractive slim tanned twenty-something-year-old guide. She wore a khaki safari suit with dark-green epaulettes on her shoulders and dark brown *veldskoens*. Her wavy sandy-coloured hair was loosely tied behind her freckled face.

"*Howzit* Stephan. Good to see you," she purred, greeting him with her flirtatious blue eyes.

Stephan frowned, "Corrine I thought you were on leave. Anyway, meet Chantelle."

"Carl's not here for a few days, so he asked me to defer my dates. He wants me to accompany you," she quipped without acknowledging me.

"That's cool thanks. You can give Chantelle more details on the wildlife rescues here. She'll be taking photos of Shumba."

Corrine glared at my stilettos disapprovingly, "You'll need better shoes than the ones you're wearing," she snorted.

Stephan directed his eyes at her in annoyance and asked, "Do you have a spare pair of *tackies* Chantelle could borrow?"

"What size are you?" she asked in her distinct Johannesburg accent.

"A six," I replied, feeling the warm blood rush to my cheeks.

"Corinne, who's looking after Shumba and the Cheetahs?"

"It's actually feeding time for the Cheetahs now, so let's do that before I take you to Shumba," she pulled on a khaki baseball cap.

"Will you kindly fetch those *tackies* for Chantelle first?" Stephan insisted his eyes narrowing.

"*Ja,* okay," her voice was tinged with reluctance as she marched off to the office.

"Take no notice of her; she's jealous of any woman I'm with."

"How many women do you bring here?"

I was feeling a bit jealous myself.

"Apart from my cousin Debbie, just you. But I've known Corrine from Cape Town days. She used to be envious of my ex. Crazy, as I've never shown her any interest other than friendship."

"Hope she doesn't set one of the Cheetahs on me." I joked.

Corrine returned and handed me a pair of *tackies.*

"Try these—they're a 6."

"Thanks, I'm sure they'll fit me," I smiled.

* * *

Trying not to appear uncomfortable, we walked down to a huge cage in which four fawn and black-spotted Cheetahs were enclosed. An unsavoury odour accosted us from a parked truck loaded with crates of raw meat. Two game rangers were off–loading the crates. They then made their way into the enclosures throwing enormous slabs of meat onto a specially built concrete table.

"Cheetahs are the cleanest of all cats. They'll only eat off a clean smooth surface like concrete," Corrine explained.

Stephan added to her cheetah knowledge, "And they're the fastest mammal on earth running at a top speed of 100 km per hour built for speed with long legs, a light-weight frame and a small aerodynamic head."

"We've now got a disabled cheetah with a spinal problem," Corrine added.

After the Cheetahs had gobbled down the meat, they purred contentedly. Stephan bravely followed Corinne into the cage.

"Come on boy," Stephan stroked the disabled cheetah's head.

"They communicate with each other in distinct whistles, sounding like birds," Stephan said.

"Tigers do a chuckle. I'll introduce you to our tigers, Zara and Jock," Corrine boasted.

Who was she trying to impress Stephan or me? She led us onto the next cage. Two lazy-looking tigers lounged gracefully, waiting patiently. Stephan imitated a chuckle trying to get their attention, but they took no notice. He placed his comforting safe hand on my back. I felt a gush of tingles erupt and gush through my entire body.

"Tigers are the only cats that seek out water," Corrine explained.

Stephan decided to give them a treat, spraying them with a hosepipe. Unexpectedly he started showering me playfully. Corrine watched, rolling her eyes with her hand on her hip. The spray of cold refreshing water gave me goose-bumps. I felt Stephan's gaze rake over my drenched dress. I curiously looked down to see what had caught his attention. I embarrassingly crossed my arms hoping to hide the outline to my erect nipples..

"*Phwoar* Chantelle! Miss Wet T-shirt!" he winked.

Stephan pulled off his shirt and slipped it over my shoulders, saying, "Here cover up with this."

My eyes were magnetically drawn to his bare chest with the sun glistening on his golden skin. Damn! He looked so sexy and athletic. His shoulders, broad without being too bulky, emphasised his lean waist.

"You guys ready to photograph Shumba?" Corrine's frustrated voice interrupted.

A middle-aged, bald guide approached.

"Afternoon Mr Stephan."

"Hi, Moses. How's Shumba doing?" Stephan asked.

"Growing fast," Moses answered chewing gum with an open mouth.

"Afternoon I take care of Shumba," his large hand felt rough and dry as he shook mine.

"Moses, I'm looking forward to seeing Shumba." I added, nodding.

Moses, dressed in blue overalls and black gumboots, carried a rifle.

"Let me take that for you,"

Stephan took my long-lensed camera equipment off me. We followed Moses shading ourselves from the blazing hot sun, as we moved from tree to tree. I used my hand as a sun-visor against the glare. We passed a baby elephant lying peacefully in a puddle of mud, unbothered by the little birds picking insects off its ears. Stephan indicated with his long finger.

"There's Moyo..our latest rescue."

"Oh, what happened to poor Moyo?"

His eyes narrowed and he explained, "Abandoned and stuck in a dried-out waterhole. But we managed to bring him back to health."

"Shame that's awful. He looks pretty happy now."

I watched on as he reached up to suck air into his nostrils. Then he rolled his trunk down and blew into his gaping mouth.

After walking for about fifteen minutes, we arrived at a cage with three white lion cubs.

"Can I leave you here?" Moses asked Stephan.

"*Ja,* sure. Catch you later," Stephan replied.

We were alone again. Stephan passed me my camera before opening the cage door to step inside. The bundles of white fluff knew his scent as he confidently squatted down. Stephan wasn't at all afraid when the two cubs sprang up to his face. He picked up one of the cubs and gently stroked it. It responded to Stephan's voice by purring. Holding the cub, Stephan made his way out of the cage to sit under a nearby *Marula* tree. With his free hand, he patted the ground next to him.

"Chante...Sit next to me."

My dress was dry. I removed his oversized shirt, placed it next to him and eased myself down. I was so close to a real white lion cub. Unbelievable, yet it was happening.

"Meet three-month-old Shumba."

Stephan turned him round and put him on my lap.

"Just watch those claws!"

"Am I really going to hold a white lion cub?" I asked as I very gingerly stretched out my arms as Stephan gently placed Shumba on my lap. I smiled widely. Despite being heavy, Shumba looked and felt like a live soft toy. His icy blue eyes set against his pure white furry coat, gazed into mine curiously. Playfully he nibbled my nose and licked my face. This was too good to be true sitting with two delights! I wanted this moment to last and last.

"What's the matter?" he asked.

I quietly replied. "Seeing and holding a white lion cub, a rare animal in real life, is quite something. It's a magical moment."

"We both love wildlife Chante."

"I sure do...apart from bloody snakes," I shuddered at the memory of our earlier experience.

"You just called me Chante again, I've never been called that before," I giggled.

"I know, I think it suits you, sweet, with an edge!" he winked.

He passed me my camera.

"You read my mind! We're on the same page."

I leaned back against the tree. Stephan took Shumba onto his lap, where this cuddly cub moved only to flick flies off his ears. I adjusted my settings waiting for the right moment to take a shot. It was difficult to focus with Stephan's admiring eyes watching me at work and Shumba suspiciously looking up at my camera lens. Focused tight on Shumba's head I snapped off several frames in succession. I tried to get a closer shot, but he blinked curiously at the whirr of the camera's motor wind, sniffing the air, reassuring himself all was well.

Stephan glowed as Shumba purred, rubbing his flanks against his leg. He started playing, chewing on a piece of knotted rope.

"If only they remained this small and cute?"

My eyes were drawn to Stephan's bare chest, a photo opportunity. I stood up to take a few spontaneous photos of Stephan. Having successfully accomplished a photo-shoot of Shumba and Stephan, I shut off my camera. Stephan sprang up and offered me his hand to pull me up. After straightening my dress, I brushed off pieces of loose grass and dust whilst Stephan returned Shumba to his siblings in the cage.

A drop in temperature jolted me back to the real world.

"We need to start heading back. It's starting to get dark."

He bent over to pick his shirt up from the ground, shook it off and put it back on. Whilst buttoning it up, he suggested, "Let's have a sundowner before we set off."

"It's not safe travelling at night—especially in the bush. We heard earlier on the radio how bad carjacking is—"

He cut me off, "Don't worry...You're safe with me."

Chapter Five

The cool polished stone felt soothing on my tired swollen feet. I eased back into the low-cushioned chair under a high thatched roof with an uninterrupted view of the Savannah bush.

The sun was setting slowly, a large red orb poised on the golden horizon. When Stephan disappeared to get us a drink, I checked my cellphone. Relief. I finally had a network connection. No work-related messages. Relaxing, I turned to my friend whenever I felt unsure. Kirsty was my brick. She was so outspoken and never withheld the truth from me.

This is what had attracted her to me when we first met at university. She was studying journalism and would practise interviewing her friends. I was doing photography and Kirsty was my perfect model with her confidence and photogenic looks. Not only was she good company, but she stood up for me especially when my room was trashed. Her spontaneous humour brightened my dullest day and her listening ear, picked up on finer details, enabling me to confide in her, something I'd never done before.

I texted Kirsty: *Hey darl. Hope you're having a fab day. Guess where I am?*

Her instant reply: *Where? U still with the hunk? K x*

My text: *Don't stress. We're at Nkuti Sanctuary. C xxx*

OMG. That's so cool. What's he like? K x

All I had time to text back was a smiley face. Stephan returned from the bar carrying our drinks placing my tall glass of Savannah dry cider with sliced lemon in front of me. He sat down next to me holding his can of beer.

"This Savannah's going down well!"

He took a swig from the brown and white beer can. Roaring lions could be heard in the distance. He scanned the acres of wide open space with pride.

"I feel more comfortable with animals than I do with people."

My nose twitched from a rotten odour and I asked, "What's that foul smell?"

"Raw meat. It's feeding time."

"Talking of lions. They're usually boring to watch. They do nothing until this time of day when their stomachs start to rumble. Did you know this is the best time to capture lions on film… when they're hunting?"

I reached down to pick up my camera.

"Hey, check those wildebeest!" Stephan pointed in the distance with his long index finger. There were hundreds. The leaders of the herds were sparring together, their horns clashing and hooves thumping on the dusty ground.

"They'd better watch out! The Lions will have them for dinner!" he joked, shaking his head.

* * *

It was a warm and windless as nightfall set in and we started our journey home. Once Stephan had left the remote dirt road and joined the tarred road, he started speeding, overtaking two mini-bus taxis. I glanced over at the brightly-lit dashboard.

"You're way over the 120kph speed limit."

Not taking his focus off the road, he muttered, "*Ja,* I know, but it's not safe out here at night."

Seeing his profile under the moonlit sky, wet my romantic urge. Stupidly, for a moment, I imagined this was a real date and not merely an extended breakfast prize.

"What music do you like?"

"I like what's playing now. Is this Enya?"

"Ja, *May It Be* from Lord of the Rings. Great movie. Did you watch it?"

He turned up the volume.

"I did. I'd watch it again any day."

Melancholy lyrics triggered mixed emotions of disappointment that my prize date was ending. What was Stephan's real opinion of me? Was he just being polite as it was his duty to be? If so he was a good actor.

Damn! The words of the next lyric sung by Adele *When Will I See You Again* raised more questions. Did Franco ever think of me? Why had he cheated on me after five years? What did I do wrong? How could I have been so stupid, believing he was working overtime or otherwise always on call? What does it take to find a man who would remain devoted to me?

Although we travelled on listening to the lyrics in silence, I felt comfortable. Somehow my mind harped back to Franco. He was worldly and intelligent with a great sense of humour. On the flip side, he was an arrogant cheat. My life with him had been lonely, only spending stolen moments together. Most of his time was consumed with work at the hospital, where he was the head surgeon. He never approved of any of my single girlfriends, including Kirsty. As for single men, even if they were business associates, he assumed they had ulterior motives. Losing Franco had created a vacuum of loneliness in my life. Today if only temporarily, Stephan had filled that.

"Chante, you're quiet. You okay?"

I wasn't okay. That awful empty feeling was returning as my time with Stephan was quickly running out.

"What's wrong?" he prompted.

"Oh, nothing."

I turned to smile at him.

The bright city lights greeted us. I didn't want today to end, but it soon would. He pulled up at the entrance of the Michelangelo Hotel. After parking, he jumped out to open my door and noticing I had put my stilettos back on; he scooped me out my seat landing me gently on the pavement. I felt safe in his powerful arms. He escorted me to my parked *VW Golf* carrying my camera equipment. A cloud moved over the moon leaving me to fumble for my car keys in the dark.

"Might help if you can see," he suggested hovering his iPhone over my bag using the built-in torchlight. I pulled out my dangly keyring.

"Cheers for that!" I quickly unlocked my door and Stephan casually moved in to open it for me. I turned to him.

"Stephan thanks for a great day. I managed to capture some amazing photos of Shumba."

"It was a pleasure."

His lips curved into a smile. We stood gazing at each other. My breathing became faster matching my racing heart as his tall, broad-shouldered body moved towards me. He bent to peck me with his soft warm lips on my cheek but slowly pulled back. Why did he stop?

"Chantelle!"

I spun round. My eyes strained, squinting to face a well-dressed man.

"Franco!"

Stephan's body stiffened alongside me. A pretty young blonde called out, "Darling, we'll be late for dinner. Hurry up!"

"I'm coming!" he yelled back at her, but she continued to march over towards us. Franco glared disapprovingly at Stephan when he placed his arm on my shoulder. A warm contented feeling gushed through me.

Now I knew where the saying 'sweet revenge' came from.

"I'll be back to collect the rest of my things," Franco huffed as he backed off and walked away.

"Don't bother. They're long gone in the trash!" I yelled after him.

Stephan placed his hands firmly on his hips.

"*Eish,* who the hell was that?"

I shrugged, "It's a long story."

"You sure you're okay?"

"*Ja,* I'm cool. Thanks anyway."

He bent down to kiss my forehead then moved to my ear and whispered, "Remember to lock your car and drive safely."

Feeling elated I climbed in clicking the auto-lock switch before starting the engine. He briskly strode back to his *Land Rover.* Once he was out of sight, I banged the palm of my hands on the steering wheel letting out a loud, "Yes!"

Would I ever see him again? Presumably only on TV, preparing for the Olympics. I searched for my cellphone in my bag and switched it on. Continual bleeping alerted me of voicemail and text messages, mostly from Kirsty, pouring onto my phone.

First text: *Hey, why so quiet? Text back or call.*

Second text: *Are you okay, hun? Why's your phone still off? Call me.*

Third text: *WTF! Are you okay?*

Fourth text: *Now I'm seriously worried.*

Why was she so concerned about me being with Stephan? I texted back: *Back in town. Had an epic time. Franco pitched up and saw me with Stephan. The taste of 'sweet revenge'. Hugs. C xxx*

Driving out the car park I noticed Stephan's *Land Rover* still parked. Slowing down curiously to see if he was in it, he surprised me by springing out making his way to the side of my car. My tyres screeched as I slammed on brakes.

"Chante, is everything okay? I just wanted to make sure you got away safely," he reassured me. I could feel his anxious eyes blazing right through me. I felt my face flushing with embarrassment. I hope he didn't think I was stalking him.

"I was just checking my messages," I stuttered.

"I've just heard on the radio that there's been a carjacking nearby. Do you have far to drive home?"

"Shit. I stay in Fourways."

"Fourways! I grew up there as a kid. I know the area well. I'd feel better if you'd let me get you home safely. I could follow you to the Mall," he insisted.

"Thanks, I don't live far from the Mall anyway."

He did a quick scout around before opening my door. He bent down and brushed a loose strand of hair off my face before softly pecking me on the cheek.

"Text me when you get home. Okay?"

Stephan closed my car door and jumped into his vehicle. I kicked off my stilettos, started the engine and drove away glancing in my rear-view mirror ensuring Stephan was following. I turned on the radio to Pharrell Williams, tapped my fingers on the steering wheel whilst singing along to his chorus of *Happy*. I was very happy, still buzzing. I couldn't wait to give Kirsty all the details.

As I approached Fourways Mall Stephan flashed his headlights before he turned off at the *robots*. I acknowledged by tooting my horn as he drove off in the opposite direction.

I was on my own now. I started to feel uneasy when I left the busy motorway, lit up and teaming with traffic. I headed deeper into the suburbs, quiet at this time of night, with fewer street lights. I was relieved when I finally turned into the road where I lived, releasing my tight grip on the steering wheel.

It was midnight when I stopped on my driveway leaving the engine running.

Without removing the keys from the ignition, I pressed the remote clicker to open the high steel gates. Nothing happened. I tried again. Nothing…

"Bloody useless buzzer," I swore under my breath. With the engine still idling, I climbed out to unlock the gates manually. I was aware how dangerous this was.

I had no sooner driven into the garage and locked the gates with the remote control which had somehow miraculously sprung back into life, when the sound of a vehicle approaching at full speed and screeching tyres on the tarmac, unnerved me completely. I had made it in the nick of time.

Hurrying towards the front door, I saw the lights in Mavis's quarters switch on. Wearing a loose floral nightie and carrying something, she rushed towards me and called out frantically, "Chantelle, what's going on?"

Relieved to see Mavis, I flung my arms around her saying, "Let's get inside the house where we're safe."

We hurried inside and bolted the door. Mavis switched on the lights. We flopped onto kitchen chairs and I plonked my camera equipment on the table. It was only then that I noticed Mavis had come to my rescue, armed.

"Whew, Mavis!"

"*Ag,* Chantelle. I was going to use this," she responded brandishing a long *sjambok*.

"I heard the speeding car then brakes like a squealing pig having its throat cut…"

"*Eish*, Mavis, I was so lucky," I cut in.

I explained very briefly what had just happened. She listened and after a few seconds replied, "You come home so late. You not tell me. I'm so worried for you."

"I'm sorry Mavis, but I didn't expect to be home so late…"

"Thank my God you're okay. Chantelle, we both, need a cup of *rooibos* with honey for the nerves."

While Mavis made the tea, I wondered to myself what I would do without Mavis. Tonight she had put her life on the line for me. She's much more than a maid and more than a mother to me. Mavis has been my protector and my advisor since I was a little girl.

As we sat sipping our tea, I sensed Mavis wanted to know more. Before she had a chance to question me further, I switched on my cellphone and texted: *Home safely. Had one of my best days with you Stephan. Cheers. C xxx*

I waited for a reply. Nothing.

Feeling somewhat disappointed I turned to Mavis and hugged her, saying, "Wow! Look at the time. We'd better get some sleep. Thanks so much for everything and we'll talk again in the morning."

Mavis retreated to her quarters locking the kitchen door after her. I walked wearily down the passage clinging to my cellphone hoping it would alert me of a text from Stephan…

Chapter Six

I was woken up by bleeps as text messages arrived on my cellphone. Ugh! I should have put it on silent so I could have a lie in. Did yesterday really happen? Stephan?
Maybe it's his text. I sprang out of bed and reached for my phone.

Text message from Kirsty: *You up?*
My reply: *I am now. C xxx*
Kirsty: *You alone?*
Me: *Hell yes!*

My phone rings. It's Kirsty saying, "Hey darl. I can't wait to find out what happened yesterday. Are you going to see Stephan again?"

I cleared my throat before replying, "I wish. But I doubt it."

"Give the guy a chance."

"Kirsty, it was only a prize date don't forget."

"I don't remember the prize including a day out at Nkuti Sanctuary!" she snipped.

"*Ja*, I guess."

"What you up to today?"

I lowered my voice, "You'll never believe what happened last night!"

"What?"

"I was almost carjacked. If it wasn't for Mavis who scared them off…"

"What the hell! How? Where? Are you okay? Is Mavis okay?"

"*Ja,* still in shock I guess. Feel numb."

"I'm coming over."

"Sounds good. I'll jump in the shower. See you just now."

It was good to unburden with Kirsty on Saturday. She wasted no time at all finding out what she wanted to know.

"So tell me what's going on. Tell me all about the hunk."

Her almond-shaped eyes lined with ink-black long lashes and perfectly shaped eyebrows, focused on me as I poured the wine.

"You mean Stephan!"

"*Ja*, Stephan Erasmus," she boasted.

"How do you know his surname?" I asked raising my eyebrows.

"He's more famous than you realise. Up-and-coming Olympic swimmer!"

"He mentioned he was training to get into the team. The heats are coming up soon," I said passing Kirsty a large glass of wine.

"Well, I did a bit of research on him and he's loaded…"

She took a sip of wine.

"He didn't suggest that to me. He was polite, charming and adventurous," I volunteered, curling my fingers around my glass of wine. I took a sip which cooled my parched mouth.

"Adventurous?"

"He takes me out to the Nkuti Wildlife Rehabilitation Centre, not telling me where we're going. Jeez! Then we end up in a ditch and narrowly avoid a black mamba. It all ended beautifully. I met Shumba, a white lion cub. So cute."

Kirsty sat up straight and put her glass down on the coffee table.

"In fact, I took some amazing photos."

"Cool. Let's see them," she said gleefully rubbing her hands together.

Kirsty followed me, glass of wine in hand, to my office. She stood next to me sipping her wine as I opened up the photos file on the screen of my *iMac* computer.

"Holy Moly! The white cub's just too adorable," Kirsty exclaimed with her eyes lighting up as she stared at the photos.

"Now I can see why you chose him as your date. He looks even more gorgeous than the night we met him. Lucky Shumba!"

She drooled over the shirtless photos of him in his jeans, his defined arms wrapped around Shumba.

"Chantelle, he's the perfect package. I'm jealous."

She leaned in closer to the screen to get a better view.

"This guy must fancy you. He didn't have to spend the entire day with you. It was supposed to be a breakfast date," she continued, stroking her chin as she ogled the photos.

"Nah! What would he see in me? Besides he's a perfectionist and cannot doesn't exist in his vocabulary."

"Stop that!" she scolded me in a firm tone.

"Come with me."

She took my hand and led me to the bedroom.

"Take a good look at yourself," she commanded as she faced me directly in front of the full-length mirror.

"Chantelle Swanepoel, you're more gorgeous than you realise."

My eyes dropped down. When I stood next to Kirsty I felt like a plain Jane with my mousy brown roots and chunky thighs.

"Take a good look at your attractive face with those exquisitely high cheekbones to die for."

I felt embarrassed. I was lucky to have Kirsty as a friend. It had been good to get this reassurance from Kirsty but I was not completely convinced.

The day had sped past and I was waving her goodbye, wondering if Stephan had texted me.

* * *

Monday drifted into Tuesday and with each passing day my hope of ever hearing from Stephan diminished. Mavis picked up on my mood swings but said nothing. Her advice was hard to follow when she told me, "If he wants you to be his friend, he will not let you go." But did he want me? It only takes a minute to send a text. The more I thought about the situation, the worse my mood. Had Stephan also dumped me? Two wounds of rejection were festering viciously in my being. My self-confidence was slipping and I wanted to withdraw, shut out the world around me.

On Wednesday Kirsty texted me: *Chantelle, wanted to make sure you're okay. What are you up to tonight? I can come over to your place for a glass of wine and a catch-up. K x*

I replied: *I'm okay, thanks. Can't wait to see you. Still, shit scared after my narrow escape. Come over now if you can. C xxx*

Kirsty replied: *I'm not surprised. Took me weeks to get over my carjacking experience last year. I've got some gossip for you to take your mind off things. I'm leaving right now. K x*

Kirsty was always in the know as she was a journalist and had a nose for any new information. An hour later the intercom buzzer rang.

"Is that you Kirsty?" I asked on the intercom.

"*Ja*, open up!" she said impatiently.

"Come in," I replied as the electric gates slid open when I held down the switch. The flood lights came on when Kirsty drove her car through the gates and up my driveway.

The gates closed automatically as I walked out to greet her. She climbed out her *Mazda* still wearing her gym outfit. Her black Lycra leggings and matching skimpy crop top accentuated her slim body. Her glossy brunette hair was tied in a sleek high ponytail with cascading curls down her back. Kirsty was not short of male attention.

I flung my arms out to give her a hug. We stepped inside locking the door.

"Would you like a glass of wine? I'll open a bottle of *Stellenbosch Shiraz*," I offered.

"Sounds good."

I went through to the kitchen opened the fridge door and removed a bottle of wine and grabbed two glasses with my free hand. Kirsty was slumped on my white couch when I entered the lounge.

"You're looking fit," I smiled at her.

"Well despite your ordeal a few days ago, you're glowing girl," she teased in her strong Joburg accent.

She sipped her wine and said, "I forgot to tell you. You know that cute guy you work with?"

I frowned, asking, "You mean Adam?"

"That's him. Well, he's been seen around town flashing cash and snorting coke. Looks like he's had a serious pay rise!"

"It can't be Adam. It must be some who looks similar to him."

"It's Adam. I'm telling you."

"Nah! I like Adam. He's a nice guy."

"Come on. How well do you know him?"

"I've worked closely with Adam for almost a year now. He's never come in hung over or speeding out from coke. In fact he asked me to dinner when I first started at *Afrika Fashions*. Put it this way. If I'd not been with Franco, I would've gone."

"Chantelle Swanepoel" You fancy Adam!"

I felt my face flush and giggled.

"He's rather cute. He's got a sexy smile. He always offered to make coffee and tea. He did not mind fetching lunch for me from the cafeteria. Adam and I often munched on our sandwiches together and laughed at silly jokes."

I paused as my thought wandered back to the last time I was alone in the office with Adam. That day the air-conditioning wasn't working. It was hot and sticky. He looked particularly desirable with his top shirt buttons undone; sleeves roughly rolled up and his brown hair tousled. He was so unlike Franco who never had a hair out of place and who was constantly washing his hands or using sterilising hand-gel. Adam had just returned with our wrapped-up tuna rolls for lunch. Fumbling in my purse for change, some coins tumbled down onto the floor. I crouched down to pick up the money and slipped onto my bottom. Adam squatted down in front of me. His
fingers gently moved a piece of my hair from my face. Our eyes locked.

From that moment onwards the magnetic energy between us intensified.

"Chantelle," Kirsty's voice snapped me back from my reverie.

I shook my head.

"Nah, Adam is NOT the guy you saw flashing cash or snorting coke. Definitely not."

* * *

A week had passed since my prize date and I just could not stop thinking of Stephan. It was driving me crazy, so I decided to put all my energy and focus into work. I had a degree in photography. I was presently contracted to a flamboyant fashion house, *Afrika Fashions,* as a freelance photographer. They were based in Rosebank, an affluent suburb of Johannesburg. This leading South African fashion house, proud of its celebrity clientele, was the brainchild of an attractive, smart and driven woman, called Tandeka Thebe.

Turning on my *iMac* I checked my emails. One from Tandeka had just arrived
in my inbox.

From: Tandeka Thebe (tandekat@Afrikfashions.co.za)
To: Chantelle Swanepoel (ChantelleS@freelancephoto@co.za)
Subject: Re: new project

Good morning Chantelle. A new job has arrived on my desk. Interested? Please let me know ASAP. Tandeka.

This was just what I needed, a chance to throw myself into my work. I immediately replied immediately:

Hello, Tandeka. Good to hear from you. I can call in the office today to discuss it. Let me know what time best suits you. Chantelle.

Her swift reply:

Hello, Chantelle. I'm in the office all day today so please do come by and see me. BW Tandeka.

I hastily changed out of my sweatpants and slipped into a fitted white linen dress and open-toed kitten heels. I touched up my make-up, grabbed my camera bag and my iPad and headed for my car.

I always felt I was in New York City as I arrived at the glass skylight entrance of the multi-storey contemporary office building. It was obvious that *Afrika Fashion's* offices were based there, by the large photos of glamorous fashion models posing in outlandish outfits.

Before reaching the elevators, I had to check in at the security desk, where a bald man handed me a security pass. As I reached the sixth floor, the lift door swooshed open and I stepped out into the lobby where Tandeka was talking to a tall, willowy model. She noticed me immediately.

"Darling! Good to see you! Come through to my office," she greeted me in her well-spoken voice. Her divine flowery perfume lingered ...oozing class. Tandeka was in her mid-thirties, gorgeously flamboyant. She bubbled with enthusiasm and energy. She was wearing an expensive beaded turquoise dress which accentuated her flawless beautiful black complexion and slim physique. Her makeup had been applied perfectly highlighting her exquisite high cheekbones, dark-brown eyes and glossy full lips.

We walked straight past the reception area into her office. She closed the office door behind her offering me a seat. I eased down into a chocolate brown leather chair.

"How are you?" she asked sitting down at her immaculately polished oak desk.

"Good and you?" I smiled.

"Busy and so stressed, Chantelle. I just hope you're up for this?" she arched her groomed eyebrow. When she got down to business, her demeanour changed. "An employee of mine's leaked some of our best ideas."

"Oh, my God! Who? What happened?" I asked as I tucked my hair behind my ears.

"Some imbecile. This is where I need your help," her eyes narrowed.

"Tandeka, that's terrible."

Taking a deep breath, she continued to give details in her calm voice. "I've hired a private investigator, who specializes in company espionage."

"This is serious. What actually happened?"

Tandeka vented, "Our biggest rival, *ZuluZaka,* launched our winter range last week, as *theirs!"*

"How the hell did they get their hands on that?" I hunched forward resting my elbows on the desk.

"I have my suspicions. Adam, my senior designer often disappears for long lunches after brain-storming." She tapped her pen with her perfectly manicured red painted finger nail.

"Not sweet Adam?" I clasped my hand over my mouth.

"*Ja*, darling. Rumour goes Adam developed a coke addiction, got himself into drug debt and paid his way by selling our winter range."

I shook my head saying, "I can't believe this!"

"What else am I supposed to think?"

She shrugged and carried on, "We've arranged a huge fashion show next week to launch our winter range with important celebs already confirming they're attending. Darling, we're talking big bucks. I've even got the contract here for you to be our chief photographer for the evening."

"*Ja,* count me in."

I eased back into my chair, relieved that this was the job she had bought me here to discuss.

"But, I have another job which I can only trust you to do."

"Oh, depends what it is, Tandeka."

She paused then whispered, "I need real evidence. Catch Adam on your camera."

I sat up dumbfounded. What the hell had I got myself into? This was going against my grain. Where would I get another job in today's employment climate if I don't do as Tandeka tells me? How will I pay my bills? I wouldn't be in this mess if Franco hadn't left me for that bitch. Now what choice do I have?

Chapter Seven

It was Friday and I was feeling deflated. I was coming down from the high of being with Stephan. Would I ever see or hear from him again?

"Get a grip Chantelle," I muttered. It was a date I'd won, so what was I getting all sentimental for? I guess a part of me wanted to believe he wanted to see me again, but my voice of reasoning quickly crushed that idea.

My thoughts were interrupted by my cellphone bleeping, alerting me that a text had arrived. I reached over to read the text from Kirsty.

Have you made plans for this evening? If not, do you want to go for drinks in Rosebank? K x

I was not a group sort of girl. I had a few close friends from various backgrounds. I wanted to see Kirsty, so I quickly replied:

Ja! Sounds good. Is 7 okay? C xxx

Spot on. See you in a few hours. K x

* * *

The trendy upmarket cocktail bar in Rosebank was lively and heaving with twenty and thirty-something year old's celebrating the beginning of the weekend. There was no getting away from the sports fanatics who were excitedly waiting for the live international rugby game to be aired on a big screen at the far end of the bar. Boisterous men were drinking beer and would soon be spurring on the South African *Springboks* playing against the New Zealand *All Blacks* in Australia.

Kirsty oozed sex appeal as her sensual figure perched on a stool at the bar. She was holding her purse and cellphone in one hand. She looked gorgeous and clearly proud of her rock-hard abs. She was wearing a barely-there backless white crop top and sheer skirt with a slit up one side. I felt all wrong in my jeans. I'd tried to add a bit of flair to my outfit with a loose white singlet top and several delicate gold necklaces. She'd had her hair styled into some high maintenance bob. Kirsty looked happy and relieved to see me as I made my way towards her through the crowd. She jumped off her stool to give me a warm hug enveloping me with her expensive perfume and then shrieked in my ear. "Good to see you. I've ordered a bottle of our favourite *Sauvignon Blanc*," she gestured towards the barmaid who was pouring two glasses.

"Thanks. Good thinking," I replied as I reached for my glass.

As we clinked our glasses Kirsty toasted, "To Chantelle and finding herself!"

"Er...now that's thought-provoking!"

Agreeing I raised my glass then took a sip of the refreshing fruity wine. I was hot and thirsty, so I took another gulp.

"My taste-buds adore this heavenly wine." I purred relaxing my back against the bar.

"I do love your hair. Who did it?" I moved a stray stand of hair off her eyelashes as I could see it was irritating her.

"Thanks hon. For a minute I thought an eyelash extension had fallen off into my eyeball."

"I thought they were your own. I would never have guessed you had eyelash extensions. Who suggested you get them?"

"Tristan, of course. He did my hair as well. I'm still getting used to it though."

Tristan, a gay drama-queen and our friend-cum-hairdresser, was a heavy pot smoker. Depending on how stoned he was, determined how good or bad his clients' hair turned out.

"Don't worry hun. You got him on a good day. Your hair looks amazing." I giggled.

Happy with my response she teased, "Chantelle you're wearing your come- hither stilettos tonight! What've you got in mind?"

Kirsty and I had the same sense of humour, which is another reason why we were good friends. We laughed louder as our wine bottle emptied. Our confidence soared the more the flirtatious men chatted us up

"Have you heard from Mr Sexy Swimmer?" she probed.

"Nah," I shook my head.

Handing me her cellphone she insisted, "Here phone Stephan, I bet he's very interested in you."

"No way. If he's interested he'll call," I snapped.

Almost immediately my cellphone started vibrating in my back pocket.

"Who'd be calling me on a Friday night?"

"Quick answer it." Kirsty said peering over at my phone.

"Damn! Missed it. Oh, it was a withheld number," I mumbled.

"Keep your phone out. They may call back."

Kirsty was becoming inquisitive. She didn't like to miss out.

It started to vibrate again in my hand showing a landline number this time. I hastily swung my hair out of the way, put my phone to my ear whilst carefully avoiding my silver hoop earring.

"Hello."

I could hear someone on the other end but couldn't decipher what they were saying.

"I can't hear you. Hold on whilst I go outside where it's quieter."

I mouthed to Kirsty I'd be back, and then attempted to push my way through the crowd of attractive women and loud, buff men engrossed in conversations and holding drinks in their hands.

After struggling to get out, I leant against the foyer wall to keep my balance. I was tipsy! Finally, I was able to hear clearly. I doubt the caller would still be there as it took me a good five minutes to get out. I put my phone to my ear asking casually. "Hello. I'm still here."

"Chantelle, is that you?" a concerned husky voice asked.

I recognized the voice but thought it couldn't be.

"*Ja*, who is this?" I asked straightening my shoulders.

"It's Stephan! Where are you?"

My heart galloped wildly as I felt my face flush.

"Where are you?" I repeated his question. I was definitely tipsy.

"At my brother's restaurant. I was calling to ask you to join me for a drink."

"Where's your brother's restaurant?" I asked trying to be cool and not wanting to show him how thrilled I was to hear his voice.

I remembered my mother's words *"Always play hard to get. Let the man do the running. He likes the chase."* I knew this was an old-fashioned point of view, but tonight it felt right for me.

"Chante you still haven't told me where you are?" Stephan was getting frustrated.

"In Rosebank."

"Where in Rosebank?"

"Chic @ Sports wine bar."

"You're just round the corner from me. I'll come and get you."

I could hear the excitement in his voice.

"I'm with my friend Kirsty," I cut him short.

"She can join us."

I could hear the reluctance in his voice.

"I'll have to ask her. Let me call you back."

I quickly ended the call. Leaning back against the wall I breathed deeply. Why did he want to see me? The intoxicating combination of wine and his voice triggered my endorphins, infusing me with delightful tingles of euphoria.

I made my way back inside. The crowd had subsided, so it was easier to get back to Kirsty.

"What took you so long? Who was it?" she asked.

"Stephan!" I blurted.

"Stephan? What did he want?"

"He asked me to join him for a drink at his brother's restaurant."

"He fancies you! This is the real Stephan wanting to see you not the Prize Stephan." She smugly lowered her voice, "So what did you say?"

"I told him I was out with you, so he told me to bring you along. I'm supposed to call him back."

"If his brother's as hot as him then count me in," she giggled.

"I don't want him to think I'm too keen. Let's wait a bit," I said.

"Let's have another drink then." Kirsty stood up to face the bar beckoning the barmaid.

I slid my bottom onto a high bar-stool while watching Kirsty order more wine. I jumped when a firm hand touched my shoulder. I sprung off the stool, spun around to face Stephan Erasmus. He smiled, "I told you I'd come and get you."

He smelt fresh and masculine again. Damn! He looked dapper in designer jeans and an open-neck blue cotton shirt under a navy blazer.

"Stephan! You made me jump."

"Sorry, I didn't mean to."

He patted me on my shoulder adding, "The heavens are about to open so we'd better get going. Are you ready?"

His hypnotic eyes met mine.

"Kirsty's just ordered drinks,"

I gestured to the bar.

"Leave the drinks. We can get more at my brother's restaurant," he said as he moved over to Kirsty. He removed a R100 note from his charcoal wallet and handed it to the barmaid.

"Keep the change," he told her then turned round to face Kirsty and me.

"Come let's go," he grabbed my hand and led me out of the bar with Kirsty trailing behind.

Once we were outside, a loud bang of thunder roared. Stephan briskly removed his blazer and placed it round my shoulders.

"Looks like a storm's on its way. Here wear this."

"Do we have far to go?" Kirsty asked putting her hand out to feel the raindrops and moaned, "Jeez, I've just had my hair done."

"Just round the corner. If we make a dash for it we'll get there before the heaven's open up," he shouted above another crack of thunder.

I slipped off my stilettos. Kirsty did the same. She lifted up her long skirt then started running barefoot past a row of boutique shops. We made our way through the Mall, dotted here and there with patrolling security guards.

"Chante let me give you a piggy back," Stephan casually lifted me onto his back then locked my thighs into his solid strong arms as my legs wrapped around his waist. My groins tingled deliciously as they gyrated up and down his hard muscled back. He sprinted past Kirsty to the corner then entered a posh-looking. There was a hum of diners and soft music. The white walls of the reception area displayed a collage of Greek Island scenes with accents of sparkling blue and sea-green.

I didn't want Stephan to put me down, I felt secure, warm and protected. He gently slid me off as a smart clean-shaven tall blonde man in his early thirties made his way over to greet us.

"I'd like you to meet my brother Anton," he introduced Kirsty and me.

His brother took my hand and gave it a firm handshake.

"Great to meet you!"

Then did the same to Kirsty.

"Anton's recently taken ownership of *Acropolis,* this Greek restaurant."

"The restaurant's full tonight guys," Anton said as he led us to a quieter area. We were seated at a gleaming white bar counter with colourful exotic fish tanks attached to the walls. The barman hastily made himself busy when he noticed Anton. "Good evening sir."

Anton handed us each a classy menu.

"Choose whatever you want. You're my guests tonight."

I had no appetite. What I needed was a stiff drink. Something to calm my nerves. The waiter brought us a bottle of champagne in a silver ice bucket, then another. We all lifted our glasses. An endless supply of snacks kept arriving.

Anton and Kirsty knocked back most of the champagne discussing world events. Kirsty was in her element being a journalist. Stephan took his time with his drink. His mysterious eyes locked into mine every time he took a sip.

Already tipsy from drinking earlier, I was now indulging in the sweet champagne letting the bubbles linger in my mouth. I learnt that Stephan and Anton had attended the best schools and universities. Anton was an imminent attorney and this restaurant was just a side-line. I wondered how wealthy this Erasmus family were.

Stephan confided in me. "I'm a private person. I left Cape Town to focus on my swimming and the wildlife sanctuary."

"What makes you tick then?"

I wanted to know all I could about him.

"My passion is swimming."

His eyes lit up as he leaned into me.

"Hobbies?" I quizzed.

"I like to watch Stephen King horrors."

"So, no romantic *flicks* for you?"

"Don't rule out a great love story. I've watched *Titanic*. What about you?"

He arched his eyebrows and waited for my response.

"Oh *ja*, *Titanic* is one of my favourite classics! I'm a *romcom* fan."

He pulled his stool in closer straddling is legs round my stool. Anton got up and went off to speak to diners. The music was turned up and couples had taken to the small dance floor. Stephan's stool screeched as he pushed it back.

"I'm just going to the gents," he announced.

Kirsty's face was flushed from drinking.

"Woah, look at you! Your eyes are sparkling," Kirsty giggled.

Anton returned with a couple, accompanied by an attractive, tall man with unruly copper hair, in his late twenties. After Anton introduced us, the couple engaged in conversation with Anton and Kirsty. The copper-haired man pulled up Stephan's barstool and sat down next to me.

'Someone's sitting there," I said in a formal tone as I pointed to the stool.

"I'll leave when they get back. Anyway, I'm Piet. Forgive me being forward, but you're one gorgeous woman."

He softly lifted my hand to kiss it brushing it past his rough stubble.

"Thanks!" I quickly pulled my hand away and crossed my arms.

"Can I get you another one of those?" he gestured to my glass of champagne.

"No thank you," I smiled whilst fidgeting with my hair.

There was an awkward silence. My eyes darted towards the full restaurant searching for Stephan. A loud dance track started playing.

"This is a *lekker* song. Come and dance!" he stood up to put his arm round my shoulder.

"She's with me!" a furious voice bellowed. I looked up to see Stephan standing over Piet as his eyes now changed to grey, flashed with anger.

"Sorry bro," said Piet as he backed off. Stephan clenched his fists as he moved closer to him.

"*Jislaaik,* there's no need to *klap* me. I was just talking to the lady," Piet replied before quickly turning to join the others.

"Who's he?" Stephan snorted pointing his finger at Piet.

"He arrived with that couple," I pointed in Anton's direction.

"I was only gone for five minutes and already other guys are making a move on you," his eyebrows lowered.

Feeling awkward I quickly changed the subject.

"Stephan I'm confused. You're eyes have changed colour."

"You do have an eye for detail. They change colour depending on my mood. Sometimes they even go dark grey, but that's only when I'm pissed off."

I felt a burn sizzle in my stomach, so I took a gulp of champagne. Before I could swig it down Stephan took the glass from me and placed it back on the table.

The lights started to dim and Anton leaned over and whispered something to Stephan. Stephan nodded. What were they discussing?

Kirsty was ready to go home. We had planned earlier that she would drive us home after the drinks, but now she was over the alcohol limit.

"Let's get a taxi. You're over the limit."

I reached my phone to call a taxi.

Stephan insisted he drive us home, but we stood our ground and ordered a taxi. He walked us to the cab when it arrived. Stephan opened the door to let us in. Every fibre of my being wanted him to kiss me. Was he going to kiss me? I had to restrain myself from pulling his head down to press his lips onto mine. Bold from the endorphin rush and excessive amounts of champagne, I pressed up against him and reached up to kiss his cheek. He pulled me into his hard body holding me tightly. I felt his heart thumping rapidly against my ear. He looked down at me then softly cupped my face into his warm hands.

"Come on Chantelle. The meters running," Kirsty slurred her words.

Damn Kirsty's timing.

"You'd better get in. Thanks for a great evening," Stephen whispered in my ear.

He held me for a few seconds, pulled away and pecked me on my forehead, then closed the taxi door for me.

Chapter Eight

I was alone and curled up in bed. Flashes of lightning lasered through my bedroom curtains. Blasts of thunder roared as the rain pelted down. Strong gusts of wind howled causing the windows to rattle loudly. I pulled the white sheet over my head as the storm lashed out. I longed to be cherished, held and protected. As my eyelids became heavy, I closed them to allow my thoughts to drift. I dreamt of Stephan that night.

I wasn't sure what woke me my throbbing head, dry sand-paper mouth or the sun glaring through my thin cotton curtains. I crawled out of bed and made my way to the bathroom. The cool-tiled flooring felt refreshing on my swollen bare feet. I looked disapprovingly back at myself in the mirror. I looked awful with dishevelled hair, puffy face and blood-shot red eyes. The mint toothpaste tingled on my tongue as I gave my teeth an extra brushing. I held my forehead trying to alleviate the pounding.

I could see Franco in my mind's eye disapproving of last night's over indulgence of alcohol, then prescribing his successful hangover formula of a high carbohydrate meal washed down with ibuprofen, paracetamol and plenty of water. I grabbed his recommendations from the medicine cabinet and glugged them down with a large glass of cold water.

It was another hot day. I pulled on my comfortable loose pale blue cotton shorts and strappy white vest. My thoughts kept going back to last night with Stephan. I can't believe I tried to make a move on him by kissing him. I was out of control after a drink too many. I cannot allow myself to drink like that again. I held onto my throbbing head.

"Morning Mavis," I greeted her as I entered the kitchen to make myself a cup of strong coffee. She could see something was wrong but she didn't want to pry.

"Morning Chantelle. Would you like some *rooibos* tea?" she asked in her tongue–clicking accent. *Rooibos* tea to Mavis was the solution to all life's problems.

"Ah thank you, but don't worry Mavis. I'll make myself some coffee. I'll need a few cups after the amount of champagne I drank last night."

I grabbed a bottle of cold water from the fridge, refilled my glass and gulped it down.

"That's the last time I drink like that again. I've never drunk like before!"

I moaned sympathetically to myself, nursing my throbbing head.

She disapprovingly shook her head and gave out a deep sigh.

"Please let me make you *rooibos* tea. It'll help you feel better."

"If you insist." I patted her affectionately on her back.

Mavis was a huge comfort to have in my life. I lethargically strode to the lounge, curled up on the couch and flicked through the TV channels before stopping at Sky News. Catching up with the news first thing in the morning was a habit I'd inherited from my parents.

There was no current breaking news. I moved over to the South African News to catch up on the weather. A smartly dressed weather reporter pointed to a map of South Africa and announced, *"Sunny conditions with a high of 35 Celsius, with no expected rain."*

My thoughts jumped back to Stephan Erasmus. I kept replaying last night in my mind's eye. He was protective and possessive over me. He became jealous when that Afrikaans Piet guy sat chatting to me at the restaurant. The more time I spent with Stephan, the more I became consumed with him. He wasn't like any other guy I'd ever met before. There was something mysteriously intriguing about him and I desperately wanted to get to see him again. The memory of his body scent and feeling his firm arms envelop me as he said goodnight, made me tingle between my legs.

The rattling of teacups perked me up when Mavis entered the room carrying a tray of *rooibos* tea and toast.

"Thanks, Mavis, it smells good."

"Mavis worried for Chantelle. Lately you not laugh and be happy like you were when …" she stopped abruptly realising that the mere mention of Franco's name was opening up a raw wound.

"You spoil me, Mavis. Thanks," I said pleased to have Mavis with me.

Her cheerful chubby face and nurturing nature was comforting. The tray was neatly set with a china teapot, jug of milk and teacups. There was a plate of fresh toast, butter and slices of cheese on the side. Feeding me was her way of mothering me. She always claimed I need fattening up.

I started to feel a bit more normal as the pain-relief medication kicked in. I reached over to the coffee table and poured myself a cup of *rooibos* tea. It tasted delicious...just what my body needed. After a bite of my crunchy buttered toast, I picked up *The Times* newspaper, which was delivered weekly. It was the same stories of doom and gloom, carjackings, murder, thefts and political rows.

On the front page my eyes were immediately drawn to a photo of a dead baby rhino. My grip tightened on the paper as I read the accompanying story. This innocent baby rhino was one of many that had been shot by ruthless poachers who sold their horns to satisfy the demand for ivory from a greedy illegal market. I wish someone would put a stop to it.

I turned to the entertainment section of the paper to see what movies or plays were showing. I enjoyed going to the cinema or to the theatre. What am I going to do today? I wonder what Kirsty's up to. She had a swimming pool in her garden and a cool refreshing swim would have gone down well. I reached for my cellphone to call Kirsty, but it went to her voicemail. She's probably still recuperating from last night.

Weekends used to be enjoyable but were now depressing. Couples were spending time together, or singles were out having fun. I was doing neither. I hated the weekends since Franco had left a few months ago. I lost my appetite, so even food was no longer a comfort to me. I would watch sad romantic DVD's, stupidly looking for possible reasons why Franco left me for someone else.

What was she like? An academic or dumb blonde? Was she putty in his hands, easy to manipulate this way and that?

Taking photographs and work were a great diversion. Stop self-wallowing I told myself, things could be worse as I reminded myself of some of the health scares I'd had in the past. Feeling much better, I stretched out my arms, poured another cup of tea and made my way out of the lounge.

"Thanks for the tea and toast Mavis. I'm going to do some work in my office," I said as I popped my head round the kitchen door.

I walked on down the passage to my north-facing office, which was gloriously bright and cheerful. But today it was too bright for my sensitive eyes. Glancing out the window I saw Lucky, my Zimbabwean gardener mowing the lawn. The smell of freshly-cut grass drifted through the open window. I closed the blinds to cool the room down. After switching on my *iMac* computer, I checked my emails. There was a new one from Tandeka. Damn. I hope she's not still asking me to spy on Adam. I did make it clear to Tandeka I didn't feel comfortable doing it even if that meant I jeopardised my contract. I had avoided her calls since our last meeting as I know how nasty she can get when she doesn't get her own way. I was so relieved to read it was only details of the winter collection which she wanted me to photograph.

I briefly went onto Facebook and did another search for Stephan and his brother Anton Erasmus but couldn't find either. I clicked out of Facebook and opened up my iPhoto album file to do some preparation work, but my eyes diverted to the album marked: *Franco and Chantelle/Mauritius trip.*

I clicked it to open. Scrolling through the holiday pictures, I remembered how happy we were. I zoomed into my favourite one of Franco that complimented his olive skin, fine features and straight, dark brown hair. His slim, six-foot physique looked well-groomed.

That was the first night he whispered he loved me over a bottle of *Moët et Chandon*. He poured his heart out to me which included his plan for us to grow old together once he had qualified as an orthopaedic surgeon. Five years later, having qualified two years earlier and working excessive overtime, he cut me off whenever I questioned our future, asking, "What type of house would you fancy?" His standard reply, "Not now Chantelle. Can't you see I'm busy," became his way of avoiding conversation involving our future together. We were drifting apart but I was too naïve to see it.

I closed the file and intended to go back to my work events album, but ended up opening the file marked: *Nkuti Wildlife Rehabilitation Sanctuary/October 2015*. With just a click, Stephan was staring back at me. He was the epitome of male beauty. This photo confirmed he was out of my league and besides, he was a couple of years younger than me I reminded myself. He could have his pick of women. I stared at his eyes. What were they hiding? Could I face being dumped again?

I moved onto the next photo of the adorable lion cub Shumba – a day I will never forget. I continued ogling blissfully at the photos of my day at the wildlife sanctuary. The buzzer went interrupting my thoughts.

Mavis answered it and opened up the gate. I presumed it was someone for her. I peered through the blinds to check who it was and saw Franco climbing out his silver *Mercedes*. My heart raced as I watched him make his way to the front door.

I hadn't seen him since the night at the carpark when I gleefully told him, "Don't bother. They're long gone in the trash!" referring to his belongings he intended to collect. Prior to that meeting the last time I saw Franco was the morning when I had no inclination whatsoever that he wouldn't be returning.

I quickly switched off the computer. By the time I was out my office, Franco dressed in blue scrubs, was already in the spare room randomly pulling his clothes from the cupboard and throwing them into a suitcase.

"What the hell are you doing?" I blurted standing in front of him with my hands on my hips.

"What does it look like? I'm taking the rest of my things," he snarled.

"You're not welcome here. Get out!"

I felt my jaw tighten and a lump form in my throat.

"You're lucky I didn't throw them in the bin, where they belong," I flung back at him as my eyes started to sting when tears formed and trickled down my cheek.

"I just couldn't face you after what I did to you," his voice softened. His cellphone rang. He answered formally, "Dr du Preez."

Then he walked out the room and down the passage to continue his conversation. After a few minutes, he returned.

"I'm on call this weekend," he informed me putting his phone back into his top pocket.

"Let me get this out," I vented. "I really don't know what our relationship was to you, but to me, we were a couple setting up home together."

"Chantelle because–"

I cut him off. "What sort of a man ends a five-year relationship with a text? You hurt me, Franco. I believed you were working overtime, not in another woman's bed."

"I'm so sorry Chantelle. I made a terrible mistake. I know I can be selfish and arrogant."

"Wait. Stop right there. The past few months have been hell for me," I hissed as I felt the blood fuel my face with anger.

"I'd do anything to go back to that moment. I screwed up. I'm not that same man."

"And I'm not that same woman anymore."

There was a brief silence before I continued, "Franco, Did you ever love me?"

"Yes, Chantelle and I still do."

He reached in his top pocket for his cigarettes.

"Read this; I'm going outside for a smoke."

He handed me the newspaper. I sat on the bed next to Franco's packed suitcase. On page 2 was a photo of Franco in his blue hospital theatre scrubs, stethoscope draped round his neck and a bold headline:

Johannesburg Surgeon, Dr Franco du Preez joins the London's top orthopaedic team.

The article went on: *Dr du Preez has been chosen to join Professor*

Peter Jones and his team. This charismatic orthopaedic surgeon trained at University of Cape Town, medical school. He did his internship at Pretoria Hospital and completed his community service year in the surgical department of Makafobi Hospital. Dr du Preez is presently the consultant surgeon at Millbank Clinic, Johannesburg.

I read on holding the paper tighter. Why do I always choose unavailable men?

I slapped the newspaper back into Franco's hands as he walked in.

Franco in London. The finality was slowly sinking in. Did I really want to know? I could not restrain myself from asking, "So when do you leave?"

"As soon as possible. There's so much paper work. I have to organise a work permit, rent out my house, you name it." His tone softened, "Chantelle, it was a tough decision to make. Just give me one more chance. Come to London with me. I'll find you a good job there."

Franco knew exactly how to lure me. He was so cunning even to promising to find me a job in London. Had he forgotten that it was he who dumped me? What makes him even think I'd consider coming back to him? Oh no! There's no way I was prepared to take the risk of being dumped by him a second time, in London.

I lowered my eyes shaking my head.

"Zelda and I are no longer together," he moved closer to try and hug me. I took a step back.

"You broke my heart, you know that. Don't you? You can't just walk back into my life and expect things will be back to normal."

Trying to maintain the upper hand, he zipped up his leather suitcase and apologised, "I'm sorry. I'm just taking my clothes. You can have the other things."

Was there a hint of tears in his brown eyes? I was numb and speechless. Then I choked as I tried not to sob. I didn't deal with goodbyes very well. This time Franco was walking out of my life for good. I wondered if I was to blame. So when he turned his back to walk away from me, my tears started flowing uncontrollably.

Chapter Nine

I cried myself to sleep that night as sorrow and loss spilt onto my pillow. I felt isolated, deflated and betrayed.

Waking up on Sunday morning I realised this was Mavis' day off. I leant over to my bedside table and reached for my cellphone to check the time. I called my mom hoping to catch her before she went to church. After two rings she politely answered, "Swanepoel residence."

"Mom, it's Chantelle."

"Chantelle! I was about to call you. Why don't you come over for Sunday lunch?"

I wasn't hungry but I also hadn't seen my parents for a few weeks.

"*Ja,* count me in. Do you want me to stop at the shops?"

"Hmmm...No. Just come over. I'm on my way to church now, so I'll see you later."

"Okay, mom. See you in a few hours," I said ending the call.

After a light breakfast and browsing the Sunday papers, I had a cool shower. I pulled on a comfortable sundress and slipped my feet into flip-flops. I layered concealer under my puffy eyes to hide any signs of sobbing. I grabbed my cellphone. Setting the alarm, I locked the house, which now felt like a vacuum without Franco yet so many reminders of him haunted me.

There was very little traffic as I drove down the main road, lined with crimson-leaved flamboyant trees reminding me it was summer. Mom and dad had downscaled to a two-bedroom, gated townhouse nearby. Using my set of keys, I let myself in through the front entrance and walked through a bougainvillea archway into their neat garden sprinkled with roses, pink and purple petunias and bright yellow sunflowers. Dad was a chartered accountant for a corporate company. Mom was a primary school teacher.

The aroma of roasted garlic chicken greeted me as I entered my parent's kitchen. I spotted a freshly-baked milk tart, sprinkled with grated nutmeg and lemon zest, on the kitchen table. Not able to resist, I grabbed a piece on my way into the dining-room where mom was setting the table. She was a petite slim 5ft with a flawless olive skin. Today she wore a hint of red lipstick.

My mother rarely wore make-up apart from when she attended church. Her salt and pepper hair had been curled and sat just above her shoulders. Mom was still dressed in her church outfit, a smart knee-length floral dress. The odour of her perfume, lavender mixed with hints of musk, filled the room.

"Wait till after lunch before you eat that tart!" she scolded me as she looked up. Nothing escaped my mother.

"What's wrong with you my girl? You've been crying! Is it that bloody arrogant Franco again!" Mom hissed as her eyebrows arched into her mildly furrowed forehead.

From the living room, Dad peered over the newspaper his specs perched precariously on the tip of his pale nose. He was fair-skinned, freckled, with patches of what was once-ginger hair now faded to grey, dotted on the edges of his balding head. Dad was emotionally absent and had always been. I don't ever remember him telling me he was proud of my achievements at school. He had never said he loved me. He showed no affection, emotionally or physically.

Mom tried to make up for it with hugs. A few years ago when I was stranded, his reply was, "You're old enough to take care of yourself."

"He's moving to London," I blurted out bursting into tears.

My father remained expressionless but my mother's eyes narrowed when she responded. "About time. Pointless wasting another tear on that man."

There was not even a hint of compassion. I stood there helpless.

"Please, Mom! I'm sick of people dropping in and out of my life," I whimpered through salty tears.

"Pull yourself together Chantelle. You know it's for the best."

She went on, "I told you it would never work. He's a womaniser. God knows how he ended up in the medical profession. He's selfish."

Her hazel eyes narrowed even more.

"Enough! Besides, he's gone now forever."

"I don't know what you saw in the man."

"Mom, it's pointless me being angry with Franco. Like Nelson Mandela quoted: *Resentment is like drinking poison and then hoping it will kill your enemies.* When I was at my lowest, riddled with bulimia, Franco understood. He gave me hope, courage and confidence to be myself despite my shape and size. Without me being fully aware of it, he played a huge part in helping me to overcome my eating disorder."

"How?" she snorted.

"By not reprimanding me like you constantly do," I retorted.

Mom interrupted, "What are you talking about?"

"If I didn't stick to a diet, you'd criticize me."

I paused then continued, "I was already angry with myself and drowning in guilt which triggered me to binge. I was my worst enemy."

"Chantelle! I was trying to help you. When life knocks you down, you have to bounce back."

"Mom, Franco taught me moderation, how to listen to my body."

Dad interrupted us. "I see Bon Jovi is heading to SA in a few months!" He read from the paper.

Too steeped in self-pity, I ignored my dad as I remembered what had started my eating disorder. In those days I would stupidly allow myself to get so hungry. This would force me to break my diet. By indulging my taste buds in delicious, sensual food I created feelings of short-lived pleasure and bliss only to come crashing down to feelings of utter failure. The following days and weeks I'd punish myself by having just one meal of bland boiled chicken and dry lettuce leaves. My life had become a roller-coaster ride of emotions, flying high with euphoria then drowning deeply in guilt. I was ashamed. My father was aware of my problem, but he just could not understand why I could not eat normally. But what was normal? I had lost all concept of normal eating. Mom had tried to help me in her own way.

I returned home feeling drained. Falling asleep that night I concluded. I had survived another Sunday and had a busy week ahead of me.

* * *

I was running late for work and was hastily gulping down my last sip of coffee, when my cellphone rang. I didn't recognise the number. It must be Tandeka. Only she would call at this time of day.

'Hello." I answered in my business voice.

"Chante it's me, Stephan "

"Stephan!"

I froze. There was a brief silence which felt like hours.

"You sound surprised. Hope I didn't get you at an inconvenient time."

"No you haven't, I was just on my way to work. How are you?"

"Well at the moment I couldn't feel better! I've been short-listed for *Sportsman of the Year* award."

"Wow, congrats."

"And I'd like you to accompany me!" he paused waiting for my reply. I wanted to shout yes before he changed his mind, but I didn't.

"When's the event?"

"Saturday evening. Please say YES Chantelle!"

"Maybe," I flirted. "I'll text you the venue, time and..."

"Hmmmmm! I don't know for sure yet," I interrupted him holding my phone to my ear with my shoulder and using my free hand to lift my camera bag over the other shoulder, whilst I rummaged in my handbag looking for my car keys.

"Oh come on!" he insisted.

I could listen to his sensual voice all day instead of rushing off to work.

"I'll collect you," his tone sobered.

"It's okay. I can drive there."

"No ways! It's not SAFE. Chantelle."

"Stephan! I still haven't said yes!"

"But you've just said you wanted to drive yourself there!" he teased in a confident tone.

"You don't give up!"

"I'm a competitive swimmer don't forget!" he chuckled.

I was beginning to like the feeling of being chased.

"Okay, email me all the details. Shit! What am I going to wear?' I was suddenly becoming anxious now that I had agreed to go.

"You'll look good in anything!" he flirted.

"Haha! Thanks. I'll text you my email address."

"And your home address. I'll be at your place for six, so we can be there for seven," he insisted.

"What's it with you and safety?"

"Chantelle! Carjackings are rife in Joburg. You know that."

"Okay, I'll go, but on one condition I drive myself there." I insisted.

There was an awkward pause.

"You win. But you'll struggle to find parking. If you insist on me not coming to your place, park at Anton's restaurant and I'll collect you from there."

"Okay, that's a plan then."

"Be there for seven, but go inside the restaurant. Don't hang around the car park. I'll get Anton to look out for you." he ordered.

"Stephan, I've got to go now. I'm running late for work."

"Okay, I'll see you on Saturday evening at seven. Don't forget to text me your email details."

Stephan Erasmus had just invited me to accompany him to the awards? It still had not sunk in. I must look the part for the awards ceremony. Especially if he wins! I could feel my breathing become shallower and harder as I visualised myself on the arm of Stephan. I called Kirsty whilst walking down the street to *Afrika Fashions* but it went to her voicemail.

I sent a sent her a text: *Darl call me ASAP. I've got some exciting news! C xxx*

I was bursting to share my thrilling news. I knew how to get her attention. Kirsty wouldn't miss out on any gossip!

Relieved that Tandeka was away on a business trip in Cape Town searching for fabrics, I would be able to focus on editing the winter collection. My thoughts were interrupted by Kirsty ringing.

"Sorry I missed your call," she whispered.

"Why you speaking so quietly."

'I'm in the ladies loo. I had to sneak out of a meeting. So tell me this news."

"Stephan's asked me to the sports awards on Saturday," I exploded with enthusiasm.

"Oh my God! I've just heard he's on the shortlist! You're dating Mr Sportsman."

"It's only a date Kirsty and he's not won yet!"

"Damn girl! This will be a real date and not just a prize. The TV cameras will be there. It's a huge event. Chantelle you'll be on the other side of the camera this time," her voice became louder with excitement.

"What the hell have I let myself in for?"

'You'll be fine. I'll come over to your place after work tomorrow. I'll bring some smashing dresses for you so that you can choose an amazing outfit. You'll outshine all the others."

"I'd love that. I feel like I'm going on a prom date."

"*Eish*! Let me get back to the meeting," she said.

"*Ja,* you naughty girl!"

I screeched my chair back and started pacing the small office. Thoughts and visions of Stephan sparked excited feelings as my head swirled with serotonin spiked with adrenaline. My thoughts were consumed with Stephan. I spent my lunchtime sat at my computer searching for the ideal outfit. It had to be classy and glamorous. I tapped and tapped away on the desk with the end of my chewed pencil.

My next phone call was to Tristan, our gay hairdresser. He was busy with a client but his receptionist managed to find an appointment for me on Saturday.

I read and re-read Mondays Daily Inspirational Quote. Was the universe trying to tell me something? *You have to be uncomfortable in order to be successful, in some ways. If you stay in your comfort zone! You would never do the things that you need to do."* (Lights Boxleitner)

Chapter Ten

I ran myself a bubble bath. As I eased down into the warm water, all the tension of the day seeped from my body; I relaxed. The sweet fragrance from the jasmine flowers oozed through the open top frosted bathroom window. I caught the last glimpse of the full moon as my tired, heavy eyelids slowly closed. My mind drifted through the day's events.

Stephan! What makes this man tick? What lies underneath his exterior of power, authority and confidence? Does he think of me? I secretly hoped so! Why could I not get this man off my mind?

I melted into my mattress wearing a silk cameo nightie, with a crisp white cotton sheet covering me. It was a hot, dry night, silent apart from the gentle whirl of the ceiling fan and the usual annoying buzz of mosquitoes. I tossed and turned that night, constantly checking the clock next to my bedside.

"Stop this Chantelle," I said to myself as horrendous visions relating to the 9mm black pistol which was hidden in the cubby hole of Stephan's *Land Rover,* surfaced.

* * *

On Tuesday night Kirsty came over to visit. She was determined to make me dazzle and arrived with an armful of dresses and shoes.

"You're a size 14 still I hope!" Her eyes twinkled.

"Damn girl! You've bought the shop with you! Where did you get all those dresses?" I gasped.

"They're from *Lipsy* on appro."

"*Lipsy London* here in South Africa?" I asked.

"*Ja,* they launched it last month. Their dresses ooze glamour." she replied

"*Eish*, I'll never fit in any of those," I shrieked with excitement.

"Maria, a woman I work out with at the gym, is the manager. She organised them for us, but we must return the goods tomorrow."

Kirsty sounded breathless. I gave her a hand carrying some of the dresses.

"That's the one," Kirsty shrieked.

"Look I googled it on their website yesterday. It read: *electric-blue, full-length bandeau maxi dress, featuring pleated bust with embellishment, side split and exposed back zip fastening. Perfect for adding Hollywood glamour to your wardrobe this season.*" Kirsty added.

"Kirsty, I'll need to get my spandex out for that!"

By midnight, after much changing in and out of dresses and shoes, we finally agreed on the right one. Various colours and styles of dresses were sprawled over my bed. Despite both of us being exhausted, we carefully folded the dresses back into their individual plastic covers and the shoes back into their boxes.

"Thanks darl for helping out. It means a lot to me. You're a star." I said.

"Anytime hun, just wish I could also be there."

"See if you can get hold of a ticket," I suggested.

"I did, but they're sold out."

'*Jislaaik*! The place will be buzzing."

"*Ja*, with celebs." she giggled.

"Stay over tonight. It's too late to drive home," I suggested.

"Good idea. I'm knackered."

She made her way to the guest room where she usually slept when she stayed over.

"I'm going to bed now."

"You'd best get plenty of beauty sleep for Saturday!" Kirsty called out.

"See you in the morning," I answered, yawning.

After removing my make-up and brushing my teeth, I flopped into bed. My body was exhausted, but my mind raced with thoughts of Saturday night. I rehearsed the possibility of him winning. I was excited, happy and overwhelmed so tossed and turned the entire night.

I must have finally fallen asleep because when I awoke, sunlight was stream-ing through my curtains. Kirsty's high-pitched voice called out, "Wakey, wakey!"

I looked up and she was standing at the bottom of my bed, dressed smartly for work in a buttercup yellow, sleeveless shirt tucked into a fitted, black pencil skirt.

"Morning. What's the time?" I asked, rubbing my gritty eyes.

"Time to get up. Are you able to return the dresses today?" she asked.

I nodded and yawned.

"Cool thanks. Please return them before they close at five."

She looked relieved.

"Of course, that's the least I can do after you so kindly organised everything for me."

"Sorry I have to rush. I'm late as usual. Call you later."

She scurried down the passage.

After a shower and breakfast, Mavis and I bundled the dresses and shoes into my *VW Golf.* I sensed Mavis' confusion because she always warned me not to be extravagant or wasteful. Her purchases demanded careful evaluation and were always driven by absolute need. I had some explaining to do, but right now I had to return the goods to *Lipsys*.

* * *

The week dragged by. Saturday finally arrived and the first thing I did was to drive to *Lioness Maine* hair studio. Tristan wasn't difficult to miss in his tight, black leather trousers and zebra-print shirt. He was standing outside puffing on what I hoped was a cigarette and not a spliff. Today was not the time to experiment on my hair. His face lit up as I walked up to him.

"Darling! Good to see you," in his sing-song Johannesburg drawl.

"You've bleached and straightened your hair," I noted.

"Well, what's left of it! Doesn't it look good against my coloured skin?" He spun round showing me his new short haircut.

"Suits you," I smiled truthfully. His bleached hair did accentuate his caramel skin.

"I'm extra busy today so let's start on your hair before my next client pitches up."

Tristan made his way back into his neat salon. I followed closely coughing on the potent smell of hair dye. The walls were sprawled with pictures of models with high-maintenance hairstyles. He sat me down on a black hairdresser's chair then morphed into work mode.

"What am I going to do with this mess? Look at your roots!" he snorted. Outspoken Tristan went on, "I told you to keep it trimmed and coloured regularly."

Before I could respond, he was showing me various shades of blonde on a colour chart.

"I think N9 alternating with G8 with a few N10," he suggested.

"Tristan, you know I haven't a clue what those codes mean. Just describe the finished colour," I replied feeling frustrated as I battled to be heard above the loud dance music.

"Darling! Leave it to me. I'll transform you into a honey-blonde sun-kissed bombshell."

"Do you want a coffee?" he asked.

"*Ja*, please. Milk no sugar."

"Nesta!" he shrieked.

I pitied anyone having to work for Tristan. No wonder he had such a high staff turnover. A young apprentice emerged from the back of the salon.

"Get a coffee with milk and no sugar for my client. And turn that music down," he ordered in one breath.

Tristan handed me a pile of magazines.

"Here's some juicy *goss* to read darling. I'm going to mix your colours."

Minutes later the apprentice returned with my coffee, nicely presented on a polished silver tray accompanied by wafer-thin chocolate biscuits.

Tristan followed pushing a squeaky trolley with bowls of hair dyes, brushes and strips of tinfoil. He got straight to work on my hair, painting the dye onto various sections before wrapping them in tinfoil.

"Is it true you have a date with Stephan Erasmus tonight?"

There was no hiding anything from the queen of gossip,Tristan.

"*Ja,* where did you hear that?" I felt my face flush.

"Darling! I'm a gay hairdresser and nothing gets past me! Where did you meet him?" he quizzed.

"It's a long story you know, but he's asked me to accompany him to the Sportsman Awards Ceremony tonight."

"F…k!" he shrieked in his camp voice. "Even more reason for me to put in some extensions for added glamour."

"Extensions?" I asked.

"Darling, hair extensions. They're all the rage. Most celebs are sporting them. What are you wearing? A sexy number, I hope!"

"Of course!" I winked.

"Damn! Can I come with you? All those buff sportsmen! Lucky bitch!" he went on, excitedly wiggling his hips.

Three hours later my hair was finished.

"Wow! Your hair looks so pretty."

Nesta's eyes twinkled and she admired me.

Tristan held a mirror, showing me the back. I didn't recognise my hair; a cascade of long golden curls tumbled down my back. This couldn't be me. It just confirmed why I continued going to Tristan, despite his bluntness.

"See what a difference a few hair extensions can make!" he assured me with his brown eyes lighting up.

"Enjoy tonight and send me pics or even better put them on Facebook," he added giving me one huge tight hug.

* * *

My stomach tightened nervously as I realised that in less than six hours I would be in the arms of my handsome date, Stephan Erasmus.

Stephan was punctual and waiting for me in the reception of his brother's restaurant. It was the first time I'd seen him dressed formally. He was absolutely gorgeous and dapper in a black designer suit, a pristine shirt, silver cufflinks and a navy tie. His aftershave engulfed me when he bent down and kissed me on my cheek.

"Wow, you look stunning. I love your dress," he said with his striking hazel eyes glowing.

"Thank you. You're looking good yourself," I replied, smiling.

With a beguiling smile, he handed me a bouquet of freshly-cut long-stem red roses saying, "These are for you." His eyes held my gaze.

"Thanks, Stephan. I adore roses."

"Shall we be on our way? Kevin, my coach, is already waiting for us."

"Here let me take those from you," he suggested.

After taking the bouquet from me, we made our way outside to the car park.

He was in another car tonight, not his *Land Rover* where he kept his black 9mm pistol in the *cubbyhole*. He opened the passenger door to an immaculate two-seater red sports car. I hadn't seen one like that before. The smell of new leather upholstery greeted me as I climbed into the low-slung coupe. The luxurious, black bucket seat hugged the sides of my body. Once Stephan was in the driver's seat, he pushed a shiny button. The engine roared into life, evoking an ecstatic glow on his face.

"Is this yours?"

"*Ja*, I only got it this week. It's my new toy." He revved the powerful engine.

"Wow, what is it?"

"It's the new *Audi R8 V10.*"

He proudly pulled away at full speed. I was thrown back into my seat. I wasn't sure if the butterflies in my stomach were from the acceleration of the sports car or sitting next to Stephan. I was snugly cocooned in my seat as we turned sharp corners

"Are you nervous for tonight?" I asked.

"Me? No!" he replied in a cool, controlled tone.

"How was your week?"

"Busy. How's Shumba?" I probed.

"He's okay."

His lips curved into a smile.

"I've been swimming and gym training every day. I was down at the pool this morning and the press pitched up interfering with our routine. They'll be swarming all over the place tonight."

"Tell me about it. Will your mother be there?" I quizzed.

"No, they're at the Vic Falls. My step-dad is in the process of buying a business franchise."

His cellphone rang. He glanced at the caller display. "Talking of which it's my mother."

He answered the call. "Hi mum, you're on speaker-phone because I'm driving."

"Okay son, hope you're not speeding," she replied sounding like a mature elegant woman.

"No, I'm not."

"We wanted to wish you good luck," a deep male voice in a strong Afrikaans accent joined the conversation.

"Thanks, Hans."

"We'll be thinking of you," his mother butted in.

Then the phone went dead.

"Shit! We get cut off whenever they call from there. The bloody networks in Zimbabwe are a nightmare."

I grabbed hold of my seat as he weaved in between cars.

"Do you consider driving at this speed a sport?" I blurted.

"Sorry, I got carried away with my new toy." He immediately slowed down.

"I'm afraid we'll crash."

"I won't let anything happen to you," he reassured me with a pat on my knee.

Driving through heavier traffic, he became quiet. I couldn't even fault his profile. Straight nose, square jaw and clean-shaven.

My stomach tensed as we drove into the venue. I slipped my lipstick from my clutch bag and slicked on a final coat. The minute the car stopped, a uniformed valet rushed up to open the car doors.

"Good evening ma'am. Good evening sir," he greeted politely.

After handing his car keys over to the valet, Stephan clasped his warm hand over mine sending electric sparks through me.

"Ready?" He smiled.

"I nodded," taking in a deep breath. My mind was racing with questions. Would I fit in socially? Was I wearing the right dress? Would Stephan abandon me to hang out with his team mates?

My knees shook as his grip tightened. He proudly walked beside me into a brightly-lit large auditorium. Camera flashes blinded us. This was all new to me as I was used to being on the other side of the lens. TV crews and more cameras were strategically placed and ready to film the awards. I kept reminding myself to look natural and to smile.

Whiffs of expensive perfumes and aftershaves mingled in the air. Men in dress suits were accompanied by young and mature women, dressed in glamorous designer evening gowns.

"Stephan, over here," a smart sun-crisped middle-aged man beckoned. We made our way to him.

"*Howzit!* You and your guest will be sitting near the front with us," he gestured towards the stage.

Stephan introduced me saying, "Meet Kevin, my coach. Chantelle...Kevin."

"Hi, Chantelle, good to meet you. Let's hope our boy wins tonight."

"Have you got your speech ready?" he asked Stephan.

"No!"

"Positive thinking Steph."

"Just kidding, Kev!"

He whipped out a neatly folded piece of A4 paper from his pocket.

"Okay, put it back, so you don't lose it. Chantelle, have you seen Stephan in the pool?" Kevin asked.

"Not yet."

"Let me tell you this guy has incredible speed and focus. Not so Steph?"

"That's cos I'm at home in the water."

They spoke briefly about swimming but Stephan insured I was included in the conversation.

"Can I get you both a drink?" Kevin changed the subject as he raised his bushy dark eyebrows.

"A glass of white wine please."

"And you Steph?"

"Just water, for now, Kev."

"Good lad. You shouldn't be drinking much anyway with your new intensive training programme." he said patting Stephan on the back.

"Just going to the ladies," I whispered to Stephan.

There was already a queue forming; I glanced around to see if I recognised anyone. A model from *Afrika Fashions* was in front of the queue. Her tall physique towered above everyone. She flicked her waist-length black hair around as she chatted loudly on her phone.

Did she also have hair extensions like me? When it was her turn to use the cubicle she spent ages in there, constantly flushing the toilet. She was still in there by the time I'd finished. What was she doing?

After I'd washed and dried my hands, I stepped back from the mirror, smoothed down my fitted evening dress trying not to pull off the diamantes, which were meticulously glued on. I had worn the correct outfit. I touched up my eye make-up and slicked on more lip-gloss.

The model strode out the cubicle wiping her nose.

"Chantelle! I didn't recognise you all glammed up. Girl, you look stunning!" she sniffed as her dilated pupils glistened.

"You look gorgeous yourself as usual," I answered hoping she hadn't noticed I'd forgotten her name. Long gold, sparkly earrings glistened against her beautiful flawless black complexion.

"Thanks, darling. So are you one of the photographers tonight?" she purred whilst bending over to wash her hands. She chatted to me whilst confidently admiring herself in the mirror.

"No, I'm here as a guest with one of the finalists."

"Oh who?" her elegant eyebrows arched as she spun round to face me.

"Stephan Erasmus."

"Oh my God! That handsome creature. You've got to hook me up with him," she shrieked loudly catching the attention of ladies washing their hands at the basins.

"Shhh," I put my finger to my lips. She was obviously high.

I turned to leave with her close behind. Damn! How am I going to lose her? All I needed was for Stephan to be smitten by her magnetic beauty. Thankfully her attention was diverted by friends who were waiting for her.

The chatter and laughter became louder as the auditorium started filling up with more guests.

"Stephan! You look amazing," gushed a pretty mixed race, young woman in a low-cut silver mini dress. I bristled as she edged closer to him.

"Bianca! Long time," he answered looking surprised.

"How the hell have you been since moving to Joburg?" she flirted with her body language and played with her brown curly hair. Bianca blabbered on, "That's so cool. You're a finalist!"

Her dangly earrings swung around as she lunged in to hug him. Stephan swiftly pulled back. Her face flushed with embarrassment.

"Got to go," she muttered and abruptly moved on.

"Awkward!" Stephan muttered, rolling his eyes.

Smartly dressed waiters and waitresses swarmed around the guests serving them from trays of delicious snacks. Kevin returned with our drinks before he disappeared back to the bar.

"*Howzit bro*," a suave guy slapped Stephan playfully on the shoulder. His grey trousers and fitted black expensive shirt accentuated his lean torso. His matching bow tie sat just below his clean-shaven copper-coloured complexion.

"Lucas! Good to see you man."

Stephan shook his hand.

"Meet my girlfriend, Deepa."

He introduced an exotic, slender Indian girl wearing a red thigh-slit, long evening dress.

"I've finally got to meet you. Lucas goes on about you."

He gently shook her slim hand with scarlet painted nails.

"Guys, meet Chantelle," he smiled, edging me forward.

"Ah, so Stephan Erasmus finally pitches up with a gorgeous woman at his side," Lucas bantered. Lucas pecked me on both cheeks.

"So *bro*, we're up against each other tonight," Lucas said.

"Swimming vs. athletics. May the best man win!" Stephan toasted with his glass of water.

"Ladies and gentleman please take your seats. We will be commencing in twenty minutes," the compere announced.

The hum of chatter subsided. Stephan grabbed my hand leading the way to our table ensuring I was comfortably seated.

"I'm just going to the gents," Stephan breathed into my ear.

After fifteen minutes Kevin joined me sitting on the other side of Stephan's empty seat. He leant over to make conversation, "Chantelle you must be special. You're the first young woman Stephan's introduced me to," he confessed.

There was such a contrast between Franco, who concealed me from his friends to Stephan, who appeared to be proud to be seen with me. This heightened my confidence. The very thought of Stephan wanting to be with me also induced ripples of excitement in my body. But I was just an ordinary woman. What did he see in me?

"Why is Stephan taking so long?" Kevin asked.

"He's worse than a woman taking that long in the bathroom!" I joked.

"*Jislaak*! What's he doing in there? He'd better get back before the ceremony starts."

Stephan returned looking abnormally elated and fidgety. The lights dimmed and the drums started to roll. The Master of Ceremonies dressed in a black tuxedo walked onto the stage.

"Good evening ladies and gentleman, I'm John Mbula and your host for tonight's Sportsman of the Year Award Ceremony. Tonight we're celebrating a fantastic sporting year applauding all nominees," he announced.

"This has been a great year for sportsmen and women," he continued. He became quite emotional when he described how a wheel-chair racer finalist had inspired a generation.

"I now welcome our local dance troupe, the *Gauteng-Movers*, who are here to entertain us tonight."

Drumming started as energetic agile dancers draped in the colours of the South African flag, yellow, green, red, blue, black and white, moved in rhythm to the beat. The louder the music escalated, the faster they danced. The audience applauded loudly.

We were also entertained by a striking singer. A fitted, green evening dress accentuated her vivacious curves and ample bosom. Large gold earrings complimented her dark-brown complexion. Her strong voice resounded through the auditorium.

"Tonight, we have rolled out the red carpet for our champions," the Master of Ceremonies announced. There was a short silence as a large cinema screen came down. The ambience changed as Queen's track *We Are The Champions* played to snippets of the six sports finalists in action.

My heart somersaulted as I watched Stephan in another world. His athletic body was crouched on the slanted starting block. He was extremely focused and ready to push off into the Olympic-sized swimming pool. He was poised in a black, tightly-fitting *Speedo* costume. He wore goggles strapped over a green swimming cap bearing an emblem of a small South African flag. When the buzzer sounded, he dived into the water, streamlined himself before resurfacing into freestyle. His powerful muscular arms circled the water at speed as he raced to the end.

The audience was captivated watching various competitors, including Lucas sprinting at cheetah speed, excelling in their respective sports.

"Stephan Erasmus is South Africa's newest swimming sensation. He has been chosen to represent South Africa at the Commonwealth Games. Stephan is currently shortlisted for the forthcoming Olympic trials," he continued. He gave a short history of the each of the other finalists.

"We have six finalists, who all deserve the award, but it can only go to one," he went on. The Minister of Sport and Recreation was introduced to present the award. She was handed a large white envelope.

"I'm about to disclose the biggest award of the night," she said.

"The winner will be walking away with a cheque worth Two Million Rand which will be given to the charity of their own choice."

Stephan squeezed my hand. He'd gone quiet and pensive watching anxiously as she removed a card from the envelope. She stared at the card for a moment before announcing, "And the winner is..."

She looked up at the audience and smiled pausing for what felt like an eternity.

Chapter Eleven

"Stephan Erasmus!" she revealed.

Stephan triumphantly punched the air with a fist then sprang to his feet. Kevin followed, throwing his arms up and shouting, "Yes!"

The audience rose to their feet applauding. Goose bumps covered my arms as I watched Stephan make his way onto the stage to the theme music from *Chariots of Fire*.

The Minister congratulated Stephan as she presented him with the silver trophy. Stephan was handed the microphone and the room went quiet.

"I don't have a speech prepared like my coach Kevin Nel presumed."

Stephan paused. He then removed the A4 white sheet of paper from his jacket pocket. He lifted it up to reveal blanks on both sides of the paper. The audience roared with laughter.

Stephan continued in a confident voice, "Sorry Kev, but thank you for having faith in me and for getting me this far. I'm honoured to receive this prestigious award and want to thank all who voted for me. This means a lot to me."

The Minister asked, "So Stephan, are you going to reveal your choice of charity?"

"The Wildlife Conservation Trust which focuses on the prevention of poaching, particularly rhinos and elephants. Apart from swimming, of course, my other passion is the preservation of wildlife," he replied.

"Fantastic. Any plans for your future sporting career?"

"To win a gold medal at the Olympics for South Africa," he exclaimed and raised the trophy above his head, beaming with excitement.

Wolf whistles and more clapping drowned the auditorium. Crowds swarmed around Stephan congratulating him. TV sports commentators rushed up to interview him. Kevin muscled his way to Stephan's side, not wanting to miss out.

"Stephan! Wait we need photos for tomorrows papers," photographers barked commands as they anxiously scrambled around him.

I stood back allowing him to enjoy his moment. But would all this change the Stephan I had met? His eyes scouted around for me.

"Chante, over here," he beckoned.

I obediently joined him. His confident presence must have rubbed off on me as I agreed to pose with him. The photographer positioned us on the red carpet. Just Stephan and I. He proudly draped his free arm round my waist whilst showing off his trophy with his free arm. The photographers darted around us taking numerous shots.

I secretly hoped Franco would see the photos in the papers to show him what he was missing out on. Think of something funny then look slightly above the camera lens, I instructed myself. This was the same advice I gave the models I photo-graphed. The whole nation will see these. I prayed I would look good in these pictures next to Stephan.

"Stephan, well done! I'm thrilled for you," I whispered kissing him gently on the cheek. He responded by embracing me. With his warm hard body held close to me he whispered, "Thanks for your support."

After many scenes of hugging, fist-shaking and trophy-lifting, things started to get a bit weird. Every time Stephan disappeared to the toilets, the rugged captain of the Springboks rugby team staggered up to me with a beer in his hand. Then he desperately tried to chat me up.

"You're sooo sexy," he slurred as his half-closed eyes drifted down my cleavage. Rolling my eyes, I smiled and turned to walk away as Stephan reappeared.

"What does that piss-cat want?" he scowled. From then on Stephan kept me close to his side. The laughter and music became louder. Guests were swaying from excessive drinking. Others were hyperactive and over-talkative, obsessively sniffing and wiping white powder off their nostrils. Men flung off their jackets and ties. Others had shirts which were hanging out. Women's guards were now down as their high slit dresses flashed naked thighs. Faux furs and pashminas were removed to reveal deep cleavages and outlined full breasts through flimsy tops. With glasses of champagne in one hand and stilettos in the other, glamorous women congratulated and flirted with Stephan.

As the celebrations wound down, Stephan squeezed my hand.

"Let's get the hell out of here," he said in a low voice.

We made a quick escape out the backstage door leaving the other guests hanging on. The ambience changed the moment we stepped outside. It was quiet and dimly-lit with a potent smell of *dagga*.

"Someone's been smoking weed," Stephan sniffed.

He checked around but couldn't see anyone. He gently pressed me against the wall between his defined arms. I breathed in the orgasmic aroma of his aftershave as he eased closer into me. I swallowed hard as his smouldering gaze locked into mine. His hot breath tingled down my neck as he softly nuzzled into it. I relaxed into Stephan as he traced a line round my lips with his slender finger, and then cradled my face. He looked deep into my eyes.

"Babe, I want you so badly!" he murmured placing his soft full lips onto my mine. I could taste the fruit champagne he'd been drinking as we morphed into a passionate kiss. I throbbed with desire as his lower body tightened and his hips flexed.

A blinding torchlight abruptly flashed on us. Stephan spun round and stood protectively in front of me.

"What the fuck!" he yelled.

"Sorry sir, I thought you were a *tsotsi!*"

A burly dark skinned man dressed in security guard's uniform apologised as he lowered the torch. Damn! Bloody security pitching up at the wrong moment, I silently cussed.

"Do we look like *tsotsis*?" Stephan vented in a frustrated tone.

"Sir, it's not safe these days," the security guard explained.

"*Yebo*, you're just doing your job," he tried to be friendly.

"We're leaving now, what's the best way to get to the car park?"

"Follow me and I'll take you there," the security guard offered.

"Jump on my back. I don't want you to trip in those heels."

I hitched up my long dress before Stephan scooped me up effortlessly with his muscly arms and gave me a piggyback. I wrapped my thighs securely around his taut, lean waist as he walked closely behind the security guard who used his bright torch to guide us. Stephan put me down gently when we reached his red *Audi*. As my stilettos touched the ground, I noticed my dress had ridden up to my waist. I yanked it down before stepping back.

The valet was sitting on the low wall of the car park, smoking a cigarette.

"Sir!" he jumped to his feet when he noticed us then hovered by the sports car whilst Stephan turned to the security guard and discreetly passed him a hefty tip.

"Thank you Sir!" the security guard beamed revealing his white gappy teeth.

The valet opened the passenger door for me whilst Stephan moved away to make a phone call.

"Thanks, bro. You mean Twitter was the first to break the news! *Ja*, I know. Don't stress. I'll phone mum tomorrow. She'll be sleeping now. Sunday it is. I'll tell Chantelle."

Those were the bits of his conversation I heard. He climbed in next to me still holding his cellphone to his ear.

"Okay bro. Speak later," and he ended the call.

When we were alone Stephan placed his hand gently on my thigh, turned to me and said in his raspy voice, "Sorry about that. The security guard sure was a passion killer. But thanks for coming with me tonight babe. It meant a lot to me."

Mmm, it's now 'babe' I inwardly smiled.

"That was Anton on the phone and he's asked you to join us for a *braai* to celebrate," he went on.

"Cool, that'll be nice. When?"

"Next weekend. Then you can meet the rest of my family."

"*Ja,* I'd like that," I smiled.

He revved up the engine letting off steam as his tyres screeched around the car park. I gripped my seat as we careered onto the main road where he floored it. His focus was on the road. We zoomed into the car park to where I had parked my nippy *VW Golf*.

"I'll get you safely on the road and I'll follow you as far as the Mall," he insisted.

"Don't forget your roses," he went on, grabbing them as he climbed out.

I felt protected and safe with Stephan. I liked the feeling. I didn't want to leave his side. He did a quick scout around before opening my door, then with his arm tucked round my waist he ensured I was safely in my car. He bent down and brushed a loose strand of hair off my face before softly kissing me on my lips.

"Text me when you get home. Promise."

Then he closed my door. I kicked off my stilettos, started the engine and drove away glancing in my rear-view mirror ensuring Stephan was following.

As I approached Fourways Mall, Stephan flashed his headlights before he turned off at the *robots*. I responded by tooting my horn. He drove off in the opposite direction. I was on my own now.

I started to feel uneasy as the traffic and street lights became sparse the deeper I drove into the suburbs. I was relieved when I turned into the road where I lived and finally, behind locked security gates and a remote-controlled garage door, I was safe at last.

It was long past midnight and I was exhausted. My text to Stephan.

Home safely. Thanks for a great time with you. C xxx

His text to me: *Sweet dreams, Babe. S xxx*

What an evening it had been. Stephan had been a perfect gentleman

and was showing an interest in me. With these warm thoughts, I curled up and was soon fast asleep.
    * * *

My cellphone rang waking me up from a deep sleep.
    "Hi," I croaked and tried to clear my morning voice.
    "Hi, babe,"
    "Stephan, have you checked the papers yet?"
    "No, but perhaps we could do that together?"
    "Good idea."
    "Would it be okay if I come over? I'm longing to see you again."
    "Give me an hour to shower and dress. Does that sound good?"
    "*Ja*, See you soon babe."
    Stephan's phone call certainly put a bounce into my step and much faster than normal, I was dressed, my face was made-up and I was standing in the kitchen awaiting his arrival.
    The sound of a car on my driveway, sent shivers down my spine. Why was he having this effect on me? After opening and then locking all the security gates and doors, we stood in the entrance hall, wrapped in each other's arms.
    "Coffee? Tea?" I enquired my lips still moist from his kiss.
    "No thanks. Let's go see what the story is."
    I led him to my office. The sun was streaming through the windows. Whilst we
waited for my iMac to start up, Stephan's eyes darted around the spacious room.
    "Did you take these?" he pointed to two large oak-framed photographs of lions displayed on the wall.
    "*Ja*," I flushed.
    "Wow, babe! You're really talented. They're spectacular!"
    "Thanks," I purred and relaxed into my black leather office chair. The leather seat was sticking to the back if my thighs. Stephan hovered over me. His wide bare-chest enveloped me from behind. I felt like a schoolgirl with a crush. My scrambled brain tried to remember how to google.
    "Let me take over," he suggested before kissing the top of my head. I felt giddy when his biceps brushed past my face and he placed his hand on the mouse before googling the *Daily News*.
    We both gasped at the headlines. A large photo of Stephan, brandishing his trophy in the air, covered the entire front page.

"Stephan you look amazing. You're the nation's poster boy!" I giggled.

"I was unknown until now. I don't feel comfortable being catapulted into the spotlight like this. I wish I could escape," he sighed.

"But you don't have much choice if you want to be an Olympic swimmer."

On page two was a huge picture of Stephan with his arm around me. I flung my head back into his hard chest in disbelief.

"They've portrayed us as a couple!" I shrieked.

"Listen to this," Stephan exclaimed and read aloud. *"Last night at the South African Sports Award Ceremony, a red-carpet event shimmering with lashings of glitz and glamour, charismatic Stephan Erasmus (28), wowed everyone looking suave. The newcomer swimming champion, Stephan, was one of ten nominees vying for the prestigious 'Sportsman of the Year' award."*

Stephan continued: "Now they got this right. *Stephan was accompanied by an unknown blonde, Chantelle Swanepoel (29), who was the belle of the ball in a dazzling electric-blue gown. The silver diamantes complimented the dress beautifully."*

"Oh my God," I gasped and read on, *"The strikingly couple are clearly happy together."* My entire being tingled.

"Nothing wrong with that. I'm proud to have you at my side. You do look beautiful," he smiled staring at the photo of the two of us.

The ringing of my cellphone interrupted us. Damn! I looked down to check who it was. Franco!

"What does he want?" I moaned and let it ring; I refused to take his call. However, Franco wasn't going to give up. My cellphone rang again.

Stephan scowled and asked, "Aren't you going to answer it?"

I reached for my cellphone in my bag and switched it off. No sooner had I done this when my landline rang, echoing through the house. No, this can't be happening?

"It's not important," I rolled my eyes.

"You don't know that," he sounded irritated and then added, "It could be your folks calling the landline!"

Breathing in sharply I jumped off my stool to answer the call. I picked up the receiver and snapped, "Hello!"

"Chantelle! Why are you not answering your cell?" Franco's voice stabbed into me.

"I'm busy," I snapped.

"Busy with that swimmer? I saw you in today's paper, having a good time," he snarled.

"You're the one who left me. You can't have it both ways."

My grip tightened tightly on the handset of the telephone.

He instantly changed his tune.

"I was calling to say I've arranged a job interview for you with medical illustrations as a medical photographer at the same London hospital I'll be working at."

"I'm not coming with you to London."

"I'll pop over later and bring a bottle of wine," his voice softened.

"No!"

My breathing picked up speed as I started to sweat profusely, visualising two alpha men, Franco du Preez facing Stephan Erasmus. I was fully aware of Franco's possessiveness and his volatile temper which would oppose Stephan's protective-ness and brute strength. The combination a recipe for a full-on fight. All hell would break loose. These two men must never meet again.

"I'm busy," I hissed.

"With that swimmer?" his voice dripped with sarcasm. "I won't stay long," he persisted. Franco wasn't going to let up. I had to stop him.

"I won't be here."

His hospital bleeper went off.

"I have to take this. I'm on call again and the only surgeon here. I'll call you again during the week," his voice had transformed into his professional medical voice and he ended the call abruptly. I leaned back onto the lounge wall feeling emotionally drained. I remembered Stephan in my study and hoped he had not heard.

Stephan was back in the kitchen sitting on the stool leaning back against the wall with his arms casually folded.

"You look like you've seen a ghost," he said raising his eye-bows in surprise.

"*Ja,* you could say that," I muttered.

"You look upset," he replied in a voice softening with concern.

"It was my ex," I sighed.

"What did he want?" he bristled. His demure instantly changed.

"Nothing. It's okay," I shook my head.

He stiffened as his eyes narrowed.

"I don't like the idea of him still sniffing around."

"I've given him the brush-off."

He screeched the stool back as he stood up.

"I'd better be going," he said.

Stephan stood watching me. I was trying to procrastinate the moment. He was keen to leave and I wanted him to say. Suddenly an invisible rift had lodged between us and my fear of losing Stephan intensified. It was happening all over again. One moment I was overflowing with happiness and the next, my doubts re-surfaced and filled me with sadness. I could feel the tension building up between us. I waved goodbye to Stephan not knowing when I'd see him again.

Chapter Twelve

I was angry with Franco. I marched to my study, retrieved my cellphone and sent Franco a text: *Don't ever contact me again. C*

My hands shook. Bleeps went off alerting me I had new text messages. I scrolled down curiously to read the one from Kirsty's first: *I'm so proud of you!!!! This is badass. You guys got so much column time! And I totally wanted to reach inside my computer screen and join you guys! K x*

The next text from Tristan : *Darling, you looked fabulous. I want to meet that hottie Stephan. Tell him from to come in for a freebie haircut. Details and all the gossip of last night please! T.*

Another from Tandeka: *Chantelle Swanepoel! Since when did you start dating Mr Sportsman? You looked stunning in that glamorous gown you wore. I would've lent you one of my creations. See you at the meeting tomorrow."*

I listened to a voicemail message on the landline from my mother: Chantelle, You never mentioned you were attending the sports awards. I would never have known had Aunty Myrna not called me. I must say you looked lovely, but your dress would've fitted better, if you had lost a few more pounds. He looks heaps better than that arrogant, cheating surgeon. Call me."

What could I have done to stop Franco from creeping back into my life? I was torn between two men in my life. Should I take a risk and accompany Franco to London? I would never be given this opportunity again. Or should I put all my hope in Stephan? What if he dumped me like Franco had?

How could I get out of the quandary I was in? Tandeka's demand to get me to find proof concerning her suspicions about Adam clashed with my own flirtations with Adam. I was being pulled in different directions. Who could help me sort out these mounting problems? I felt alone, confused and deeply depressed.

* * *

It was late Tuesday afternoon as I eased my body back into the cool leather chair waiting for my iMac to fire up. Will Stephan contact me before I meet his family on Sunday? That was only a few days away.

"Get a grip, Chantelle!" I scolded myself and sat up straight to check my emails. A new one from Tandeka was in my inbox.

From: Tandeka Thebe (tandekat@Africafashions.co.za)
To: Chantelle Swanepoel. (ChantelleS@freelancephoto@co.za)
Subject: Thursday meeting
Chantelle,
Just a quick email confirming that Thursday's meeting will be held in our executive offices at 10am. Attending will be yourself; Anita Patel and Bonang Malema, the newly-appointed editor of South Africa Vogue. We will be finalising our Christmas collection for the November issue. Adam will be joining us. Trust you have given my proposal some consideration.
Look forward to seeing you. Tandeka

No! How do I seem to get myself into these awkward situations? It's like I've got 'desperate' plastered over my forehead. I thought Tandeka had found a professional PI to do her dirty work. Why me? I drummed my fingers trying to come to a decision. If I turned down Tandeka, I knew she would conveniently find a way to end my contract. I had bills to pay. I owed money on my credit cards, thanks to Franco not paying his share of the household bills.

I shuffled uncomfortably on my chair. I had no PI training. I was a photographer. Where do I start? What exactly did Tandeka want me to do? I couldn't even talk it through with Kirsty. I was on my own with this one.

I abruptly pushed the chair back and marched off to the kitchen to make a cup of coffee. Mavis was hovering in the kitchen.

"You can go early if you've finished Mavis."

"Can I make you *rooibos t*ea before I leave?"

"No thanks, I'm going to make myself a strong coffee."

"Chantelle, I'm going to the township to see my aunt. They want me to bring money," her eyes moved down to the ground.

"Again? How much do you want to borrow this time?" I frowned.

"R500," she mumbled, keeping her eyes fixed on the floor.

"Well, I'll deduct it off your weekly wage again. How are you ever going to get anywhere in life if your relatives keep draining your wages?"

"Because I get accommodation, food and transport money on top of my wages, they think I'm rich," she shrugged.

"Oh Mavis," I patted her on her shoulder. "Let me see what I've got."

Returning to the kitchen I found a *rooibos* teabag in a teacup, coffee in my favourite mug engraved with wild horses and some shortbread; all set out on a tray.

"Here's R500. Watch out for those dam *tsotsis* in the overcrowded mini taxis."

I handed her a thick brown envelope with banknotes.

"Thanks, Chantelle. I'm hiding the cash in here," she smiled broadly, folding the envelope in half and pushing it into her large white bra under her uniform."

"See you Monday morning, Mavis."

"Goodbye," she added, closing the back door behind her on her way out.

Sitting back in front of my iMac I opened up my emails again. I clicked into

Tandeka's latest one and replied:
From: Chantelle Swanepoel.
(ChantelleS@freelancephoto@co.za)
To: Tandeka Thebe
(tandekat@Africafashions.co.za)
Subject: Thursday meeting
Hi Tandeka,

Everything's in order for the meeting on Thursday I hope the images meet to your approval. I'm looking forward to meeting Bonang Malema. I've given your proposition some thought. Could we meet up after the meeting to discuss it in more detail? See you Thursday. Chantelle.

I pressed "send" and took several sips of coffee to refresh my dry mouth. I was despondently staring at the screen when Tandeka's email popped into my inbox.

Hello Chantelle,

Great to receive your email. I am relieved that you are loyal to me and my

company. I'll get Suzi to book a discreet table for just you and me at Da Vinci's Restaurant for lunch. That way we will be out of sight from any prying eyes. I will give you all the latest information I have to hand then. Oh, and do   NOT tell anyone we are going for lunch. This is Top Secret from now on.

Looking forward to seeing you Thursday. Tandeka.

I re-read Tandeka's initial email and her words, 'Adam will also be joining us', leapt off the screen. Damn. Adam will be there. Will he realise what Tandeka and I are up to? I was scared. I felt sick in my stomach. I felt that tingling sensation in the back of my neck which usually alerts me when something is not right. I knew. I just knew ...

* * *

On Thursday after lunch at *Da Vinci's* with my eyes lowered and fixed on the dusty dry dark-brown earth, I strolled solo back to the office through the park. It was the long route, but I couldn't face Adam. My mind swirled with excuses to escape Tandeka's control. Her words throbbed in my head: *If you do this for me and photograph Adam in the act, I will promote you to chief photographer.*

The pressure was on. Why can't I just say no? I lifted my heavy head giving me a view of the cloudless blue sky.

"God, please tell me what I need to do?" I prayed.

Reaching my desk, I flung my bag onto the chair and switched on my iPhone. The first familiar text alert was from Stephan. Should I open it or delete it? What did I have to do to stop myself from opening his text? His handsome face came to my mind's eye. What was I thinking? It's not his fault that Franco was trying to manipulate and upset my emotions.

How's your day going? Mine's been hectic! Fancy joining me tomorrow night for the opening of a larney restaurant, Plenty of Seafood? S x

Just hearing his voice again, triggered a warm fuzzy tingle. Then realising he had asked me, even after his rapid exit on Sunday, lifted my spirit. I kept the conversation brief not wanting to seem too keen. I texted back: *Mine's been interesting! I've not heard of that new restaurant. C xxx*

Eish no! This restaurant is seriously upmarket. S, he texted back.

"Chantelle!" Tandeka hissed before her eyes narrowed and darted towards Adam.

"*Ja!*"

I dropped my cellphone into my bag before I looked up. The wine from lunch had given me the courage to slowly walk over to Adam's desk. He was engrossed with drawings on his computer screen. Actually, Adam was handsome. Today he was dressed smart/casual in a blue shirt which flattered his cappuccino-tinted skin. His dark eyelashes rolled up beneath his brown eyes. He smiled at me.

"Chantelle! You okay?"

I paused, smiled and walked away from Adam. Even thoughts of my high overdraft didn't stop me from feeling uncomfortable, dirty and deceitful. I couldn't do it. For the remainder of the afternoon, Tandeka hovered around me. I yawned and day-dreamed of being in Stephan's arms as the effects of the wine wore off. I daren't annoy her anymore by using my cellphone, so I didn't get an opportunity to reply to Stephan's last text.

* * *

1700 hrs. Relief. I shut down my computer, slipped my iPad into my bag and swung it over my shoulder. I marched over to the lift with Adam close behind. The lift was full of sweaty businessmen, their sleeves rolled up and their top buttons undone. I managed to squeeze in. When the lift stopped at the ground floor, I was first to step out into the fresh, crisp evening. I was free.

"Where are you parked?" Adam's deep voice caught me by surprise.

"Across the road."

"I'll walk you to your car."

"Thanks, but there's no need," I shouted back as I zipped over the road through a gap in the traffic. I climbed into my *VW Golf* and Adam walked up smiling. His sporty aftershave smelt good as he put his head through the window.

"Drinks after work tomorrow?"

I paused...he was interested in me.

"Well?" he pressed.

This was a perfect opportunity, but I couldn't do it.

"I have plans tomorrow."

His tone changed. "That's a shame. I'd better head off as it looks like a storm's brewing."

The sky darkened. A chill was in the air and gusts of wind scooped litter from the streets. Adam jogged off carrying his brown briefcase.

I wanted to get home. I turned the starter key. Nothing. I tried again. Nothing. "Damn you car! Not now," I yelled.

Crowds of city workers were running to catch buses and mini taxis to beat the approaching storm. My heart pounded at the thought of being alone, stranded and helpless. I fumbled for my cellphone with one hand whilst constantly trying the starter key but it was dead. Stephan's caller ID flashed up.

"Hello."

"Chante. You ok?"

"My car won't start. I think the battery's dead."

"Where are you?"

"Parked outside my office," I gabbled.

"Stay put. Lock your door. I'm leaving now."

There was silence on the other end.

"Stephan...you there?"

Nothing. Dead.

There was a loud crash of thunder followed by flashes of lightning. Hail and rain pelted aggressively against the windscreen. My eyes squinted as I desperately tried to see through the steamy windows. I jolted upright when I heard loud knocks on my door. My head spun round and a face was pressed up against my window.

"Adam! You scared me to death."

I clutched my heart.

"You okay?" he mouthed.

Biting hard on my lip, I rolled down the top half of my window. He blinked as his slender fingers wiped the dripping water from his eyes.

"*Ag bliksem*! Pop the bonnet and let me have a look."

"But you're soaked."

"*Ja*, but the rain's easing off."

Adam shivered as he rolled up the sleeves of his wet shirt which clung to his lean torso. He rushed over to the front and effortlessly lifted the bonnet with his taut, tanned arms. The rain stopped as I climbed out the car. The storm had passed, so I walked over to Adam. His head was still buried under the bonnet.

"What do you think the problem is?"

He stood up, pulled a handkerchief from his trouser pocket to wipe his hand. "Your battery's dead," he sighed.

"Damn. Now what?"

"I've got some jumper leads with me."

"Thank God for that. Are you parked close by?"

He gestured to a few cars behind me.

"*Ja*, over there. Jump into your car while I get them."

My heartbeat and breathing returned to normal as I eased into the driver's seat. A white *Nissan* Twin Cab screeched round the bend and pulled up right in front of me. Adam jumped out carrying jump leads. His opened up the bonnet of his car. My neck stretched as I watched him in action. He attached the jump leads from his battery to mine. I hoped my battery would spark?

"Chantelle, fire her up." Adam loudly instructed.

I took a deep breath and turned my starter key. Nothing. I tried again.

Nothing. I rolled my eyes. Not again.

My car door swung open and Adam leaned over me saying, "Let me try."

We both spun round to screeching brakes, revving and hooting. A red *Audi* sports car pulled up close.

Adam yelled, "Who the hell is that?"

My heart hammered in my chest when I looked up to see Stephan muscle in. His chest was puffed out and his fists were clenched. Adam pulled away and quickly backed out my car.

Stephan's eyes narrowed as he glared at him. I chewed my thumb nail. "Stephan, meet Adam, my work colleague. He's trying to start my car."

Adam replied, "*Howzit*."

Stephan's jaw clenched.

"I even tried my jump leads," Adam said, shrugging his shoulders.

Stephan tucked his head under the bonnet, whipped Adam's jump leads off my battery and shoved them into Adam's hands.

"Yours are useless. Chantelle needs manpower to kick-start her battery."

The hair on Adam's neck bristled.

"Thanks Adam for all your help," I smiled.

"You okay now?"

I nodded.

"Sharp, sharp. See you tomorrow at the office."

Once inside his twin cab, he put his foot down and zoomed off.

"You ok babe?"

"You shouldn't have been so rude to Adam. He was only trying to help me."

"Come off it. He couldn't take his eyes off you."

"You're jealous," I laughed.

His lips pursed, "So this is the the reason you threw me out on Sunday?"

"Hell no!" I yelled, "I only work with the guy."

"Sorry for being jealous. I didn't like seeing him all over you."

He pulled me into his warm body. I felt something hard protruding into my ribcage. I leaned back to look at his jeans.

"You mean this?" Lifting his T-shirt, a black pistol was tucked against his washboard stomach.

"That's so bloody dangerous. It could've gone off," I shrieked backing off not taking my eyes off the pistol.

"No ways. The safety catch is on."

"I don't care. I could've been shot."

"Chantelle, I've told you before I carry the gun to protect you and me. No sane person goes anywhere without a firearm," he said, raising his voice.

"Why is it not in a holster?"

"It usually is, but I was in a hurry to get to you."

He shoved the pistol back down into his trousers.

"Babe, let me take you home and I'll organise your car to be collected by the AA," his tone softened.

I looked up at his chiselled face and smiled, "Thanks."

After locking up my car, Stephan gently took my hand. He led me to his sports car and opened the passenger door for me. When I had climbed into the low-slung coupe, the luxurious black bucket seat hugged the sides of my body. Once we were both in, he immediately activated the auto-lock system. He casually removed the black pistol then leaned over to place it in the *cubby hole*. Stephan pushed a shiny button. The engine roared to life and he pulled away at full speed. I was thrown back into my seat but snugly cocooned as we turned the corners.

Chapter Thirteen

Leaning forward in my office chair, photographs of the *Afrika Fashion's* Christmas collection were sprawled over my desk in front of me. My mind was wandering aimlessly. The local radio station played in the background. I tapped my marker pen in time to Beyonce singing *Rocket*.

"What's your favourite part?" Adam asked in a flat tone.

I looked up from my desk, "Favourite part of?"

He cocked his head to one side and smiled, "Chantelle?"

"All of it! I know what you're trying to drive at and I'm not going to fall for it!"

"I was only asking you which is your favourite part of the song?"

"The bit about touching and starting to scream! Anyway Adam, what are you trying to achieve?"

"I'm trying to lighten you up after last night's drama."

I felt my face flush.

"Don't remind me. Thanks anyway for trying to help."

Xolani usually worked in the printing room, but today he was in the open-plan office with us. His tall, lean body was hunched over the photocopier, attempting to fix it. He stood up, scratched his bald head and asked, "Guys what happened last night?"

"Chantelle's car battery died, so I tried to help her. Well, that's before that arrogant piece of shit pitched up," Adam rattled on.

"Who?" Xolani frowned.

Adam looked directly at me and continued, "Ask Chantelle."

I cut Adam off, "Now's not the time to talk about it."

Xolani quickly changed the subject, "Guys, do short men or taller men get more sex?"

"*Eish*, Xolani! How would I know? Ask Adam!"

Xolani burst into a deep laugh.

"*Ag*, you guys talk such rubbish," I stretched back into my chair. My cellphone rang, to my relief, as the conversation was getting awkward. I reached into my bag to answer it.

"Babe? You still at the office? Are you okay?" Stephan sounded impatient.

"*Ja*, why?" I rolled my eyes inwardly. Mr Paranoid was at it again I thought.

"Rosebank Towers is trending on Twitter. There's been a shoot-out there."

"What?" I jumped off my chair and marched towards the ceiling-to-floor window.

"Half an hour ago at the Post Office."

Cold chills rippled from the nape of my neck to my fingertips as I peered through the window, searching the street below.

"I can see the Post Office from here. Was anyone hurt?"

"Chantelle, stay put. Don't leave the office."

"Guys, turn on the news. There's a shoot-out in the street below..."

I gestured to the portable radio near the water fountain.

"When?" Adam asked, sprinting towards the radio.

"Is that *loskop* with—"

I cut him off, "Stephan, I'll call you back."

"Listen to this," Adam's deep voice blasted. He turned up the volume on the radio. We absorbed every word of the newsreader's pacy voice: *"We're crossing over live to the offices of Rosebank Towers."*

A young woman's high-pitched frightened voice gabbled: *"At eleven today my colleague witnessed a shooting at the Post Office. She was too horrified to talk. Then she saw one of the shooters following her."*

She paused before she went on: *"I've just heard that some of these armed men were having coffee at the Wimpy. They were waiting for the security guard carrying the cash boxes which they had collected from the Mall."*

The newsreader asked the young woman, *"Are you still at the office?"*

"We're all terrified. We haven't left the office as yet."

The newsreader cut her off, *"Are the cops still there?"*

"Ja, but we're too scared to go down to the shops as we've heard the two suspects are still at large."

The newsreader asked, *"When you say the suspects are at large, are they still in the Mall?"*

"I'm not sure, but we're scared stiff because these gunmen could be hiding in one of the offices. I' saw one climb through the ceiling."

"Very scary stuff. Thanks for talking to us Edna."

My heart hammered against my chest. I jolted when I heard my cellphone ring,

"Hello."

Stephan blurted, "Chantelle, I'm driving over to get you now."

"Don't be stupid. The police have cordoned off the Mall. You won't be able to get through."

"Is that *loskop* still there?"

I looked over at Adam.

"Who else is there?"

"Stephan, come off it."

Adam glanced at me. I walked over to the coffee machine, out of earshot from Adam.

"Stop it! What's with you and Adam? I told you I just work with him."

"I was only asking because if there is a man with you, it's good. It's some sort of protection until I can get there," he rattled, his words shot out like a machine gun.

A loud gunshot made me jump, loud enough for Stephan to hear. My phone dropped as Adam grabbed me and pulled me down onto the floor with him.

"Quick! Hide under here," he ordered as he shoved me under his desk.

He ensured his body enveloped me, shielding me from any potential harm. Despite my racing heartbeat I could barely breathe.

The newsreader announced, *"We're now crossing over to Bogani Mbeke at Rosebank Towers as more gunshots have been reported. Hello Bogani, are you there?"*

After a Long pause, Bogani replied, *"I'm here inside the Wimpy as the Towers are still cordoned off."*

"What's the latest down there Bogani?"

He replied, *"No one has been reported injured. The police have apprehended one of the suspects, but the other is still at large and was last seen fleeing the scene in a black Toyota Hilux. Mercy, I've just heard they're opening up the Mall so shoppers and staff can leave, but no one can enter. However, all the roads in that area are still cordoned off."*

"Thank you Bogani."

Adam and I crawled out from under his desk. He picked up my phone and handed it to me as it began to ring.

I answered, "Hello."

Stephan replied, "Thank God you're okay. They've opened up the Mall now so I'll come and get you."

"*Ja*, but the roads are still cordoned off. The police will be escorting us to ensure our safety. Stay put and I'll let you know when we leave."

"Please stay safe, babe."
"I will. See you later," I replied.

* * *

What am I letting myself in for? This is going against my grain. Where am I going to find another job in today's employment climate if I do not do as Tandeka tells me? How will I pay my bills? I would not be in this mess if Franco had not left me for that bitch. Now what choice do I have? But maybe Tandeka is right. Maybe Adam is a secret coke-addict and he is selling off our ideas to our rival company. Am I blinded by my attraction to Adam? Do I really want to know?

I will have time before meeting up with Stephan at the Seafood Restaurant. He would meet me there. If only I could get this behind me, I could really enjoy my evening out.

If Adam should notice me following him, I would pretend Tandeka sent me with some extra work. My mouth was dry. My hands were sweating. I gripped the steering wheel tightly. I drove a few cars behind his white *Nissan* Twin Cab. He travelled at a steady speed. He is most probably going home.

Then suddenly he took a left turn. I hoped he had not noticed me. I backed off slightly. I did not want my strained eyes to leave his vehicle. I could not risk losing sight of him.

Where were we? I could not recognise where we were. Where was Adam heading to? I felt uneasy as we drove into a shanty town with an occasional street light. It did not feel safe. What was he doing in this ghetto-type place? We passed bottle-stores where drunken men staggered around swigging from beer bottles. Loud music blasted from parked cars. Youths with hoodies huddled in groups smoking *dagga* and goodness knows what else.

I reluctantly continued to follow Adam's vehicle. But the road became more desolate as we left the township behind. I was frightened, very frightened. I remembered the shoot-out at the Mall earlier on. It was at that moment I decided to abandon this mission. I turned round and drove back to the main road.

* * *

Our evening went far too quickly at the Seafood Restaurant. I was getting to know Stephan who insisted again that he follow me as far as the Mall where he would head home in the opposite direction. I remembered my earlier journey following Adam and felt relieved to be heading towards Fourways again. Reassured that I was nearing my house, I sighed.

However, not far from my home, fear gripped me as I stopped as the *robots* turned red. A car seemed to come out of nowhere and my head spun at the sound of screeching brakes. I was briefly blinded by glaring headlights, then squinted to see if I recognised anyone. Who the hell was this? I didn't know these two dark men in the front seat *of a Madza*.

The doors opened and two bulky men waving pistols ran towards my car. I instinctively forced down the auto-lock button. I just made it! One thug pressed his scarred, scowling face up against my window, yelling. "Open the fucking door!" Venomously spitting on my window before he tried to force the door open with a crowbar. He gave up and swung the crowbar at my side window. I was showered with glass and put up my hand to protect my face. The second even bigger man thumped on my windscreen with his large knuckles waving a gun in his other hand.

"Get out or I'll fucking shoot you!"

A black hand grabbed my arm and pulled at me; my dress rode up to my thighs, but I clung on to the steering wheel. I saw him look at my legs and just knew…

"Come on get her out. Put her in the boot," the second man yelled.

My scalp hurt as the first man moved his grip to my hair and tugged, trying to get me to crawl through the broken window.

"Get out," he hissed. His breath was foul, beer and vomit in equal parts.

Panicking I realised there was no escape but I had to survive this. I remembered the advice from a lecture I had once attended on 'How to Survive a Carjacking.'

"Don't resist, learn to surrender your car and not your life," were the words of the lecturer which had stuck in my head.

"Take my car, but please don't shoot me!" I yelled realising I would have to give up my grip on the steering wheel.

I heard the sound of another vehicle approaching and heavily braking to a halt behind their car. I couldn't see. I was dazzled by the bright headlights. It must be the rest of the gang. I was overwhelmed by terror. I feared for my life and struggled to swallow. My legs went numb. Feeling utterly helpless, I froze stiff like a marble stature. Having absolutely no respect for life, I knew these thugs would stop at nothing.

The driver jumped out and moved towards us. Two deafening shots were fired. God help me, this is it. I shut my eyes tightly waiting for the bullet. I heard footsteps crunching on gravel as the thugs scrambled into their car and with a loud screeching of tortured tyres, sped off.

"Chantelle!" Stephan's voice called.

Was I hallucinating? I opened my eyes in disbelief and saw Stephan running towards me tucking his black pistol into the front of his trousers and tried to open my locked door.

"Are you okay?" he mouthed.

My hands shook as I fumbled to unlock the door. Stephan yanked the door open and swooped me out of my seat. I clung to him shaking. My legs were numb. I couldn't have walked if I'd tried.

"I told them to take my car," I sobbed, gasping for breath.

"Your life's more important than any car," he said softly whilst cradling me in his arms.

After a few minutes he cupped my face in his hands and looked into my eyes.

"We can't stay here, do you think you can drive if I follow?"
I felt reassured by his manly presence.

"Yes, let's go now."

I managed the drive quite well, no scares and it was good for me to have to get behind the wheel – even if the window was smashed. I stopped at the gates. I'd had enough.
Stephan had pulled in behind me, ran to me and held me for a moment.

"Let's get inside. We need to report this."

He had the situation under control. He opened the gates. I watched him drive my car into the garage before he went back and parked his *Land Rover* on the driveway. Stephan ensured the gates were locked. As we approached the front door, the flood lights automatically flicked on as bright as daylight.

Once we were safely inside the house with all the doors locked, I quizzed Stephan, "What made you come back?"

"I noticed a suspicious-looking car following you as you turned off. Alarm bells rang. That's when I turned round to check up on you," he explained.

"Stephan, I can't thank you enough for saving my life," I whispered.

"What's it with you and carrying a gun?" I asked the question which had plagued me for so long.

"Why do you think? To protect myself from bastards like tonight and anyway most South Africans do these days. You'd better report the carjacking to the police," he prompted.

"What're they going to do?"

"Probably nothing as usual, but you never know."

Retrieving my cellphone from my handbag, I dialled the police. Once I'd been transferred to the carjacking incident office, I relayed the horrendous event.

"Did you get a registration number? Can you describe your attackers? What was the make and colour of your assailant's vehicle?" The questions went on and on.

After pausing to yawn, Inspector Magwena garbled loudly. "Miss Swanepoel, I've documented everything you have told me. Please write down your case number. It is CS976523. There's nothing we can do right now, but we will contact you when we have any further information."

Stephan had his secure arm around me as we sat on the couch going over the event. Venting about it, gave me some relief. "I'm staying here till daylight to ensure you're safe from those bastards."

I was safe now. Stephan had made it so.

I woke up to the aroma of good coffee and abruptly sat up. Was this Mavis making coffee? Then I remembered she was off and would only be back on Sunday. I rubbed my sleepy eyes before checking the time; it was already 9am. Why was I on the couch? I looked down to see I was still wearing my dress from last night! I flinched as I moved my legs.

"Eina!" I winced. A painful reminder of last night's terrifying experience. Stephan. It must be him brewing coffee. I followed the welcoming strong coffee aroma into the kitchen where Stephan was cooking. He was bare-chested, a small white bathroom towel wrapped around his waist.

"Food's the way to a woman's heart!" I softly greeted him still rubbing my gritty eyes. He spun round holding the egg flip.

"Good morning Chantelle! How are you feeling?" he asked in a compassionate voice.

"Er I'm okay. Still shell-shocked from last night." I answered seeing a neatly laid kitchen table. Holding the egg flip, he bent down to peck me on my cheek. The side of my face tingled as his morning stubble bristled against it.

"What happened last night? Did I fall asleep on the couch?" I asked.

"Ja, you were sleeping like a baby once you took those painkillers. I didn't want to disturb you," he continued cooking.

"Thanks for saving me and for staying over to support me."

My mouth went sticky and dry with the memory of the harrowing experience.

"I'd never have forgiven myself if anything had happened to you."

"So where did you sleep?"

"On the other couch. I didn't like to leave you alone in case those bastards followed us."

I shuddered at the thought.

"What about you?"

"I'm fine babe. Wait till I catch those bastards. I'll sort them out for what they did to you last night."

"It's in the hands of the police now."

"The cops had better find them. They have to be stopped from carjacking innocent victims," he vented in an angry voice.

"Let's hope so."

I glanced down at his taut torso noticing how the white towel accentuated his tan saying, "Are you watching the toast!"

My toaster had the habit of burning the toast because it often never popped up, but just then the two slices popped out of the toaster.

"Don't worry, Chante. Coffee?" his husky voice suggested.

"Ja, please. I'll just brush my teeth first."

"Don't be long. I don't want your breakfast to go cold."

I squirted plenty of toothpaste onto my toothbrush. Whilst moving the brush around, I scrutinised my eyes which were smudged with make-up. That was so un-like me. I was so meticulous about removing my make-up before going to sleep. Just goes to show how traumatised I had been.

I found ibrufen painkillers in the medicine cabinet and swallowed two down with cold water, followed by numerous drops of my powerful homeopathic *Rescue Remedies* to help calm my nerves from last night. How could I stop thinking of those scary thugs? *Rescue Remedies* combined with Stephan's warm protective presence.

Not wanting to wet my hair I covered it with my shower cap. It was a relief to get out of the uncomfortable clinging dress and clamber into the warm shower. After a refreshing shower, I dried myself and checked for bruises and cuts. I only found one a graze on my thigh, so I dabbed it with tea-tree oil.

My started to feel calmer as the *Rescue Remedies* kicked in. I dipped my painted fingernails into a pot of perfumed body cream and smoothed it onto my body. I pulled a yellow halter-neck top over denim shorts, and shoved the *Rescue Remedies* bottle into my pocket. With a spritz of fragrance, I went to join Stephan.

"Woah you smell good," he inhaled deeply before pecking me on my lips. "Sit down for your breakfast!" he gestured to the kitchen table.

I perched myself on the stool while he poured steaming hot coffee for me.

"Milk?" he asked.

"Just a splash thanks."

This was an indulgence for me as Franco had never cooked. He always expected me to do the cooking. Stephan served me with a perfectly formed poached egg on buttered rye toast topped with asparagus.

"Enjoy!" he said before dishing his up. He sat down opposite me.

"Did you know breakfast is the most diverse meal on the global menu?" he announced.

"I've heard that before. Have you been watching MasterChef?"

"I wanted to conjure up an awesome breakfast for you."

"You have been watching MasterChef. I recognise the lingo! Well, you've cooked this egg to perfection, not too soft or too hard," I giggled whilst still munching.

I sipped on my coffee waiting for him to finish eating. Next, he placed a white plate of well-presented fresh strawberries and blueberries on skewers sprinkled with cinnamon, on the table.

"Try these," he seductively offered me. As I nibbled on a piece of strawberry the succulent spicy sweet fruit melted in my mouth.

"Hmm refreshing and moist, I can taste a hint of alcohol?"

"Your taste buds are spot on! I soaked them in white wine."

"Seriously Stephan...this is yummy," I swallowed.

He screeched his stool back to stand up and reached over to wipe off some juice with his thumb from the corners of my mouth before licking it off.

"Food is about enjoyment and seeing a smile on your face."

"You sure have put a big one on mine," I brimmed.

The ringing of my cellphone interrupted us. I slipped off my stool to answer, but it stopped. "Damn! What if that was the police with more info on the carjackers?" I sighed with frustration.

"They'll call back if it is. I'd better turn my cellphone on. I know I'm going to be bombarded. I checked it earlier and I've already been asked to do various interviews! It's hectic."

"Stephan, don't stress, It'll settle down!"

"I like my privacy. Most guys would be chuffed to be in the spotlight!"

I slipped the *Rescue Remedy* bottle from my pocket for another dose as I followed Stephan to the front door. Our eyes met. Our mutual feelings drew us together and with a quick embrace and kiss on my forehead, Stephan, said, "I need to get to training. See you tonight, Chante.. Keep Rocky inside to protect you."

I melted inside and could barely speak.

"Yes, thanks Stephan for everything. See you later."

Chapter Fourteen

"Are you there?" Tristan's camp voice shrilled down the phone.

"Hi," I replied as I inwardly rolled my eyes with disappointment. I assumed it was Stephan and not Tristan, who was probably calling for a gossip.

"Chantelle, I've been trying to get hold of you," he panted. I knew he was irritated because he only called me when was upset or was after gossip.

"Tristan! What's wrong?"

He couldn't get his words out fast enough.

"It's Sonja. She's in her final stages of labour, about to give birth, but the baby won't come out. The midwife says the baby's in distress and Sonja may need a Caesarean. They can't find a fucking gynaecologist in this hospital. I know you're good friends with the gynae, Dr Anderson," he shrieked sounding desperate.

"What do you mean? There has to be another gynae on duty. Which hospital are you at?"

"There's so few staff here, most of them with half a brain cell in this shit hole," he snorted.

"Tristan! Slow down. You have to tell me which hospital you're in."

"Makafobe Koppies!"

"What! How the hell did Sonja end up in that government hospital? Makafobe must be one of the worst hospitals in SA."

No wonder Tristan was in a state.

"We've had shit luck all day. We were in the industrial site early this morning visiting a fabric clearance sale, when Sonja's waters broke and Makafobe was the nearest hospital. Her hubby, Leon is away on a business trip in Cape Town. So it's only me and her." I could hear the panic escalating in his voice.

"Tristan, calm down."

"I've never seen a fanny before. The midwives put a hospital gown on Sonja leaving the front wide open with a full view of her item. Oh my God! What an ugly sight. Thank fuck I'm gay."

"Listen to me carefully. You're no help to Sonja if you're having one of your panic attacks."

He went silent. All I could hear were the clinical sounds of monitors, bleeps and Sonja wailing in the background.

"Now breathe with me. Breathe in. Breathe out. Breathe in, breathe out." I calmly instructed. I kept talking. "Are you okay for now whilst I try and get hold of Freya Anderson?"

"*Ja,* I'll be okay after a couple of spliffs."

I scrolled through my iPhone for Freya Anderson's number. I hadn't spoken to her for over a month. Freya and I were close friends. We'd met at UCT (University of Cape Town), where she was studying medicine and I was studying photography. It was through her that I met Franco when she worked at the same hospital as him. He was a guest at her wedding and I was her maid-of-honour. Finding Freya's cell-phone number, I pressed the call button.

"Hi, Char. I always did believe in telepathy. I was planning to call you, later on, today after I saw photos of you in the Sunday Times. How come you didn't tell me you had a new man in your life?"

"It's all been a bit of a whirlwind, to be honest. I was going to call you later in the week and suggest we have lunch."

I felt the blood rush to my cheeks out of embarrassment as I was calling for a favour instead.

Freya pulled up outside my home in her new silver SLK Mercedes. I climbed into the passenger seat and leant over to air kiss her soft cheek. I heard the reassuring click as Freya pressed the central locking switch and settled myself into the luxurious black leather.

"You smell good. What perfume are you wearing today?" I asked.

"Thanks. It's a new one by *Lancome.*"

"It's good to see you Freya. Thanks for collecting me and seeing my friend's sister on your day off."

"I was in the vicinity anyway. I don't make a habit of seeing patients when I'm not on duty. Oh Char, please put your seatbelt on. I see too many fatalities in casualty caused by passengers not buckling up," she said in her thick Joburg dialect.

When she turned to face me, I noticed she had lost weight as her cheekbones were more pronounced than usual. She was very attractive with brown eyes, milky skin and shoulder-length curly black hair. Her formal choice of clothes hadn't changed. She wore an expensive cream shirt tucked into dark grey trousers.

"Oooh! New glasses as well. You look super intelligent," I commented.

"You think so? They're *Ted Baker.* I need bifocals now. You're looking radiant. You must be in love," she commented as her full lips curved into a wide smile.

"Haha. I'll fill you in with all the details later," I giggled.

"I look forward to it."

There was a distinct difference in the scenery as we sped deeper into the south of the city. Derelict flats, littered surroundings and potholed roads. Buses and mini-buses sped past.

"I'm not risking stopping here hey. This area's notorious for carjacking."

Freya leant forward peering right and left before she gave way instead of stopping at the red robots. Vagrants and hawkers looked on.

"It's shocking that there's no gynae on call at Makafobe. Saying that, their working conditions are disgusting from what I've experienced during my training," she added, pursing her peach-coloured lips.

We were assailed by a potent stench of stale vomit as we entered the reception of this old unkempt hospital. Abandoned and rusty wheelchairs were scattered about. The corridors were overcrowded with scruffily-dressed patients queueing all the way to the entrance door. Others sat or lay on rows of chairs in an overcrowded waiting room. Many toddlers were crying and one woman was wailing uncontrollably.

Two men, in their thirties, were arguing with the security staff. A hospital clerk sat tapping her pen on the desk listening inattentively to a dishevelled old man wobbling about on a crutch. Blood poured down his leg. She was clearly fed up and not interested in listening to this patient.

I followed Freya down a long dirty corridor lined with unused beds. Cockroaches scurried across the floor. We followed a worn-out sign which read: Labour Ward. We reached the nurses' station, which resembled a reception desk behind which a couple of attractive nurses were seated. Unattended phones were ringing constantly interspersed with sharp bleeps.

A pleasant looking young intern dressed in blue scrubs with a stethoscope draped round his slender neck, stood at the desk rummaging through a thick file. He briefly looked up at us over his glasses which were perched on the end of his freckled nose. His young fair-skinned face was already engrained with frown lines.

A weary-looking nurse in her late forties and dressed in a faded pale-blue uniform with white shoulder epaulettes and a name badge indicating she was the sister in charge, glanced up and asked in an authoritative tone, "Can I help you?"

"Good afternoon, Sister. I'm Dr Anderson, gynaecologist from Morningside Clinic. I'm here to see a patient, Sonja Nel," Freya replied politely, yet sternly.

She slowly stood up answering, "Good afternoon, doctor. I'll get her file."

She reached over to a pile of files and searched through them before handing Freya a thin khaki folder. Freya read through Sonja's notes.

"Not much in here," she sighed venting her frustration.

"Sister, is there facility for epidural here?"

She shook her head, "No doctor."

As they continued discussing Sonja, my eyes drifted to a large bay comprising ten occupied beds with the surrounding curtains half-hanging off the rails. Relatives and friends were huddled round one bed.

Char!" Freya nudged me.

"Follow me please," the sister in charge instructed as she waddled ahead.

We walked down a small corridor where gun-metal paint was peeling off the walls. A whiff of cannabis drifted nearer as we stopped to enter a side room. The small room reeked of weed, laced with aftershave.

We were met with the sound of Salt-N-Peppa blasting *Push It* from Tristan's silver disco-flashing glitter iPhone. He was dressed in very tight zebra-print trousers and a white fitted shirt. He sat next to Sonja and joined into the chorus of the song.

As he slurred his way through the lyrics he stood up and emphasised the push movement. It was embarrassing.

"Tristan. Shut up man! You're stoned," Sonja yelled, holding tightly onto his brown, slender arm.

He stopped and spun round as he heard us enter. His eyes were bloodshot, puffy and glassy. He was clearly high as he slurred, "Dr Anderson, thanks for coming on your day off."

As he moved in to give me a hug I whispered sternly, "You can't smoke that shit in here. You'll get us into trouble."

"Could you switch off that music," she sternly ordered Tristan. He reluctantly picked up his iPhone from the side table to hit the stop button.

"Hello, Mrs Nel. I'm Dr Anderson, a gynaecologist. Would you prefer me to call you Sonja or Mrs Nel?"

"Sonja," she replied sitting upright in her bed.

"Sonja. How are you feeling right now?"

"I'm in terrible pain," she winced holding her large protruding stomach.

"That's the labour contractions. Try and take deep breaths," Freya continued whilst writing up Sonja's notes.

"And I've also had a dreadful headache since this morning," Sonja groaned, clutching her head with one hand.

"You do look puffy. We'll need a urine sample from you. I'm going to get your obs checked again and then see how far your cervix has dilated. Are you allergic to anything?" she asked with her pen in one hand and the file in the other.

Sonja shook her head, "Not to my knowledge."

Freya turned to the midwife standing next to her,"Sister, please take her obs."

Suddenly Sonja let out a blood curdling scream., 'Doctor! Give me something for the pain, please."

She flung her head back and screwed up her eyes as she gripped tightly onto the side of the bed.

Freya ordered, "Sister, get me 100mgs of pethidine and some gloves."

The midwife grabbed a syringe off the trolley and drew up fluid from an amber glass vile then passed it to Freya. She then drew the grubby curtain around the bed.

"Sonja, I'm giving you an injection for pain relief. Could you roll over onto your side for me?" we heard Freya say.

"Ouch," Sonja winced.

Tristan flinched, "Fuck! Did you see the size of that needle! Poor Sonja. That's one hell of a long jab."

"Sister, please get some KY jelly, sterile gloves and the ECG scanner."

"*Ja* doctor," she answered before reaching through the curtain for a large kidney bowl, containing medical instruments, a pack labelled 'Sterile', which were on a nearby trolley.

Tristan and I stood aside to let the one of the midwives push through a blood pressure machine."

"We're here Sonja, if you need us," I shouted.

Tristan looked pale and became unusually quiet. His head was huddled down distracting himself on Facebook, Twitter and texting.

"You okay?" I turned to ask him.

"I'm shit scared for Sonja."

"She's in good hands. Try not to worry," I squeezed his cold hand.

Two more midwives wheeled into the room what looked like an ECG machine and pushed it behind the curtains. All I could see were shoes shuffling around the bed.

Sonja blurted, "I need to pee."

"I'll get a bed pan. Then we can do your urine sample at the same time," responded a midwife.

Freya said in a worried tone, "She's still only 4cms exactly like the previous exam done by the midwife ."

The sister commented, "And that's when she was first admitted!"

"Lets see what the ECG says," Freya said.

"Doctor, look her protein is two pluses," the second midwife interrupted.

"What's her BP?" Freya asked.

The sound of the blood pressure machine started up. A short silence.

Freya said loudly, "Jesus! BP is very high,"

There was a serious conversation going on behind the curtain.

"Right, we have a foetal distress here. Sister, get the anaesthetist on call for an emergency C-Section," she ordered.

Everyone jumped to attention, running in and out of the room. It was frightening to watch. Thank heavens Freya was there. I admired her as she morphed into work mode and calmly and confidently took control of the terrifying situation. I felt so helpless just standing there. The curtains whisked open.

Freya faced Sonja and said, "I'm going to be frank with you. Your cervix has only dilated 4 centimetres and you need to get to 10 centimetres. You've stuck at 4 centimetres. You baby is in danger, so I'm going ahead with an emergency Caesarean."

Sonja cried, "I'm going to be vomit."

A midwife swiftly handed a brown sick bowl to her.

"Try and not worry Sonja, but we do need to act quickly."

I closed my eyes and prayed for a divine intervention as I felt tears forming.

"Will my baby be okay?" She sobbed.

"I can't promise anything, but I'm going to do my upmost best. I have to rush now. I'll see you upstairs in theatre," Freya said rubbing the nape of her neck. After patting Sonja on the arm, she turned to me. "Char, can I have a quick word outside?"

I followed her out the room then closed the door. She whispered, "I'm telling you this in confidence. This is serious. Between you and me, if I don't get this baby out soon, it may not survive. Can you keep an eye on your friend Tristan, as he's a serious drama queen and could have a breakdown? He needs to be there for his sister. Time is of the essence. I'm waiting for them to find a bloody anaesthetist. I'll call you with an update when I'm finished in theatre." She air-kissed me on both cheeks before marching off.

I paced the floor of the waiting room. Tristan fidgeted as we stood by for any news. I was holding tightly onto my cellphone when a text message came through from Freya.

Char, I'm out of theatre. All went well. Sonja and baby boy okay. Both r in recovery so the brother won't be able to see them for an hour. Will call when you can both come up F.

I immediately told Tristan the good news.

"Thank God!" he hugged me tightly.

"Dr Anderson's fabulous. She's got VIP status to free hair treatments for life. Sonja must call her son, *Tristan*!" his voice shrilled with excitement.

"Tristan, really now! We can't see them for an hour so let's get a coffee." I suggested, smiling.

"Coffee! A spliff more like it! We've got some celebrating to do."

I rolled my eyes. Typical Tristan, any excuse to have a party.

Another text came through, but this time it was from Stephan. My heart raced faster. I read it immediately.

Howzit beautiful. How was your day? I'm finally home after a hectic day of training and interviews. I'm missing you. Let me cook supper for you tonight. S xx

I replied: *Hello! Sounds like you've been seriously busy. Hope the interviews went well. Thanks for invite, but can't make it tonight. Sorry. C xxx*

"Who's that from?" Tristan asked whilst peering down at my text.

"Stephan."

"Oh ja! What does gorgeous Mr Sportsman want?" he leaned his bleached head forward.

"He's invited me to his place for supper tonight."

"Holy Moly! You were only with him last night. Darling he's besotted with you."

"He can get any woman he fancies. I think I'll play it a bit cool," I smiled widely.

"I heard some scandal about him yesterday," he winked.

"Have you been picking up *stompies*?"

"This one's from his past," he raised a perfectly manicured dark brown eyebrow.

My phone rang. I answered it immediately thinking it was Freya.

"Hello."

"Chantelle!" Stephan's words rolled seductively over my name.

"Stephan!"

My heart beat rapidly and my cheeks flushed.

"You're turning me down tonight."

"Maybe," I teased and moved out of earshot from Tristan.

"Well, this man hasn't stopped thinking about you and wants to see you again soon," his husky voice set off a spiral of last night's delicious memories.

"This woman's tied up at the moment."

"Chantelle, where are you? Sounds like you're in a hospital," he asked in a concerned tone.

I explained to Stephan briefly why I was there.

"It's dangerous that side of the city. I'm coming to make sure you get home safely," he insisted in a masterful voice.

"Stephan, stop! I'm not a small child."

"Look what happened to you the other night. Please babe. I care too much about you to let anything happen," his voice softened.

"I'm really grateful that you saved me, but I can't live my life in fear."

Did he really care about me or was he just being a possessive control freak? I closed my eyes in thought.

"Babe, let's have dinner tonight. I'm really missing you."

I desperately wanted to see Stephan.

"Come over to my place later for coffee."

"Can't wait beautiful. Text me when you're home safely."

"See you later.," I smiled enigmatically at the thought of being with him again.

I walked back to Tristan who was gossiping on his phone. He ended his call as I reached him.

"So tell me what you know about Stephan's past," I asked.

"I need a spliff. Let's go and sit in my car and I'll tell you all the scandal on Mr Sportsman of the Year."

I rolled the passenger window down for two reasons. Firstly, I needed to cool down from the dry, dusty summer heat and secondly, to avoid getting stoned from the fumes that enveloped me from Tristan's thick dagga joint. We were discreetly and safely parked behind the hospital in the staff car park. His CD player was blasting the tunes from Afroman, *Because I Got High.* Tristan's head moved back and forth to the beat. At the chorus, he joined in singing. It was awful, off-key and too much too loud; but he obviously thought it was great.

"Turn down the bloody volume. We won't hear Freya ring back," I said sighing and inwardly rolled my eyes.

"Darling chill," his camp voice was starting to slur. He picked up the cover of a CD decorated with green marijuana leaves and a bold heading which read: *Twenty Smokin' Tunes About Weed.*

"Oh, Sean Paul's on the CD," I said.

"*Ja*, he's spunky, sexy and hot like your Mr Sportsman!" Tristan's face lit up.

"Every guy's hot to you!" I laughed.

"Come on! Have a draw," he enticed holding out the joint.

"You know I don't smoke that stuff. Besides, I already feel stoned on your damn fumes and my clothes and hair probably reek of the stuff," I snarled.

"Darling, you really need to relax."

After taking a long draw on the joint, Tristan exhaled a puff of smoke through his full lips. He encouraged me to have a go. I was tempted and he was right I did need to chill, but I hadn't tried it in my 29 years and I wasn't going to start now. I stood my ground and shook my head.

"Listen to the lyrics of Snoop Dogg." *Live Young, Wild And Free* began playing,

"Enough of these weed songs. Look those security guards are walking this way. They probably smelled your spliff."

"I think that falls into the category of *tough shit*!" he snorted whilst raising his perfectly shaped eyebrows.

"Actually they're not coming to us. The guards are making their way to someone else's car." I sighed with relief.

Still curious to know about Stephan's past, I reminded Tristan again, "So are you going to tell this gossip you heard?"

"Well, Stephan was only fifteen at the time. His father was away for a week on a business trip in Zimbabwe. Unbeknown to Stephan and his brother, his mother had a boyfriend, who happened to be sleeping in her bed that night. Well, the meetings were cancelled so his father flew home early. He wanted to surprise his wife, Stephan and his brother." He took another long drag of his spliff.

"His father tiptoed into the house, not wanting to wake the kids up as it was gone midnight. The lover, in the meantime, heard someone creep up the stairs and thought it might be one of the children. When the footsteps became heavier and more solid, he realised it wasn't a kid. He grabbed his firearm hastily, climbed out of bed and reached for the door, opening it slowly.

He saw a tall, thick-set figure walking towards the bedroom. Alarm bells started ringing thinking it was an intruder. Consumed with fear, the lover randomly fired the gun twice at Stephan's father, killing him on the spot!"

"What! That's awful. Poor guy," I said shaking my head.

I was saddened as I visualised a helpless young Stephan. Now I knew why he didn't trust women. My phone rang. It was Freya.

"Char, are you still in the hospital?"

"I'm in the car park with Tristan. How's everything going?"

"Mother and baby are stable. They've been transferred to Ward F now."

"Ah, that's good news Freya. Can we come up and see them?"

She replied in a tired voice, "*Ja*, come up now as they need to get some rest. I've just got to write up my report before doing a handover. Do you want a lift home?"

"*Ja,* please."

"Okay, meet me at reception in forty-five minutes."

"Cool. See you just now, Freya."

Tristan slurred, "Is my sister okay?"

I smiled, "*Ja*, Freya says they're both stable and going back to the ward.

He held me. "Thank God. I can't wait to see *baby Tristan*!"

"*Baby Tristan*? Seriously! Is she calling him after you? "

"She insisted on naming him Leon, after her twatty husband. But I think he should be named after me. I can dress him in leather zebra pants like mine!"

"Eish! You're stoned! How much of that shit have you smoked?"

We clambered out his car and excitedly dashed back into the hospital. After visiting Sonja and her baby boy, I left a high Tristan with them.

I quickly made my way back to reception to join Freya. I was relived as we sped off in her Mercedes.

"Here's our song Char," she turned up the volume to Enigma singing *Return To Innocence*; we both joined in the chorus:

As we sang I realised then that genuine caring relationships were more important than money and appearances. Freya, Kirsty and Mavis were important people in my life. Tandeka was unscrupulous. She didn't give a damn about me, Adam or any of the staff. Like Enigma says: I didn't care what others say. I had decided I would be myself and tell Tandeka that I was not prepared to do her dirty work for her.

And Stephan. I couldn't stop thinking of what poor Stephan had experienced as a vulnerable young teenager. It explained his obsession with security. As my mother always said: *Never judge a book by its cover!* At last, I had come to the conclusion that it was no longer important I wasn't a perfect size 10!

Stephan was now my priority.

Chapter Fifteen

Rocky continued barking. Gripping tightly onto his collar I yanked him back as I used my free hand to open the door.

"*Howzit*. Come in quick. I don't want Rocky to get out."

Stephan closed the front door behind him then bent down to pat Rocky, "Good boy! It's only me."

"You're out of breath, babe." He kissed me on my cheek. I pushed my dripping wet hair off my face. "I've just come out the shower."

"I know I'm early. I have a fear of being late. It was drilled into us in my swimming training days in the States: *Never ever be late for a swimming competition.*

"Sounds good advice to me. My father's always early for everything in life."

His eyes scoured the kitchen. "I didn't see Mavis when I came in."

"She's gone home to sort out some family problem."

"When will she be back?"

"Sunday afternoon."

"Shit! No ways are you staying here on your own."

"I'll be fine. I've got Rocky."

"Haven't you heard? They poison guard dogs these days. Giving them meat laced with a deadly toxin."

"That's wicked. Poor dogs."

"Babe, come and stay at my place. I'll make supper then we can watch a movie."

"I won't lie. I don't feel safe anymore after last night's ordeal."

"Don't worry I've got you " He hugged me tightly.

"Pack your bag so we can get going."

Stephan made me feel safe secure and special.

Stephan opened the passenger door of his sports car for me. Once we were inside, he immediately activated the auto-lock system. He casually removed the black pistol from his trousers which had been tucked against his washboard stomach. Then he leaned over and placed the gun in the *cubby hole*.

"Do you have a licence for that?" I gestured towards it.

"Of course," he muttered, frowning and firing up the engine.

"Stephan, the first rule of owning a gun is safety. It should be locked in a gun-safe!"

"Everyday someone's shot or has mace sprayed in their face. I'm not risking my life for a cellphone or for a few hundred Rand," his eyes narrowed as he focused on the road.

"I know all that, but don't you think you're being paranoid?"

"No one can rely on the police these days. Take last night. The cops still haven't come to take fingerprints at the crime scene. Which is why I need a gun for protection," he said and physically stiffened.

"You're so right," I let out a sigh.

Stephan was sadly correct.

"Babe, you know we live in a gun culture here," he reassuringly patted my thigh. His jaw clenched and his look intensified as he raced through Johannesburg. He only relaxed when we reached , a wealthy suburb. He changed gears to slow down as we approached speed bumps. We drove up to a security-guarded entrance protecting a prestigious, walled residential estate.

A security-guard, wearing a blue uniform with epaulettes on his short-sleeved shirt, lifted the boom and waved us through. Stephan raised his right hand to thank him.

"*Eish*! Security's hot here. I've already spotted two CCTV cameras!" I noted.

"That's the reason I live here!" he smiled somewhat smugly.

His sports car purred as he took off and drove up to the luxurious entrance of his modern multi-million Rand house. His black *Land Rover* was parked in the driveway.

Stephan placed the pistol into his trousers and he climbed out. An excited bull-terrier dashed up to greet him. He crouched down to stroke the dog's stomach as it rolled onto its back.

"Hello boy! I'm home now."

After opening the large double doors to his home, Stephan stood aside to let me enter a well-lit entrance hall. My heels clattered on the polished, white marble floor as I strode in. He placed my bag in a corner, saying, "I'll take this upstairs for you and lock up my pistol in the gun-safe while I'm there."

He walked upstairs carrying my bag calling after him, "Make yourself at home."

Moments later I was in the large open-plan lounge/dining-room, with floor to ceiling windows. Palm trees in pots were scattered around. Framed pictures of wildlife on the walls caught my eye. Stephan draped his arm around my shoulder, which aroused in me a rush of sensation. I gestured to a photo of Stephan posing with a lion.

"Is that you? Where was that taken?"

"*Ja*, it's me with Zion taken at *Nkuti*. We released him into the bush after he had been nursed back to restored health."

"Interesting. You should let me take some photos of you there next time." I suggested.

Dropping his arm down to hold my hand, he led me into a cosy living room with an enormous plasma television screen attached to the wall and surrounded by a stereo sound system. An elongated, red leather couch, which could seat several people, faced the screen.

"This is where we'll watch a movie one day."

Stephan, I realised, owned a beautifully stylish home highlighted with touches of white, black, grey and red décor, giving it a homely feeling. It felt expensive yet relaxing. I couldn't wait to find out what his bedroom was like.

"How many bedrooms do you have?"

"Four! The last time I counted."

It was pretty obvious to me how obsessive Stephan was with health and fitness. His shelves were lined with large tubs of creatine and protein powders. A small glass-door fridge was filled with bottles of energy sports drinks. On one end of the grey marble worktop, a bowl overflowed with fresh fruit. The current issue of *Men's Health and Fitness* was open on the breakfast bar.

"We've got the place to ourselves now!" he grabbed my hand again.

Moments later we were standing at the end of his lounge, which discreetly opened up into a bar. There was a masculine feel to the room with a ?table tucked away in the corner. The main feature was a long oak wooden bar with matching stools. Displayed on the shelves were swimming trophies and medals won by Stephan along with photographs of him swimming races and holding his trophies.

"Would you like a drink?"

"A glass of cool white wine would go down well." I licked my dry lips.

I glanced around when he poured the wine. Stephan was clearly highly motivated and a devoted swimmer. Inspirational posters spread around the room.

Evaluate the people in your life,
Then promote, demote or terminate
You're the CEO of your life.

He noticed me reading the words and added, "My favourite's a phrase from Michael Phelps, the American 22-time Olympic medallist: *If you want to be the best, you have to do things that other people aren't willing to do.*

"They do say South Africans are enthusiastic generally and keen to say yes." I giggled.

His eyes dazzled as he laughed aloud, exclaiming, "*Ja,* I'm up for anything."

"Let's have our drinks outside." I suggested.

"After you," he gestured towards the open French doors. We made our way into the fragrant fresh evening air, smelling the jasmine planted in hanging baskets on the secluded patio overlooking a sparkling pool.

"This is the entertaining area," he announced, pulling out a deckchair for me.

After putting our drinks down on the poolside table, he bent down and gently pressed his soft lips on my forehead. "I'm going to change into my swimming shorts. Why don't you put on your cozzie?"

"Great idea. I need to cool down. I'll change after you."

After Stephan disappeared inside, I relaxed in my chair, sipping the chilled white wine. I watched the light from the moon sparkle on the crystal-blue pool water and it enticed me to jump in. After finishing my drink, I kicked off my sandals and sat dangling my feet into the cool water. Hurriedly I slipped into my bikini and eased myself into the pool, waiting for Stephan.

The water was refreshing; I felt weightless. The tang of chlorine took me back to my synchronized swimming days at high school. The pool lit up as two underwater lights automatically came on.

"Why is he taking so long?" I muttered feeling the urgency to see him.

Then the patio lights flicked on. Stephan strode through the French doors.

He stopped abruptly, baffled.

"Where's she gone?" he murmured.

Giggling to myself at his puzzled face, I teased him playing hide-and-seek. I ducked under the water holding my breath. All was silent apart from bubbles from my nose and mouth which shimmered in the underwater lighting. Gasping for air, I shot out of the water to the sound of the outside world, wiping my eyes before opening them. I looked up to see Stephan standing at the edge of the pool with a towel draped around his waist. He was holding a *Speedo* sports-bag.

"You can't hide from me. I'll always find you," he said locking eyes with me. He dropped the sports-bag and placed his hands on his hips.

"Come and get me then!" I flirted, smiling.

He looked magnificent in his green swim shorts. Water splashed my face when he dived in.

"Come here," he said. His hands caught me by the waist and pinned me against the side of the pool. I wound my arms around his neck. Our faces nearly touched. I felt we were alone and that nothing existed outside our bubble.

"Chantelle, I want you so badly," he said in a smoky voice.

I'd never felt this kind of magnetic attraction before. A part of me wanted to yield to my desires but part of me, knowing the deep pain of rejection, held back. But desire overcame caution.

"Tonight I'm yours," I whispered, feeling this strong attraction was so right. Stephan caressed my chin with his thumb gazing longingly into my eyes.

"You're driving me crazy," he murmured against my lips. He pulled me closer and caressed my neck. Taking a fistful of hair he gently tugged it igniting waves of euphoria through my body. It was the right side of aggressive to turn me on wildly.

He longingly sucked on my lip before kissing me deeply with his agile tongue. His mouth tasted salty and sweet. I erupted in goose pimples when the air brushed against my naked breasts as Stephan gently removed my bikini top.

His eyes glanced longingly down as he moved his soft warm lips over my nipples making them tingle, tighten and harden.

"You smell so good, I want to kiss you all over," he whispered.

I traced my fingers down his firm chest, I wanted to explore further. My body trembled and my muscles clenched as Stephan's tongue glided further down to my mid-riff, stopping as he reached the water level. He cupped my face in his hands then went back to kissing me but harder this time.

"Ah!" I moaned into his mouth.

The pool water swirled around us lubricating our bodies as we rubbed against each other. I felt his erection. Both our breathing became more intense as he gently pulled down my bikini bottoms, moving his hand over my buttocks. Not breaking eye contact I glided my hands down into his swim shorts letting them drop as his hard erection sprang out. He groaned as I stroked it softly with my fingers.

I wrapped my legs tightly round his waist as we submerged under water. He gyrated me up and down his firm torso as I gripped onto his hair. I didn't want him to stop as it all became mind-blowingly intense …

Stephan's biceps flexed as he gripped my waist and lifted me onto the edge of the pool. He pulled himself out effortlessly. Water dripped from his golden body.

"Where can I find a towel?" I asked, desperately wanting to cover my naked body.

"Hang on. I'll get you one from my sports-bag."

He shook the water from his hair before he grabbed a large beach towel and wrapped me in it. Tenderly he dabbed my face dry. "You're beautiful, Chante."

I smiled and placed my lips on his. He took control and hugged me tightly with his towel draped round his waist.

"Time to move inside," he suggested.

With our wine glasses topped up we settled next to each other on the leather sofa.

"I've got a romance and a thriller for us to watch…which one first?" Stephan stroked my hair.

"What's the romance?" I smiled.

"You mentioned *Titanic* was one of your favourites, so I managed to get hold of it!"

"Cool! Thanks hey. Let's watch that first. But what's the thriller?"

"*Cold Harbour!*"

"Ah! I've been waiting to see that. That's set in Cape Town starring Tony Kgoroge. Damn! Now I'm torn which one to watch first?" I rubbed my hands together.

"Let's toss for it. Tails for *Cold Harbour* and heads for *Titanic*. Tails or heads?" he asked whilst picking up a coin from the coffee table.

"Tails!" I giggled as it spun high into the air, then grabbed it as it fell.

We both looked into his open palm.

"Heads!" he winked.

"*Titanic* it is then. But I still want to watch *Cold Harbour.*"

After slipping the DVD into the player he cuddled in next to me, wrapping his arm round my shoulder.

I wiped a tear from my cheek as Celine Dion crooned *My Heart Will Go On,* the theme tune from *Titanic.* "This movie always tears at my heart," I whispered.

Stephan pulled me in closer and pressed his lips onto mine. We melted into one another discovering the beauty of each other. Love radiated between us. I was in heaven, cocooned in Stephan's arms.

Much later, after the flame of passion had been turned into a gently glowing ember, we fell asleep, sated by our experience.

* * *

I was on a high when I woke up on Sunday morning. The world was a better place. The sun shone brighter, the birds twittering was music in my ears and the smell of coffee lured me to the kitchen.

We enjoyed croissants and fresh coffee, exchanging loving looks and soft kisses. After a late night, we'd slept in and were not very hungry, preferring to savour our appetite for the impending braai.

The kitchen door opened and Stephan's middle-aged domestic, wearing a grey apron smiled as he entered the kitchen.

"Good day Stephan," he grinned, looking up.

"Chantelle, meet Enoch. He keeps my place spotless."

"Morning Chantelle," he nodded. I smiled acknowledging his greeting.

Enoch immediately left through the back door.

"I'll lock up before I leave," he murmured, sensing our need to alone – but very much together.

Chapter Sixteen

Stephan wasn't his usual self. Something's wasn't right and I couldn't put my finger on it. He was withdrawn despite making an effort to entertain his guests. Stephan and Anton were standing over the *braai* cooking man-sized steaks and *boerewors*. Next to Stephan was a sun-crisped, thirty-something neighbour. With a beer in his hand, he turned to Stephan and remarked, "Well done *oke*. It must've taken a life-time of training to qualify for the Olympics?"

Kevin replied, "Stephan pushes himself so hard. He's training six hours solid a day."

He asked, "How many lengths a day?"

Stephan softly replied, "At least fifty lengths a day."

"*Eish*! That explains your solid muscle."

Anton added, "Stephan's so focused and devoted. It means the world to him. He's exceeded everyone's expectations."

He patted Stephan on the shoulder.

"Are you going to get some medals for South Africa?"

I walked up and whispered, "Babe, where's the bathroom?"

"Come I'll show you," he passed the *braai* tongs to Anton and led the way up to the large house. I smiled at his mother who was engaged in a conversation with her friend. She looked up and did not take her steely grey eyes off us as we walked hand in hand towards the house. I had a strange feeling his mother did not like me. She was very cool when Stephan introduced me to her. But why?

"Stephan, you sound stressed."

"I am."

"How come?" I tenderly gave his firm hand a squeeze.

"I need to get away for a few days so I'm escaping to the sanctuary tomorrow. Why don't you come with me?"

"Monday's a bank holiday. I'll have you back home by Monday night."

I paused. I loved my experience last time and I wanted to see Shumba and Moyo again.

"So you joining me?" he pressed.

"*Ja,* count me and my camera in."

"We're going through the back entrance via the kitchen so I can grab some of the best biltong."

He stood back for me to enter a spotless kitchen. We were greeted by the sweet aroma of pastries, cinnamon and nutmeg. Numerous plates of delicious puddings were neatly lined up on the worktops of the large sunlit kitchen. Two muscular swimmers were leaning against the kitchen hob chewing on sticks of dark-brown *biltong*.

"Henk! Carl! I wondered where you guys had got to. I see you're enjoying the *biltong* my uncle made."

Henk, the taller swimmer, highly competitive, with a shaven head to gain a nano-second on his swimming times, greeted, "*Howzit bro*."

Stephan smiled and grabbed a handful from a large canister.

"*Ja*, your mother offered us some. Steph, this stuff's *lekker,*" Carl replied with a mouthful.

"It's the best source of protein for your training diet," I said.

"*Ja*, but egg-whites are the perfect source. I start my day with six egg-whites mixed with a protein drink.

"Guys check you later. Got to get back to braai the meat."

Stephan pointed down a long deeply-carpeted passage. "Chante, the guest bathroom's on the right. See you just now."

Making my way back to the kitchen I overheard Henk's venomous words, "He's a fucking cheat. I don't like him at all."

"Who are you talking about?" Carl asked.

"Stephan! He needs to be brought down a peg or two. Every time I see him he's showing off with all his money and endorsements," he hissed.

"Hell! No ways."

"*Boet*, I checked him out in the toilets at the Sports Awards."

Carl whistled through his teeth.

They're supposed to be his friends. Why were they talking about him like that? Why's Henk accusing him of being a cheat? What did he see Stephan doing in the toilets at the awards ceremony? Could it have been the young pretty blonde, who was flirting with him? No wonder he took so long. Why even Kevin had noticed. Nausea overwhelmed me as I listened on.

Carl replied, "I haven't seen Steph showing off his money —"

Henk cut him off, "And that Chantelle's just another bimbo of his. Probably just with him cos he's the new Mr Poster boy. I wonder if she knows what a cheating bastard he is?" he spat.

"Bimbo? I bet you'd have done her if you'd had the chance," he laughed.

I didn't want to hear anymore, so marched outside to find Stephan.

"Chante! Come and meet my cousin, Debbie," Stephan beckoned.

"Cuz meet Chantelle," he swigged on a bottle of beer. Why was Stephan drinking alcohol now? All the other swimmers were drinking fruit juice or energy drinks?

"Hi Debbie," I faked a smile. It wasn't her fault her cousin was a cheat.

"Nice to finally meet you."

She pecked me on the cheek.

"Stephan, we need to talk," I blurted.

"Now, but —" he frowned.

I cut him off, "Now!"

Feeling the tension, Debbie interrupted, "I'm off to get myself a drink. "See you both later."

He grabbed my hand and pulled me out of hearing distance.

"What's got into you?" he snapped with a beer breath.

Glaring at him with my hands on my hips, I snapped, "Why—"

Appearing from nowhere, his mother cut me off saying, "Son, you're supposed to be mingling with the guests. I suggest you sort your love life out after the braai."

She narrowed her eyes at me.

Rage tore through me as I ripped my arm away from Stephan's grasp. Grabbing my handbag, I marched down the tarred driveway to my *VW Golf.*

"Chantelle stop!" Stephan bellowed. "Come back."

His heavy footsteps caught up to me. Just as I opened the car door, he spun me round and snapped, "What the hell are you going on about?"

I glared into his puzzled eyes.

"You're a cheating bastard. I suspected you had something going on with that blonde tart," I spat.

"What the hell are you talking about?" he yelled.

With adrenaline ripping through my body I pushed his solid arm out of my way and jumped into the car. He looked down at me holding the door open.

"I don't know where the hell you're getting this from. This isn't like you."

"Come off it — just own it."

"Chantelle, I'm not fucking cheating on you!"

"I even fooled myself into thinking I was the only one — I'm accustomed to being used."

Tears pricked in my eyes.

"And forget about me joining you at Nkuti tomorrow. You can go on your own," I screamed at him in an absolute rage.

Stephan jerked back as I revved up the engine and sped off. In the rear-view mirror, I saw Stephan sprinting after me waving his arms.

* * *

"Chantelle, Chantelle," Mavis called knocking insistently on my bedroom door. My eyes reluctantly opened. I glanced at my alarm clock. It was eight in the morning. Shit, my alarm hadn't gone off. Then I realised it was a bank holiday.

"Coming," I mumbled clambering out of bed and pulling on my dressing gown.

Mavis was standing patiently outside my bedroom.

"Morning Mavis," I said sleepily.

"There's a strange man at the gate asking for you."

She raised her eyebrows with concern and crossed her arms. I frowned.

"I'm not expecting anyone. Are you sure he has the right house?"

'Chantelle, he's asking for you by name," she insisted nodding her head.

"Really, what does he look like?"

"He's dark in complexion, big and he has a gun," she replied in a worried tone, her eyes widened.

"Is he dressed smartly? How old does he look? Is he driving a car?"

I patted her on the shoulder as I reminded myself she wasn't good at giving details. Mavis pursed her lips deep in thought.

"I don't know...he's got a uniform. Maybe you can look for yourself, Chantelle," she replied.

"Let me get changed. Then I'll go outside and see what he wants," I sighed before heading to the bathroom.

"The sooner they come and fix the intercom, the better," I muttered.

After changing into my old comfortable beige sweatpants and an over-sized grey T-shirt, I stepped outside into the glaring sun, squinting.

"*Eina,*" I muttered wishing I had worn my flip-flops when the hot ground burnt my bare feet.

Rocky's short brown fur bristled on his neck as he snarled at the unfamiliar man on the other side of the gate.

"Rocky get inside," I ordered. He would not budge, so I struggled to drag him by his thick leather collar.

"Miss Chantelle, I'll take him," Lucky startled me from behind.

"Lucky, please put him in the kitchen for now."

Releasing my grip on Rocky's collar, Lucky's grubby, calloused hand took over from me.

I pointed the key fob towards the gate which slid ajar noisily. I cautiously put my head around the heavy metal gate. Standing to attention was a distinctive, tall and burley man smartly dressed in a navy blue security uniform.

"Morning, madam."

"How can I help you?" I asked, with a hint of suspicion in my voice.

"Thato Ndaba from Red Alert Security reporting for duty madam."

"What?" I shrieked, in disbelief.

"There has to be a mistake as I have not organised any security," I huffed, placing my hands on my hips. He handed me a brown envelope addressed to Miss Chantelle Swanepoel and took a step back.

"Wait here. I won't be long," I announced before closing the gate. I turned round with the envelope in my hand and marched inside.

"Who was the man at the gate?" Mavis was quick to enquire.

"He's a security guard."

Rubbing her chin, she went on in her tongue-clicking voice, *"Eish,* these days you have to very careful. These *tsotis* pretend to be policemen or security guards."

"Ja, but this one's not a fake," I muttered as I impatiently tore at the envelope with a pencil and pulled out a formal letter addressed to me. A contract was attached. I glanced over the A4 paper. It was a formal 24-hour security plan, detailing the hours and times a guard would be assigned to protect my property. There was a list of contact numbers and a Code Zebra in the event of an emergency.

What was going on? How did Red Alert get my name and address? Who organised this? I went straight to my landline, picked up the receiver and dialled the contact number at the top of the letterhead. Mavis conveniently hovered in the lounge, dusting the furniture.

"Red Alert," a male with a thick Afrikaans accent answered.

"This is Chantelle Swanepoel. I've been sent a security guard and a Contract with your firm, which I never organised," I blurted down the handset.

"One moment please."

There was a short silence. Then a formal business man's voice came on the line.

"Hello Miss Swanepoel, Sorry about the confusion, but the service has already been paid for in advance."

"Who by?" I demanded, holding onto the handset more tightly.

"Our VIP client, Mr Erasmus," he answered in a surprised tone.

"Stephan!" I shook my head as it all began to fall into place.

"*Ja,* Miss Swanepoel. He's paid for six months service in advance. We are highly rated and we are known to have the quickest response team in SA," he boasted.

"Thank you, I replied and ended the call briskly.

Chapter Seventeen

Pacing up and down in the lounge, my mind swirled with questions. Why didn't Stephan warn me? Besides, I'd already told him not to organise security for me. Part of me was flattered, but the other half was annoyed because he'd ignored my wishes. I felt my resolve hardening. I needed to confront him.

All fired up I called Stephan on his cellphone.

"Chante, good morning."

"Stephan, why did you organise security without my permission?" I blurted still pacing the room.

"I wanted to make sure you're protected and safe."

"I'm quite capable of organising my own security," I laughed in a sarcastic high pitch. "I don't want to sound ungrateful, but you've paid for six months in advance and I'm on a budget."

He cut me off, "Chantelle Swanepoel, let me talk. I can afford it."

"We don't even know each other that well. Besides, no one makes decisions for me. It is my choice, my choice," I replied tightening my grip on the phone. Did Mr Sportsman of the Year think he could buy me?

There was an awkward silence.

"Stephan, just cancel the contract. Goodbye."

I slammed the phone down. I was suddenly overwhelmed with regret. I must have sounded like a spoilt, ungrateful bitch. Maybe he was genuinely concerned about my safety and he was not trying to control or impress me with his money. I looked down at my cellphone waiting for him to call or text. Nothing. I probably wouldn't hear from him again. I felt sick in my stomach.

I chewed on the end of the pencil as I scowled at myself in the lounge mirror. My hair was unbrushed and dishevelled. I had no make-up on. Basically, I looked like a shabby, scruffy and unattractive mess.

I ensured Rocky was closed up in the kitchen before I stepped outside wearing my flip-flops and marched to the gate to dismiss the waiting security guard.

Once back inside the house, I checked for a call from Stephan. Nothing. I felt bereft. What had I done in a moment of madness? Slumping onto my cosy, comfortable couch I huddled into the corner, clutching a soft silk cushion close to my chest. There was something reassuring about holding onto something familiar.

* * *

"Darl, where've you been? I've been trying to contact you for days. It felt good to hear Kirsty's familiar voice.

"I know. It's been a whirlwind. You wouldn't believe what's happened in the past 48 hrs," I sighed.

"You sound really down. What's happened?"

I inhaled sharply. "I don't know where to start, but I called Stephan and yelled at him."

I started sobbing.

"What's wrong? You haven't cried since Franco dumped you for that bitch."

"I've just screwed things up with Stephan."

I ran my fingers through my hair.

"How?"

I could hear the confusion in her voice.

"He organised and paid for six months, 24/7 home security, without even telling me. The security guard pitched up this morning. In a complete rage I called Stephan impulsively. I yelled at him and I hung up," I babbled without taking a deep breath.

"Jeez Chantelle, are you crazy? Stephan's smitten with you. Can't you see it? If he didn't care about you, he wouldn't be concerned about your safety. Get a grip; he saved your life the other day."

"I didn't mean to be ungrateful. I don't feel right that he is paying such a large amount of money when we barely know each other. I'm so used to Franco being such a tight arse, counting every cent. I can't believe I allowed Franco to make me feel guilty about spending my own money."

"Good riddance to that stingy imbecile. Darl, don't feel bad about Stephan. He was rather presumptuous organising security without your permission," she sighed.

"I feel crap because I spoke to him like that. Oh well, I won't be seeing or hearing from him again." I paused.

* * *

After a miserable bank holiday, I was fired up to get to work and hopefully forget some of my troubles.

My cellphone rang, it was Kirsty. "We need a proper catch-up. Let's do lunch tomorrow at our usual spot," Kirsty suggested.

"Good idea. Shall we say midday?"

"*Ja*, I'll be a little late, but have a drink till I get there. Hey, I've got to go. There's a dead-line on this story I'm doing. Take care."

"Cool, see you tomorrow."

I rang off. I wanted to focus on anything but Stephan, so I picked up the remote on the coffee table and switched on the local news. I caught the end of the weather report: *Overall it will be a warmer day over South Africa today. Mostly dry. Temperature in Kimberly reaching 30C and in Johannesburg, Soweto and Pretoria will be 28C. Cape Town, on the other hand, will be mostly cloudy and cool with scattered rain showers and highs of 22 C.*

We're now crossing over to join Candice Prinsloo, at Johannesburg Swimming Park, for the sports headlines.

I sat upright. My eyes fixed onto Stephan wearing a fitted black *Speedo*. Water droplets glistened in the sun accentuating his broad shoulders and small waist. He moved with animal grace raising his arms to remove his olive-green swimming cap and white goggles.

My heart lurched when a pretty young TV reporter moved closer to him. She flicked her long, blonde hair and purred, "Stephan, I can see why you won the 'Sportsman of the Year' award. How does it feel?"

Thoughts of them together pierced me. Overwhelmed by jealousy and remorse, I grabbed the remote and clicked off the TV.

In my mind's eye, my mother was shaking her finger at me and, in her 'I told you so' tone, bellowed, "What do you expect Chantelle? You never think before you act."

Work for me was always a form of escapism. I had two days before meeting the deadline on the Christmas range which would appear in the November issue of *Vogue*. I grabbed my iPad and scuttled off to the *stoep*. Plonking myself on the hard French-washed wicker chair, I strategically placed my iPad against a homemade frame on the glass table. Firing it up, I put on my head-phones and clicked into iTunes. *Fast Car* by Tracy Chapman blasted into my ears. The deep-red polished floor cooled my hot bare feet. I tapped my feet in time to the strumming of Tracy's guitar.

Intending to go straight to the *Afrika Fashions* photo folder, I gave into temptation and hovered the cursor over the album marked, *Nkuti Wildlife Rehabilitation Sanctuary, Stephan and Shumba.*

I moved the cursor to the delete icon, ready and poised to press it. But I was undecided and torn. My logical head scolded:

Stop behaving like a school girl with a crush. Delete the album together with any memories of Mr Olympic Swimmer. You know he's out of your league.

Then my heart said: *Do NOT delete. Stephan cares for you and your safety.* I don't know what made me turn round. I felt someone watching me. The blood drained from my face. My heart pounded. I froze...

"Hello Chantelle," he said, casually twirling his car keys. He was wearing green tracksuit pants; the South African flag printed down the both sides with a white fitted T-shirt and *Nike* trainers.

I opened my mouth but nothing came out. I never expected Stephan to just pitch up.

"I thought it best I come over personally to continue our conversation."

His face was unreadable. He folded his arms. He paused awaiting my reply.

"How did you get in?" I gulped.

"Your gardener." He paused, waiting for my reaction.

I cleared my throat, " But he doesn't even know how you are."

"Exactly! Why do you think I'm trying to organise security for you?"

I stared anxiously up at him as he walked towards me in a predatory way. His sporty body wash engulfed me as be bent down to whisper in my ear as though nothing had happened between us.

"You're not going to get rid of me that easily."

Concern clouded his narrow eyes as he looked at me more closely.

"Have you been crying? What's wrong Chante?" he asked, frowning. Reaching his hand towards me, he tucked a strand of hair behind my ear.

"Nothing," I managed, smoothing back my hair and realising how vulnerable I was. It was all my fault I was in this mess. Could I redeem myself?

"Would you like something to drink? Some fresh orange juice?"

I tried to distract him. My situation at work threatened and who knew what the outcome of that would be. Perhaps I was using time as a means of procrastinating what I had to face at *Afrika Fashions*.

"Orange juice sounds good, but let's clear the air first."

A slow smile radiated across his face. Stephan was the most handsome man I'd ever set eyes on. He casually leaned against the patio wall keeping his hands in his pockets.

"I'm sorry I was harsh and hung up on you and ran off from the *braai* in a state," I whimpered, reaching for a tissue.

"What's with your hang-up, not wanting me to keep you safe?" he asked, not taking his mesmerizing eyes off me.

"Well...I just felt uncomfortable with you spending that kind of money on me. Like I owed you a favour. Also, you didn't respect my decision."

I shifted uncomfortably on my chair.

"I care about you. I want you to be safe even if it means spending money on top security. What's wrong with that?"

"It's a lot of money and I'm on a budget."

"Chantelle, *ja,* so what if I'm wealthy. That's what a boyfriend does. He spends money on his girlfriend."

Girlfriend? The word sounded warming, comforting and sweet.

"I know money isn't a problem for you."

"It's not. So you'd better get used to me spending it on you."

Stephan bent down and pulled me off the chair.

"Come here. You're too independent for your own good," his voice softened as he pulled me into his hard body. I let my head rest on his chest.

His cellphone rang. He ignored it. It rang again. He retrieved it from his pants pocket and without even checking to see who it was, quickly switched it off. Suddenly feeling self-conscious, I pulled away from him. I felt Stephan's hand spin me round.

"I'm not going to let you walk away from me," he said in a soft voice as he pinned me against the cool wall. A thrill went through my entire body. I bit hard on my lower lip. I wanted him even more as his eyes looked deeply into mine.

"Chantelle...I can't stay away from you." His arms tightened round my waist.

"Mavis is back from her time off," I warned, looking up at him. I pulled back again.

"Makes it more exiting. We could be caught!" he stared down at me. With just the right amount of force, not to be considered aggressive, he yanked me back into his arms. I could not resist as his fingers slipped through my hair. He tightened his grip and pulled my head back. His warm breath tingled down my neck as he started kissing it. I melted into him. He tenderly cupped my face into his hands, stared at me and softly said, "Chante, I don't want to lose you."

I slightly opened my mouth and pulled his soft lips onto mine, eagerly exploring his moist, fresh minty mouth. I wanted him so badly. I knew the feeling was mutual. I felt alive again. My nipples tingled, tightened and hardened as his hand slipped under my loose top whilst gently squeezing, stroking and soothing them. I eagerly lifted my top over my head. Goose pimples erupted through me as his mouth glided down my body.

Stephan looked even more desirable as he ripped off his T shirt, leaving his tracksuit pants to drop onto the ground.

In one sweep he cleared all my papers off the dining room table, letting them scatter onto the floor. His biceps flexed as he gripped my waist and effortlessly lifted me onto the end of the hard oak table. He was in control as he lay me down and slipped off my sweat pants. He pinned my arms above my head, clasped his hands into mine and splayed out my fingers. My eyes closed against the surge of arousal…pleasantly aching, trembling and radiating with desire. My hands gripped his hair pulling him harder into me. Our desire for each other intensified.

"Chantelle," he murmured.

I wrapped my one leg around his waist. I tightened my leg around him.

My buttocks stiffened as waves of ecstasy started to ripple deliciously through me. I was beguiled. He held my hands and looked deeply into my eyes. I felt them moisten with unshed tears of joy.

"You are mine," he murmured griping me tightly.

"Yes, all yours," I whispered into his ear.

Our bodies merged like we were glued together. I wanted the moment to last forever…

When I stared into his eyes, I saw shutters coming down, closing me out. I didn't understand.

What was his problem? Had Mavis come into the room? This shockingly sharp shutdown did not match his words or the closeness we had shared moments ago. I needed time to think.

"I'm going to take a shower," I said quietly, moving slowly away from him.

He ran his hands through his hair. There was an edge to his voice and for no apparent reason, he looked uneasy.

"I must make a few phone calls."

"What's wrong?" I cocked my head to one side.

"What do you mean?" he frowned.

"You're acting so weird."

"I'm emotionally confused," he said. I felt there was a tinge of regret in his voice. I shivered as I felt the post-coital glow evaporate.

"I've a meeting lined up as soon as I leave your place. I need a shower. Do you mind?" he asked.

"Sure. Use the guest bathroom. Shout if there're no fresh towels," I replied as I made my way to my shower room.

Stephan was standing, beamed down at me. His hair was wet and combed back. Why was he like that? He was still a mystery.

His cellphone rang, he immediately answered it and faced the window.

"*Ja*, of course I'm interested Anton. I'm aware of the legal aspects. Check when you're free tomorrow."

He waited, still staring out the window.

"Ten tomorrow's good. I'll get the *Speedo* contract from Kevin and bring it with me."

He paused, still holding the phone close to his ear. I scurried to the kitchen. Rocky's tail wagged frantically when I crouched down to pat him. I let him out the back door and noticed Mavis in the laundry, carefully pressing the steam iron onto my white cotton shirt. I cringed at the thought of her walking in on us if we had lost self-control.

Opening the fridge, I removed a jug of freshly-squeezed orange juice and filled two glasses. I put them on the glass coffee table and plonked myself onto the couch.

"Since winning, my phone hasn't stopped ringing. *Speedo* is offering me a sponsorship," a slow smile spread across his face and he shared his success.

"Woah! You're now South Africa's new sports hero!"

"*Ja*, I know, but I don't like all this publicity. They want me to do a photo shoot."

He crossed his arms, frowning.

"Come on, Stephan. You look the part. You'll get used to it."

I gazed back up at him. He sat down next to me.

"Chante, I'm so sorry I made you feel like that," he paused as his eyes bore into me and he went on, "Please let me reorganise the security for you. No strings attached, okay? Look at it as a gift."

He gently stroked my cheek.

"Chante, I would never ask you to do anything I wouldn't do."

I rolled my eyes, asking, "Is that why you're acting weird cos, I won't have you pay for my security?"

"If you must know. I'm paranoid about security," he raised his voice.

"When I was fifteen years old, my father was shot in our own home."

His voice softened, but his fists were clenched. "I don't want to loose anyone else."

He swallowed hard and blinked to hold back his tears. I'd never seen the vulnerable side of Stephan. He reminded me of a broken-winged bird. I felt helpless. I was speechless and didn't know what to do. My heart went out to him.

"I'm so sorry," I offered, placing my hands gently onto his back as a wave of empathy washed over me.

"Swimming in the Olympics is a dream my father had for me and I want to do it for him."

He took a deep breath then stood up.

"I'll do whatever it takes to take part in the Olympics. You've no idea what I'm prepared to do, to live out my late father's dream. I've waited ten years for this."

He paused disrupted when his cellphone rang. After checking who was calling, he answered, "What's up?"

He stood up and moved back to the window, facing my manicured garden. There was silence as he nodded his head, listening to the person on the other side.

"*Ja*, what now? But I've got a meeting at four!"

He ran his fingers through his wet hair.

"Okay, I'm coming over now."

He ended the call and replaced his phone in his tracksuit pocket. Turning to face me he said, "Kevin wants to have an urgent meeting with me now. He sounds really upset. He doesn't sound his usual self. Something weird is going on."

"That's not right. You could've been in the middle of something important."

I stood up.

"Exactly! Sorry babe, I have to shoot. Speak to you later."

He bent down to kiss me. I smiled back at him saying, "I'll let you out the gate."

I grabbed the gate fob and walked outside with him following me to his sports car.

Chapter Eighteen

I ploughed through the work Tandeka needed from me for the Thursday meeting. Feeling shattered, I took a break and called to Mavis for a cup of coffee.

"Please, Mavis, I'm in the lounge."

"*Rooibos* tea Chantelle?" Mavis questioned, like a stuck gramophone record.

"Mavis, you do try. Coffee will be good. Ta."

Then I grabbed the remote and switched on the television and selected the 13h00 news. I bolted upright with my eyes fixed on the television screen. My heart galloped. I couldn't swallow.

"Breaking news! Mr SA Sportsman Stephan Erasmus has been tested positive for a banned sports-enhancing drug. The Anti-Doping Disciplinary Committee of the South African Institute for Drug-Free Sport confirmed today that Mr Erasmus has been found to have Anabolic Endogenic steroids in his system and has been temporarily suspended."

I couldn't feel my body because it started to get cold. I froze as the newsreader's words continued to tear through me.

"The panel met yesterday and Mr Erasmus could receive up to a two-year ban and be stripped of his title. At the South African National championships he finished first in the men's 100m backstroke and also finished first in the 50m butterfly."

Stephan? No — this can't be true. I watched on in disbelief.

"We're now crossing over live for the latest from Ruby Thulo."

A petite attractive reporter holding a microphone continued, *"Good morning Alex. We're in Bryanstan outside the home of Stephan Erasmus, but there's still no sign of him."*

"What about his management team?"

"Alex, we've not had a response from Stephan or his team."

"Any talk of an appeal?"

"We're unsure at this moment if he's appealing...Hang on, he's coming out."

Crowds gathered at the sight of the high steel gates opening and a black *Land Rover* drove out with Stephan in the driver's seat. He was wearing a camouflaged baseball cap and dark shades. A reporter dashed up to the car and shoved her microphone towards the half-closed window

"Mr Erasmus, have you got anything to say?"

She raised her voice, *"What do you think of the drug results?"*

He ignored her and sped off.

A few by-standers chanted, "Cheat! Cheat!"

I felt awful that I'd accused Stephan of cheating with another woman. My breathing became rapid as disappointment began to drown me. I yelled at the flat-screen, "Stephan! Why did you do it?"

His erratic behaviour started to fall into place...mood swings, lack of self-control and impatience. His body was swimming with excess testosterone. Just who is the real Stephan Erasmus?

The reporter spun round adding, *"Well, there you have it folks. No comment from Stephan Erasmus."*

"Ruby! What do you make of this?"

"We've had no comment from Stephan Erasmus or his management team.

"Has there been any indication he's been using this illegal drug?"

"Alex, according to a reliable source, he was on performance-enhancing drugs whilst qualifying for the Olympic Games and they are seriously considering stripping him of his title."

"Alex, as a young boy Stephan witnessed his father being shot."

"Thank you, Ruby. We'll get more on this story."

"Alex, back to you in the studio."

How was Stephan feeling now I wondered? Just then my phone rang.

"Chantelle, switch on the news on. Stephan's been suspended. He's been caught using steroids," Kirsty sounded frantic.

"We don't know if this is true. Maybe he's been set up. I've been thinking all along he's been cheating on me with another woman. No wonder he's been acting weird and distant."

I felt sick in my stomach for behaving like a jealous bitch.

* * *

The hot still night together with my over-active mind caused me to toss and turn. I couldn't sleep. In my mind's eye I visualised Stephan as a fifteen-year-old boy witnessing his father being shot by his mother's lover. It must have been traumatic, tragic and torture for him. Part of my training as a photographer was to write a thesis on criminal photography. The sickening sights of a shot with a pistol left me with nightmares for months. I wanted to wrap the young Stephan in my arms and heal him. The full moon shone a glimmer of light through the curtains. I tried to still my mind by hypnotically staring at the mesmeric turning ceiling fan. Finally, my eyes closed and I gradually slipped into a deep sleep, dreaming of hospital, babies and Stephan.

Chapter Nineteen

The powerful aroma of freshly cooked pizza enticed me into the busy Bourgeois restaurant. A friendly bald waiter greeted me and led me to a neatly laid table. The restaurant was buzzing with laughter and the rainbow nation chatter in English, Afrikaans and Zulu. Clutching my cellphone tightly, I checked the weather forecast for the weekend on my app: Johannesburg — mostly sunny — 26 degrees C on Saturday and 28 degrees C on Sunday. Notifications splashed all over my phone: Breaking News: *Mr Sportsman of the Year, Stephan Erasmus suspended. Stephan Erasmus found positive for a sports-enhancing drug.* I wish Kirsty would hurry up as I was itching to speak to her.

"Can I get you a drink?" the waiter politely asked handing me a menu.

"Umm, yes please. Could I have a *Savanna Dry?*"

He hastily scribbled down my order, asking, "And to eat?"

"I'll order when my friend arrives."

He scuttled off leaving the menu with me. I ogled the various mouth-watering dishes. *Prawn Spaghetti* jumped off the menu. My eyes drifted further down the page to the cocktails: *Dom Pedro* (Whiskey or Amarula mixed with ice-cream and topped with fresh whipped cream).

My heart did a double beat as my cellphone rang. I answered it after two rings. "*Howzit* sweetie. I'm in Sandton as we speak. Do you want to meet up for a drink or two?"

My heart plummeted in seconds. Why does Tristan call when I'm expecting it to be Stephan? "Hi, as it happens I'm at Bourgeois waiting for Kirsty."

"Cool. I'm dying for some girlie talk. Did you see the news? Your… my hunk has been suspended! See you just now," he replied in an excited voice.

"Darling, sorry I took longer than I anticipated," Kirsty surprised me. She pulled out a chair and smoothed her fitted black pencil skirt before sitting down opposite me, removed her large dark sunglasses and placed her *Blackberry* on the table.

"Have you ordered yet? She waved at a waiter who was carrying my drink on a tray.

"A *Savannah Dry*…I needed a bit of a kick but waited for you before I ordered anything to eat."

"I'll have a *Smirnoff Spin. Jeez*, I'm starving," she said glancing down the menu.

"Shall I come back to take your meal order?"

"Just hang on. What you having darl?" Kirsty looked up at me chewing on her perfectly manicured red painted finger nail.

"The *Prawn Spaghetti*."

"*Ja*, me too. Make that two *Prawn Spaghetti's*. Oh and a green salad please." she said to the waiter.

"Shall we share a large salad?" she looked across at me.

I nodded, "I'd better get my five portions of veg." She looked up at the waiter smiling. "Make that a LARGE green salad. And don't forget my *Smirnoff Spin*."

"By the way Tristan just called and is joining us," I warned.

"This is going to be an interesting lunch. Was he stoned?" she smirked.

"Probably! He sounds like he's on a mission."

"So tell me what's going on? What's this business of Stephan being suspended?" She cocked her head whilst folding her arms.

I cleared my throat from the sharp cider taste of my *Savannah Dry* before replying, "It's news to me —"

She cut me off, "Don't tell me…he confided in you that he was taking steroids."

"No! It wasn't like that."

"Come on darl; I didn't mean it that way, Don't be sensitive —" she stopped as standing at our table was Tristan in his trademark tight zebra-patterned trousers, clutching his iPhone, "I found you both," he beamed bending down to peck both of us on our cheeks.

"Is that fancy moonbag of yours full of dagga?" Kirsty laughed.

He patted it fondly, "What are you saying! This is my fanny pack," he screeched in a high-pitched tone.

"Turn it round and it can be your bum pack," she looked up at him.

He pulled out a nearby chair and gracefully sat down at our table crossing his slender legs. The loud shrill ringtone of his cellphone went off, matching his loud screechy voice. "Listen Quentin. You gave me the shock of my life by leaving me in the thick of it.…" He waved his free hand in the air beckoning the waiter. His manicured index finger pointed to a *Double Vodka* and a *Red Bull* on the menu. Looking up he mouthed to the waiter, "Two." Kirsty and I rolled our eyes at each other.

"You are the weakest link — goodbye!" he abruptly ended the call.

"You sound pissed off," I said.

"I am. Things are tight and my business partner Quentin has been cheating me out of money."

His phone rang again. "Pauline! Turn that hair-drier off. How do you expect me to hear you?" He paused whilst listening to his hairdressing assistant. "Of course, it's 10.1 and a bit of bleach. You've done it before at 6% and you can leave it in for a bit longer. What do you think you're going to comb her hair with — your fingers?" he bitched and ended the call.

He looked back at us, "Pauline has been my assistant for a year and still hasn't got it. I can't leave the salon for five minutes and she's on the phone."

"Darling! You still with that gorgeous swimmer? I've some more *skinner* for you." His dark eyes opened wide as his perfect thin eyebrows arched.

"I hope it's no more drama from his childhood," I answered.

"So what's this gossip?" Kirsty moved in closer and looked at me, "I bet he's going to tell us something about Stephan being suspended!"

His voice lowered, "I still can't believe he's been suspended. I wonder where he's disappeared to."

I snapped, "He's only been temporarily suspended. I think he's been set up."

Kirsty shook her head, "*Eish*, this is serious. Have you heard from him since the news announcement?"

I lowered my eyes, "No."

Tristan's eyes lightened up. "They said he was caught taking steroids. Darling, you got lucky. His penis must've grown a few inches from it!"

"It's not that kind of steroids. The sports-enhancing drugs are for speed and strength," Kirsty giggled.

"Ooh, even better! Speed! You guys must've been at it like wild rabbits!"

I glared at him, "Come off it. This is serious! His swimming career is in ruins."

Well, sweetie, you don't want to hear this skinner then?" He abruptly stopped as the waiter arrived with his drinks. He took a gulp from his glass then dramatically groaned in an organismic tone, "*Ag*, I needed that." After licking his lips, he looked over at me.

"What do you mean?" I felt my body stiffen.

"It's about his mother."

"So," I shrugged.

Kirsty rolled her heavily-mascaraed, brown eyes, "For God's sake

Tristan get to the point!"

He paused, straightened up and announced in a slow lower voice, "I found out yesterday that my client, Estelle Kloppers is a close pal of Stephan Erasmus's mother." Still holding onto his glass of a double vodka concoction, he took another swig, inhaled sharply and babbled, "So Mrs Kloppers started bragging how well she knows Mr SA Sportsman's mother and how the mother wasn't happy to see YOU on the arm of her precious golden boy." His words couldn't jump out fast enough.

A lump formed in my throat. I tried to talk but nothing came out. I took a sip of my drink, cleared my throat and squeaked, "Why?"

Kirsty jumped to my defence, "The cow doesn't know anything about Chantelle."

"Did she say why," I asked feeling confused.

He wiped his wide mouth with a napkin then moved his slender fingers to slowly unzip his matching zebra print moon-bag deliberately attempting to keep us in suspense. He was clearly enjoying the drama as he removed a cigarette from the pouch, "I'm going for a smoke." He scraped his chair back to stand up.

"No man, you can't keep us on tenterhooks like that. Finish the story," I vented in an irritated tone.

Sitting down again he drummed his cigarette on the table.

"Apparently the mother already has another chick in mind. Some *larney* family friend's daughter, who is younger than you, sweetie. One thing that Estelle banged on about was the mother wasn't happy that you are older than her son. She's now determined to get this chick on the scene."

"What! I'm only two years older than him," I hissed.

He turned his peroxided head to me, looked directly into my eyes and said, "Well, sweetie, she clearly doesn't give a shit who her son wants. This chick's only twenty-three, just finished medical school, is a Miss South Africa finalist and comes from a bucked-up family."

Tristan's words fired into my heart like a round of bullets. I did not stand a chance against this obviously beautiful, brainy hand–picked doctor. Compared to her I was plain boring and old.

"Does Stephan know all this?" I crinkled my nose.

"Of course not. The *poison dwarf* is plotting this on her own."

"Who the hell is the *poison dwarf*" Kirsty asked raising her manicured eyebrows.

"The bitch of a mother. Estelle showed me a photo of them together and she's a short ass," Tristan snorted.

"The names you come out with," Kirsty laughed, shaking her head.

Kirsty added dryly, "Huh, the stupid cow thinks money is the be all and end all of EVERYTHING. I heard she only married Stephan's father for his money. That's where Stephan's wealth comes from. His late father left him a healthy trust fund and that wildlife sanctuary, which I might add, your Mr Sportsman has sole ownership of."

Kirsty looked at me. My eyes narrowed. My jaw clenched and I spat out in a rage, "Who the hell is she to talk?

Tristan butted in, " The *poison dwarf* had a lover who shot Stephan's father."

Kirsty cupped her slender hand over her mouth, "What? Oh my God, Tristan, you didn't tell me."

"It was an accident. Apparently, the lover mistook Stephan's father for an intruder."

" Oh *ja,* that's the lover's story. He probably did it to get the husband out the way," Kirsty added,

I lowered my eyes staring down at my nail-bitten fingers.
Kirsty banged her glass down on the table and looked over at me. "Darl, go. Give his family a chance to get to know you properly."

Tristan jumped in, "Wear your highest stilettos next time and show that *poison dwarf* who's who in the zoo!"

The waiter arrived with our food.

"Tristan you want mine as I've lost my appetite?" I pointed to my plate of food.

"*Ja,* I need some fattening up. That graze smells divine."

My cellphone pinged alerting me I had received a new message. It was Stephan: *Babe. Can we meet later? S x*

I stared at the screen. I just couldn't face seeing him now. I typed a text back to him: *Something's come up. C xxx*

I hovered my thumb over the send button. Do I or don't I?

"Darl, who's the text from? It's got your full attention alright," Kirsty asked with a mouthful of spaghetti.

"Stephan." I snapped.

"Are you stupid? Chantelle Swanepoel! Be a fighter, not a quitter."

I grabbed my phone and pressed 'send.'

"You need a man in your life and Stephan is smitten with you...so why not give the guy a chance."

"No, I don't. Listen we all come into this world alone and leave alone," I blurted as I picked my handbag off the floor. A barrage of texts came through. I grabbed my cell without looking to see who the sender was.

"Aren't you going to see what he said?" Tristan pointed his fork at my phone.

"What for?"

"Give me your cell. I'll have him if you don't." He dropped his fork and snatched my phone out of my hand. He opened up my messages and started reading them out.

"What's come up that's so important? S"

Next text: *Please reschedule your other plan if possible. I need to see you urgently. S"*

Tristan went on, *"Darl! Reply to him."*

Tristan passed me my cellphone. "I thought I might have a chance, but he wants you sweetie."

Kirsty laughed," Tristan! What makes you think he'd want you?"

I waved to our waiter, mouthing, "Bill."

"I've got to go guys. I need to prepare for an important meeting tomorrow."

The waiter was at our table in minutes and left the bill. "Here's my share. I've left a tip as well." I slipped R200 into the blue bill folder. I bent down to peck Kirsty and Tristan on their cheeks.

"Drive carefully and let me know when you're home," Kirsty said and Tristan blew a kiss in the air as I turned to walk out of the restaurant to the find my car.

I felt tears prick in my eyes so glanced into my rear-view mirror and tears spilt out of my eyes, flooded my mascaraed lashes and slid down my pale cheeks.

Stephan's mother's plan raced through my mind. Wasn't I good enough to stand next to her son when he won the Sportsman of the Year award? What was wrong with me? I was always attracted to the wrong men. Franco had dumped me for his pretty nurse.

I revved up the engine letting off steam. The tyres screeched round the car park. I gripped the warm steering wheel and drove onto the main road where I floored it. With the windows open, the welcoming breeze immediately cooled down the heat trapped inside the car. My reliable and nippy *VW Golf* never let me down.

My cellphone rang so I glanced down expecting it to be Stephan. The hairs prickled on the back of my neck as my caller ID showed the name, Adam. I ignored the call.

Just when I thought I could not bear anymore drama for that day I answered the next call on my cellphone automatically.

"Hi Chantelle,"

My sheepish voice asked, "Stephan! Are you okay?"

"*Ja,* you've obviously heard. I'm laying low till my initial hearing comes up."

"Stephan is it true?"

"We need to meet, but I've been given strict orders by my management not to speak to anyone. If you get any calls from the press, it's important for you not to say anything," he paused and then continued, "Can you meet me later?"

I swallowed hard. I was curious to know the whole story. "It'll have to be later this afternoon?"

"Is Fourways car park okay? At four?"

"*Ja,* I can do then."

"I'll be in an old green *Jeep* parked at the bottom of the carpark. I'll hoot twice when I see you. Drive around twice to make sure you're not being followed."

"*Eish*, this sounds serious."

"Chantelle, it is. The bloody press mustn't get wind of us meeting. Otherwise they'll hound you and make your life hell."

Then park your car and jump into mine. I'll drive to a place that no one knows."

* * *

Stephan's face looked drawn shielded under a baseball cap as he dragged his feet listlessly leading the way to a small tin shack. The smell of rain on the red earth drifted through an open window of the small room.

Stephan sat slumped looking across at me and said, "Chantelle, most of it is true."

His eyes dropped to the cold concrete floor. I swallowed hard trying to hold back all the questions I had.

"Hear me out," he lifted up his head to hold my gaze, and continued, "Chantelle, please don't judge me. I was recuperating from a bad shoulder injury, in so much bloody pain and unable to train."

"I didn't know you injured yourself...what happened?"

Massaging his temples he went on, "My doctor's instructions were to rest till my shoulder was healed. But Kevin and I worked out a training programme that would still give me enough time to qualify for the

Olympic team."

I cocked my head to one side, "And?"

"My shoulder was stuffed and I was losing the strength and endurance I needed to stay in the team. But the bloody Swimming Federation brought the Olympic trials forward by a month, so my entire training plan was thrown out of sync. The clock was ticking and the pressure was on big time."

He let out an exasperated sigh. I shuddered from a cold draft as I leaned forward asking, "But why didn't you just wait for the next Olympics to give your injury time to —"

He cut me off. "No — I would've had to wait another four years, making me too old. I'm already one of the older swimmers in the team...well was."

I nodded. "Four years is a long time to wait."

The wind started howling, "I had to make a plan or quit. It was now or never. I worked out that, before I injured my shoulder, my times were only seconds faster! "

He paused to take a sip of water. Then with his eyes fixed on the ground, his voice lowered, "I decided to do anything to get there. I took steroids for my freestyle trial. It was just to help me swim at my former times. And it worked. I still had a chance to live my late dad's dream."

"Jeez Stephan. If you'd not injured your shoulder, you wouldn't be in this mess."

He blinked back tears. "It didn't end there. I continued using the juice till my shoulder healed. Chante, I can't explain how it took away the excruciating shoulder pain whilst I was training."

"Juice?"

"Slang for steroids."

I fumbled for a tissue in my handbag and passed it to him.

"What were you thinking? Why didn't you just stop when you got better?"

He sniffed as he wiped his wet eyes. Then blew his nose. "Without swimming I'm nothing. I didn't want to risk not making the Olympic team. I have to admit I lost sight of the consequences. When I didn't take the juice, it was hard to focus with the continual pain. My confidence in maintaining my swimming standard was going down the tubes...fast."

"How the hell did you get away with it? Surely they must've drug-tested you before the trials?"

Burying his sun-darkened face in his hands, his voice muffled, "I had a contact. But somebody got wind of it and reported their suspicions to the Federation. Hence the spot check on Thursday."

I clenched my jaw. "Huh...is that why you were snappy and pissed off when I cancelled dinner?"

He cupped his large warm hands over mine. His voice softened, "Chante. I'm so sorry...I really didn't mean to. I'm embarrassed, alone and drowning in a mess I don't know how to get out of."

"Stephan, were you ever going to tell me?"

"Don't hate me. This all happened before I fell for you. I'm not who I was then. I promise. You can trust me now."

"I'd really like to believe you."

He held onto my gaze, "Please believe me. I regret ever taking steroids. I wasn't myself on them. I've flushed what was left down the loo."

I raised my voice to be heard over the hailstones thrashing down onto the metal roof, "Who do you think found out? Did Kevin know?"

"Kevin! No way. It must've been one of the swimmers."

"Well, I think I know which swimmer it was." I could feel my heartbeat escalating.

"Who?" he asked. His body stiffened.

"At the braai I overheard Henk talking to Carl about you cheating and I thought he meant with another woman! But now it all makes sense."

I chewed my thumb nail. Was I doing the right thing by divulging what I had eavesdropped at the braai?

"*Ja* well, I was the fool to think I could get away with it."

"Jealousy can bring out the worst in people." I was relieved in a weird kind of way Stephan wasn't cheating on me. He was cheating on himself.

He scraped his chair back and stood up, "Swimming is such a competitive sport."

It's time," he went on and blew air out his mouth.

"For what?" I swallowed hard.

"For you to leave."

There was crack of thunder. Rain lashed down harder. I reached for my cardigan. Noticing how cold I was, Stephan quickly closed the window.

"Looks like the storm's here to stay. It's not safe to venture outside in that.

His eyes were soft, caring and understanding. He stood up and took me into his arms. I felt the solidness of his muscles, yet the softness of his heart.

He lifted my hand to his mouth and tenderly kissed it.

"How are you going to cope?"

"I know its madness, I firmly believe in destiny," he said with real sincerity.

"I think I'm falling in love with you. You're a part of my life and I don't want you to go…I shouldn't have asked you to come. I don't want to drag you into my mess."

Stephan's jaw twisted into a knot of tension. He deserved my support. I held his gaze.

"I came here to give you the benefit of the doubt. I didn't say I agreed with what others are saying."

His gaze darkened to steel grey as they penetrated into me.

"*Ja,* but it obviously has affected your opinion of me."

"You are wrong. I can make my own mind up."

I had put aside Kirsty's disapproval, my mother's anger and public opinion. Was I ignoring all the warning signs by falling headfirst into the moment? I collected my bag and my thoughts. "Maybe I should go," my voice squeaked.

His hand darted out and pressed on top of mine. "Don't leave...but I understand if you want to go."

Stephan pulled back. He was hurting. There was a fighting tug in his eyes, a spark, and an electrical current. "I care too much for you to get hurt."

Something in the depths of his pupils jumped into my soul — a connection formed between us. I reached for his hand and gave it a warm squeeze. It was madness, but it was a risk I wanted to take. I was tired of worrying what others thought. I wanted to do something for me, to be daring and to do something I believed in.

My body leaned forward as he lifted my fingers to his mouth and tenderly kissed my hand. His eyes were gentle, caring and understanding.

"Chantelle, I'm leaving for the sanctuary to be with my animals."

"When?" I pulled my hand back.

"At the crack of dawn."

I swallowed hard. Will I ever see him again? Stephen tilted my chin back and gazed down at me. "Come with me," he whispered.

My breath evaporated as a sudden vibration pulsated against my thigh. "Someone's desperate to get hold of you," Stephan sighed.

I rolled my eyes. "Let me switch it off." Squeezing my fingers deep into my pocket I yanked out my cellphone. Tandeka's name flashed on the screen. "Damn!" I muttered.

"Chantelle, Tandeka here. It's been a few days since our meeting and I wanted to touch base."

"Tandeka, I haven't actually heard from Shiloh Patel about the prints yet," I said into the phone.

"I meant. Have you found out anything yet?"

"On Adam?"

Stephan's eyes darted at me catching my glance. I moved to the corner of the room and faced the stained grey wall.

"I'm glad you called because I needed speak to you."

"And —"

I took a deep breath before going on. "You can't expect me to do this." How was I to explain to my CEO that I had moral standards?

"You know what this means Chantelle?" she hissed.

My back stiffened and I added boldly, *"Ja,* you should be hiring a PI specialising in espionage which I have no qualifications in.*"*

I couldn't believe I finally said it.

"Where are you going with this?" she snapped and paused.

"It's not part of my contract. So why me?" my voice grew louder.

"You know why because Adam is besotted with you, making you the last person he'll suspect."

"You're asking the wrong person. I'm sorry Tandeka I can't do it."

"I'm disappointed. Weigh it up, a generous bonus or —"

I cut her off, "Or what?"

"Figure it out for yourself. You do know your contract's coming to an end next month. I'm assuming you were banking on me renewing it."

"Hello, you there Tandeka?" Nothing. All was quiet. She was gone.

Another clap of thunder broke the silence. I turned round to face Stephan.

"You okay?" he asked.

I blinked and replied, *"Ja,* office politics," I shrugged.

"Adam?"

"It's nothing...forget it—"

"So are you going to join me at the sanctuary?" he pressed.

I nodded, smiled widely and reached up to wrap my arms round his solid neck. My heart was dancing. Butterflies fluttered in my stomach. Stephan Erasmus was my love drug. The crisp scent of fresh air drifted in through the open window. The storm had passed and allowed the hot sun to reappear and soak up the wet, red earth.

Chapter Twenty

What am I going to pack, is the question I asked myself I scrutinised the rail of dresses, jeans and skirts.

"*Ja*, casual it is!" I smiled as I grabbed all my knee-length shorts, jeans and an armful of colourful T-shirts. After shoving them into a large suitcase I slung in my *tackies, veldskoens* and *slip-slops*. My toiletries, including bottles of sunblock, were hurled in before I zipped up the case and stood it in corner of my bedroom.

Mavis! What am I going to tell her? I chewed my bottom lip. I had sworn secrecy, to tell no one in order to keep the press from finding Stephan. I couldn't trust Kirsty. She was a journalist. And as for gossipy Tristan, he was out of the question. Neither could I risk telling my mother who could so easily slip up and say something to one of her many friends. If I told dad, he would definitely tell mum.

There was only one person I could trust. My secret was safe with Mavis. I scribbled on a yellow sticky note.

Morning Mavis. I hope you managed to sort out things for your family. Please keep this a SECRET. I'll be staying at Nkuti sanctuary with Stephan for a few days. I know I can trust you. You're the only person I have told. Please don't tell Lucky or anyone, not even my folks. If anybody asks, just say I'm in Cape Town on business.

Reporters will probably come to the house. Ignore them. Don't answer the gate or the landline. This is a secret number if you need me: 0791542233. I'll try and call you daily. I've left your wages in our safe place. I've left groceries for you in the pantry. Make sure you take care of yourself and Rocky. Thanks Mavis.

Chantelle x

After firmly pressing the note onto the fridge door, I poured myself a large glass of white wine. My bare feet felt cool and soothing on my parquet floor. I made my way to my own sanctuary, my cosy, comfy couch. I curled up and took a large sip of chilled wine, then another and another.

I took one last scroll through my phone. A few new notifications popped up. My jaw twisted with anger as I read the news alerts:

Mr SA Sportsman of the Year, Stephan Erasmus suspended. He has tested positive for a sports enhancing drug.

Stephan Erasmus has gone into hiding.

Mr South African Sportsman of the Year kicked out of the Olympic team after testing positive for a sports-enhancing drug.

Why don't they just leave Stephan alone or find out the truth? The bloody press! They either love or hate you. No in-between.

Then a text from Franco came through. I hovered my thumb over the delete button. But then I opened it.

My darling Chantelle, I told you that swimmer was not to be trusted. From reading the headlines he's a piece of shit. A cheat. Come with me to London. I miss you. Franco xxx

I swiftly replied.

Huh! And you're not a cheat? I seem to remember you CHEATING ON ME with that blonde tart of a bitch. Now bugger off and NEVER contact me again.

As my thumb glided over the 'off' button, a text popped up from Adam. I immediately read it: *Sorry to hear about Stephan. I'm here if you need to talk. See you tomorrow in the office. Adam x*

Do I tell Adam the truth? Do I tell him Tandeka expected me to spy on him? He is going to want to know why I've left. If I don't tell him, I would hate to think what awful explanation Tandeka will give him. I called him. After one ring he answered, "*Howzit* going?"

"I'm okay, thanks. Adam, I'm not returning to *Afrika Fashions*!"

He sighed, "Really? Why?"

I paused before continuing, "I have to be honest with you. Tandeka didn't renew my contract when I refused to do some dirty work for her."

"What? Did it involve me?"

Do I tell him?

"Chantelle, you there?"

"*Ja,* I feel shit even saying it. But she asked me to find out if you were selling off *Afrika's* new range ideas. She was convinced you were desperate for cash."

"Fucking bitch. I can't believe she scooped that low. Fucks sake! I'm not desperate for cash. What made her think that?" He yelled.

"Apparently she thought you were doing coke."

His voice became even louder, "Huh! I've never touched that shit. My cousins the one into drugs, so I'm trying to get him help. Besides, I don't need to sell any of *Afrika's* ideas. I've got my own cash. My late aunt left me money in her will."

"Sorry, Adam. I couldn't do it, so she gave me to boot."

His voice softened, "*Eish,* Chantelle. Sorry you had to leave because of me. Thanks for believing in me. I can't work for that witch anymore knowing what she thinks of me."

"Don't blame you. She just exploits her staff."

He asked, "How are you with all this stuff on Stephan?"

"I'm just keeping a low profile for now."

"Take care, Chantelle. Call if you need me."

"Thanks, Adam."

I switched my phone off.

I glugged the last drop of wine from my glass. Questions seeped into my head. Why am I protecting this man? Why am I throwing caution to the wind? Why do I no longer care what others think of me?

In bed that night my troubled mind turned things over once more. This was madness. I didn't understand the way I felt because I had only met Stephan a month ago and yet I wanted him so badly. Stephan Erasmus was a drug to me, the best high I'd ever experienced. I felt ecstatic, charged with energy and walking on air. Even my mother had commented, "You have a certain glow about you, Chantelle. You seem to be bursting with vitality."

But tonight I was going crazy. I didn't have my fix and I was paying for it. The several glasses of wine I had downed earlier, could not satisfy my craving. Nausea, sweating and sadness overwhelmed me. I curled into the foetal position to protect myself from the real world. I drifted in and out of sleep with vivid dreams of Stephan.

Crouched down on my knees pleading, " Don't ever leave me. Stephan." But then I could not see him. Where was he? I could hear his voice in the distance. He was calling me. I kept repeating, "I love you, Stephan…"

* * *

I jolted as my alarm went off. It was dark. Damn! I must have set it for the wrong time. I rubbed the sleep from my gritty eyes. What was today? Saturday? Stephan and Nkuti! I switched on the bedside light and glanced over at the alarm clock. It was already 4 am. Stephan would be here in half an hour. I scrambled out of bed and dashed to the bathroom. A quick wash with cold water and brush of teeth and I was fully awake. I glugged down cold water then pulled on my jeans.

Awake I remembered. This is the day my new life begins at *Nkuti*

Sanctuary with Stephan Erasmus. I cocked my head and listened. A dove cooed, then again and again. Our secret code. I crept to the front door and opened it for Stephan. He greeted me with a quick hug.

"I hardly recognised you in that camouflage clobber!"

"Good! That's the idea."

"Mavis didn't see you, I hope."

"No. I was very quiet. I didn't see Rocky though."

"He's sleeping in the spare bedroom."

"He's not much of a guard dog. He hasn't barked once."

"We need to leave now before it gets light. Where's your stuff?"

His wide eyes darted round the lounge.

"In my room," I beckoned down the passage.

After we'd locked up and quietly loaded my things into a dirty, dilapidated, green *eep,* we drove off. I turned round to take one last glance. I hoped I was making the right decision? Looking ahead, the streetlights had turned off and the road was desolate.

Once we had left the bleak city smog of Johannesburg behind I wrestled to wind down the stiff, rusty window for some fresh air. The sight of the golden sun rising in the distance gave me a rush of excitement. My new adventure with Stephan just had begun. Stephan's fist pumped the air. "Thank God we made it without being recognised!"

"We did it!" I clapped as we stopped at *Nkuti's* locked high steel gate.

The guard greeted us as he opened the gates and stood aside to let us in.

Moses smiled widely as we drove up to Stephan's thatched roofed chalet. I waved back.

"It feels good to be back."

"Thanks for standing by me babe," He patted my knee.

* * *

The late afternoon sun threw a shaft of light onto a small brass tin on the glass-topped coffee table. Stephan was topless, only wearing a pair of khaki chinos and sat perched upright in the chair with his tanned bare feet placed firmly on the stone floor. He pulled up the coffee table. His athletic body bent over to reach and open up a small brass tin. He dug out a packet of *Rizlas* from his pocket and started rolling a small spliff meticulously.

I glared at him asking, "What're you doing?"

"Chante, please chill," he stated as he took a long deep draw then, holding his breath, he slowly exhaled and eased himself calmly back into his chair. I recognised the familiar smell from varsity, parties and nightclubs. There was an awkward silence between us.

"Well, you sure are Mr Unpredictable!"

He faced me and explained, "I swim my worries away. You know, it's a lonely sport."

"How?" I cocked my head.

"You're constantly moving through the water. You end up in a trance."

"But why smoke?" I shrugged my shoulders.

"Natural remedy for my painful shoulder."

"What happened?"

"I stuffed it up."

"But why smoke that shit?"

"One day, Henk brought some to training and after a few hits, the pain disappeared like magic."

"Chocolates or wine are my escape!" I replied reaching for my glass of *Savannah*.

He passed the slim hand-rolled joint to me. "Try a puff. It'll relax you."

I shook my head. This was something I had promised myself I would never do. Franco had told me horrendous stories of addicts he had encountered in his medical profession. This has scared the life out of me. Why would Henk lure Stephan into starting a habit which is not easily broken?

"Well, it's been legalised for medicinal pain-relief purposes in certain parts of America."

"Mmm. But this is not America," I retorted feeling strong about my opinion.

"You've never even had a blow-back?"

"What the hell's that?"

His glassy eyes flirted, danced and engaged with mine. "You wanna try?"

I hesitated. Butterflies fluttered in my gut. He leaned closer, swept my hair aside and tenderly nuzzled my neck, breathing seductively into my ear. Was I like a moth being drawn to a candle? My carefree side was tempted to find out what all the fuss was about. I remembered how some of my friends at varsity, who smoked it raved and said it melted their stress.

"Maybe." I ventured into the unknown.

After taking a long draw and holding on to it, Stephan cupped my face in his large gentle hands. He then pressed his soft lips against mine and gently blew into my mouth. I inhaled instinctively.

"Come on. Have another one." Stephan beckoned. He breathed sharply into my mouth again. After a few more hits, my eyes closed and a feeling of calmness overwhelmed me. I felt like time had stood still.

"*Whoah*! I'm feeling dizzy."

"That's cos you're stoned! Don't stress. It's natural to feel like that. You're safe with me."

Even if I felt completely safe, giving myself to Stephan would be risky. He wasn't the type of man I could manage. I'd lose all control by letting him in. He eased back into his seat with a puzzled look on his face as he gazed into the sky. "That looks like the Star of David," he commented.

"Where?"

His taut arm pulled me into him. I could feel the warmth coming off his body in waves. With his other arm, he gestured towards the starry sky above us. There was a distinct bright cluster of stars which seemed light years away on the clear night. I had never seen the stars this bright before. Even the familiar chirping of the crickets sounded louder. What was going on?

"What's that sweet perfume smell?" I giggled.

"Oh, that's the frangipani flowers. You're only noticing it now?"

"Well *ja*!"

"Haha, that spliff's heightened your senses!" he laughed.

"*Eish*! That stuff's ugh..."

I couldn't think straight and was having difficulty forming words in my mouth. Even Stephan's aftershave smelt stronger. I drowned in all the intensified scents around me. My skin felt super-sensitive.

"Chante, you're so damn cute stoned!"

His serene face eased closer, "You want another blow-back?"

"Just one," I whispered.

Stephan took a deeper drag, this time he held onto it then again pressing his warm mouth onto mine he blew a deep puff into mine. His tongue teased and his half-lidded eyes skimmed my body. He aroused me as never before. He cupped my face in his hands and whispered, "I want you."

My flesh tingled already aching for him. Stephan's skin felt softer and warmer. I was losing control as I melted into his aroused hard body.

I wanted more of this unattainable man. I didn't want this to stop. The hurt might come later, but for the moment, it didn't matter. It felt so good being with Stephan. Being with him was like learning to fly, thrilling but scary.

* * *

I had never felt like this before. Is this what they called love or was this pure lust?

I was developing a crush on Stephan. He was like a drug to me, my ecstasy, despite his unstable nature. I couldn't rationalise my feelings in any way? He was unattainable and unpredictable. I found myself thinking about him all the time. What was wrong with me?

Stephan slipped his warm fingers through mine.

"You ready to meet Moyo?"

"Of course, I've waited over a week."

"I know babe, but he had to get over his cold first."

"I'm going to first do my daily check in with Mavis."

He released my hand, "Sure."

I punched in Mavis's cellphone number and it promptly answered, "Hello."

"Hi Mavis. Chantelle here. Are you okay?"

"Hello, Chantelle. *Ja*, I'm good and everything's okay."

"That's good to hear. Is Rocky still eating? Any calls?"

"*Ag*, he's getting too fat," she giggled. "And nobody has called yet."

"Thanks, Mavis. Call me anytime if you need me. I'll pop in this week-end. I miss you and Rocky."

"Bye Chantelle. Look after yourself, please."

Stephan looked up. "Everything okay?"

I smiled, "*Ja*."

Stephan released my hand to reach into his camouflage coloured rucksack which contained lotions and potions for rescued wildlife. The antiseptic smell of the cool gel was refreshing as Stephan pumped the clear liquid into the palm of my hands.

"Elephants are more susceptible to catching infection than humans so we always use this before handling Moyo."

I rubbed my hands together till the gel was absorbed.

"How did Moyo become a rescue?"

"We received a phone call reporting an abandoned elephant calf that was stuck in a dried-out waterhole," he frowned.

"*Ag,* shame."

"We found him badly sunburnt and dehydrated," his voice lowered.

"That's heart breaking," I said swallowing hard.

"After transporting him here he was immediately treated by the vet. And check how healthy and happy he is now. Animals share love just as much as humans do, and deserve the same form of protection as we have."

His long index finger pointed towards the passive grey baby elephant curling it's trunk in an S-shape.

"You know the African saying. *Little by little, a little becomes a lot?"*

I nodded, "*Ja.*"

"Well that's what we're trying to achieve here at *Nkuti*. We know we can't save all the wildlife but we can try and save one at a time."

"That's just so awesome," I blinked back tears.

A sweet tropical coconut aroma drifted towards us as we approached the elephant calf.

"What's that nice smell?"

"It's *lekker* hey! It's the coconut based oil we use on Moyo's skin," he explained and inhaled deeply.

"Stephan patted the grey head, "Hello boy. What's your story?"

A flexible trunk sprung out towards Stephan, playfully sniffing his nose.

"Check babe. Moyo's kissing me with the end of his trunk."

Stephan stroked the adorable baby elephant's face allowing its mouth to suck on his thumb.

"Ouch! He's chewing your hand. Doesn't that hurt?" I squealed stepping back.

"No! He's playing, babe. Don't stress. You know that elephants value good relations with humans." Stephan playfully twirled his thumb.

"I have heard that. They've got freaking amazing memories as well!"

"You telling me! Plus they're emotional, caring and intelligent."

"Some humans could learn from them. So how old is Moyo?"

"Eighteen months."

Stephan crouched down to the waist-high baby elephant and gently rubbed a large amount of white cream into the grey leathery skin, saying, "He's prone to skin cancer now, so we use sunblock on him daily. Here, try rubbing some on him."

My knee creaked as I knelt down on the soft grass to face Moyo. Stephan squeezed out the last bit of sunscreen into my hand. I gently rubbed the white sticky cream into the hard, rough hide.

"Is an elephant's skin still sensitive despite being so thick?"

"*Ja,* for sure. They notice every fly that lands on them," he replied in his raspy voice.

His slim trunk slinked into my ear. "Moyo, that's ticklish," I let out a squeaky giggle and tightly squeezed my eyes.

"It's his way of showing he's enjoying it," Stephan chuckled.

A middle-aged bald man wearing khaki overalls strode up to us. He was holding a bucket. "Morning sir?" he greeted Stephan and then glanced at me and nodded.

"Morning Enoch. Enoch is part of our Moyo team."

Enoch smiled widely as he lifted a baby bottle, full of milk, from the bucket.

"Is that baby formula? How many bottles does he drink every day?"

"*Ja,* it's specialised milk formula for African elephants. Moyo goes through a bucket a day!"

His trunk twirled around the bottle, gripped the teat and he suckled rapidly. After meeting Moyo, I never tired of studying, photographing him and watching him communicate with his trunk, his ears flapping and tail twitching.

Chapter Twenty-One

Golden sunlight streamed through the crisp cotton curtains. I looked at the bedside clock. It was 6am. Stephan slipped quietly out of bed to get ready for his habitual morning swim. I gently rubbed sleep from my gritty eyes before stretching out my arms. I gazed up at the ceiling fan blades, turning slowly in time to a soft humming sound. What had we planned for the day?

I felt a surge of butterflies in my stomach remembering that today Shumba was six months old. I had arranged to be alone with the white furry cub. This spurred me on.

Stephan bent over to kiss my forehead very gently. "Chantelle, don't go into any enclosures apart from Shumba's and watch out for Tau in the enclosure next to him," he warned me.

"What's the story with Tau?" I frowned.

Stephan towered over me barefoot, dressed casually in shorts, a T-shirt and an olive-green towel hung over his broad shoulder.

"He has a serious temper and has never formed a relationship with any of us. Stay away from him. He's bad news."

"*Eish*, poor Shumba having such a grouch as a neighbour!"

"I still don't know why you don't wait for me…"

I cut him off, "*Ag*! We went through this last night. I need to be alone to get some natural shots of Shumba."

"Well, just take care and stay away from the other lions. Even though they're rescues, this doesn't stop them from going in for the kill. They're in an enclosure for a reason."

"I get the drift," I mumbled.

"See you later babe," he walked out closing, the bedroom door behind him.

* * *

"Good morning, *sissy*."
I greeted a young woman wearing a yellow checked housecoat and white trainers. She stood in front of the kitchen sink filling the kettle. The maid slowly turned her chocolate-coloured face toward me, and said, "*Goeie more, mevrou*. Can I make *rooibos* tea?"

"*Ja*, please. Have you seen my camera bag?" I sighed.

"In there," she gestured with her chubby hand to the thatched-roof bar area.

"*Sjoe*! Thanks, *sissy*."

I smiled at her and walked over to the bar. The polished red cement floor cooled my bare feet. Stephan's maid was correct. My black bag was on the bar stool. I carefully fitted my camera, tripod, and pepper spray into the bag.

"Your tea," she called to me.

"Coming."

"Your braids look so nice," she noted smiling broadly and revealing an attractive gap in her front teeth.

I patted the tight small plaits on my head, asking, "You think so?"

She nodded then waddled back to the sink. After a few sips of the hot red tea, I set off to find Shumba.

Was life finally beginning to be good to me? *Nkuti Wildlife Sanctuary* was waking up. The cooing of the doves, the acceptance nod from the sleepy-eyed workers sweeping the yards and the warmth of the early morning sunshine on top of my head. As I neared the enclosures, a commotion broke out.

"Tau, get back! Help! Help! Tau's going to kill Shumba," shouted a worker in blue overalls beating the dry ground profusely with a long stick.

Tau had escaped from his own enclosure into Shumba's. I raced through the cloud of dust to the gate and fumbled for my pepper spray. I yanked open the unlocked gate and went in. The enormous angry beast was growling, baring his huge yellow canines as he prepared himself to pounce on the timid baby cub. A distinct lion stench overwhelmed me. It was Shumba giving off a pungent smell of fear. Blinded by rage, I ran towards the savage brown Tau, squirting spray into his face. Tau gasped, snorted and shook his tawny-coloured mane. He was momentarily disoriented, which gave Shumba just enough time to slink away. I froze.

"Chantelle. What the hell are you doing? Get the hell out of there!" Corrine yelled pressing her freckled face against the fence.

My heart hammered in my chest as Tau turned to stare at me. I could hardly breathe. Would this frenzied fully-grown lion kill me?"

A bakkie roared up to the enclosure. Stephan bolted out, aimed his tranquilliser gun at Tau and pulled the trigger. He shot a red dart into the lion's muscular flank which made the animal swivel his head frantically, in an attempt to remove the dart.

I stumbled back as Stephan's big hand locked around my upper arm and yanked me out of the enclosure. He spun me round with a beat pulsing in his neck. When he looked directly at me, I noticed his usually warm eyes had become shadowed by his brow.

"Are you trying to get yourself killed?" he yelled in a rage. "You can't fight off a lion with pepper spray."

His hair was wet from swimming and his damp white T-shirt clung to his torso.

"Chantelle, what the hell were you thinking? A stressed out lion is a danger to humans."

"I was trying to save Shumba," my voice trembled as the reality of the moment sank in. Stephan's grip softened and immediately I felt comforted.

"Come here, babe. I couldn't bear anything to happen to you." He pulled me into his arms and held me tightly.

"Stephan, looks like the tranquilliser has kicked in. What you say?" Corrine elbowed Stephan. He pulled back to look into the enclosure. Tau was disorientated, drowsy and docile. With a loud thud, his heavy frame flopped to the ground. Five bulky workers dashed in, checked Tau over and gave Stephan a thumbs-up.

"Take him back to his enclosure and make sure the bloody gate's locked." Stephan ordered with his hands on his hips. "Corrine, how the hell did Tau get in there?"

She rolled her eyes. "Who do you think? Most probably Amos. He must've forgotten to close the inter-leading gate." She gestured to a slim worker, dressed in blue overalls, walking away with his head hung low.

"Was he pissed again? I've warned him not to drink at work." Shaking his head, Stephan added, "It's time to read him the riot act. Just now someone's going to get killed the way he's carrying on."

I scanned the enclosure from the fence. "Where's Shumba? Is he ok? Is—"

Corrine cut me off, "Stop stressing. He's in good hands now, away from your bloody photo shoots," she hissed.

"Corrine, back off. What Chantelle did, took guts. How can you criticise her when she was protecting the wildlife?"

Stephan's nostrils flared. He turned to me and smiled, "Babe, you're one brave girl."

Stephan's voice started to fade. Why is my head spinning? Am I going to pass out? Why did I have red smudges of blood on my hand? I wiped my nose again as the warm fluid dripped down.

"Nosebleed?" His hand moved to my shoulder and guided me under a large acacia tree. I nodded as the metal taste in my mouth became more intense. He patted a nearby rock, adding, "Come and sit down."

He stood over me and pulled a large handkerchief from his shorts pocket. He moved it over the bridge of my nose. He paused, "You're okay to breathe out your mouth for ten minutes?"

I nodded again not wanting to move my mouth. He placed the soft cotton handkerchief over my nose and clamped down hard.

"Daniel! Go and fetch some ice!" he shouted to a tall worker, quite unperturbed as he puffed on a cigarette. Daniel peered at us saying, "Yes, Mr Stephan."

Even in the shade of the tree, we sweated as we waited for the ice. Stephan sat next to me and continued to clamp down tightly on my nose.

I reflected on today's terrifying incident. Stephan's calm and efficient response had impressed me. Once more he had saved me from danger. Stephan was smarter and more capable than I'd given him credit for. Maybe he genuinely cared about my well-being.

* * *

"It was a month today!"

"What was?" Stephan's eyes narrowed.

"Since I joined you here at the sanctuary for the first time."

My eyes shifted to the computer calendar. Running his hands through his slightly longer hair, Stephan said, "Don't change the subject, babe. Just press the button."

I looked up from the slim computer screen. "I'll be up against the pros, so much more talented than me. I don't stand a chance."

"Have more faith in yourself. Those photos of Shumba and Moyo are epic. I know you have a very good chance." He pointed at the screen. I re-read my completed application form addressed to the National Geographic African Wildlife competition, that Stephan had persisted I enter. What's the point?

"If you don't hit that button, I will." He hovered behind me.

"Okay, you win. Wish me luck," I replied, closing my eyes I pressed 'send'.

He let out an excited, "Yes!"

With that he wrapped his arms tightly round me and kissed the top of my head.

* * *

The coolness of the evening was welcoming after the searing heat of the day. I inhaled deeply, breathing in the tropical perfume of the yellow frangipani flowers. It felt peaceful, cosy and magical as Stephan and I relaxed in chairs on the open patio, gazing out into the still night. I felt serene, safe and secure with Stephan.

"I couldn't even imagine this in my wildest dreams." I disclosed downing the last drop of *Savannah* dry from my glass. Stephan placed his warm hand over mine, turned to me and said, "Everyone needs somewhere to escape to. That's why I love it out here."

I leaned forward and whispered, "I always knew there was something special about you. You were hiding your true self away."

We sat for some time, sipping our drinks and laughing louder as the alcohol relaxed our minds and bodies. A cool breeze caressed us, crickets chirped and the hypnotic beating of drums from the rural compound could be heard in the distance.

Strange, shrieking squeals from the hyenas interrupted the moment.

"Those scavengers are at it again," I said.

"*Ja*, probably fighting over a zebra carcass."

"Ag shame."

His voice lowered, "Stay away from them. They're cunning."

I shuddered, "*Eish,* I wouldn't go near one if you paid me."

Their distinctive, eerie, rapid vocals became louder.

"They even lie to each other," he added.

"*Isit?*"

His jaw tightened, "What's worrying me is the rhino poaching. It's getting out of hand. Last week the bastards killed a white rhino and her calf in the *Kruger Park*. Her two-year-old wouldn't leave her side, so they shot it as well."

I could feel my fists clenching. "That's awful. Murderous pigs."

His face darkened with contained anger. "Then the bastards used *pangas* to hack off the horns."

I shook my head. "Poaching any animal is criminal. But slaughtering rhinos does not feed their families. It's blood money. Those greedy poachers don't stop at anything to satisfy their greed for worthless ivory objects."

I noticed his grip tightening around the beer bottle. "I hate the way they use AK-47s to shoot the rhino. Merciless. These horns fetch a good price from the black market. Chante, I'd like to shoot those ruthless bastards."

"*Ja,* I know it seems horrific, but it doesn't actually hurt when their horns are cut off. So now the Rangers are cutting off their horns to save them from the poachers. No horns, no reason to kill them." I paused and added, "They're even painting their horns pink!"

He smiled, "Let's hope it works."

"Me too, *cos* if this doesn't stop them, there'll be no rhino or elephant left in twenty years' time."

"The supply of ivory to Asia should be prohibited."

"I agree. Are the animals at *Nkuti* safe from poachers? Shumba, Moyo, Tau?"

"*Ja*, no sign of poachers this side. Besides the high-tech, electric fences would *zap* the shit out of them."

The exuberant African drums grew louder, faster and somewhat erratic.

"Why do they do this evening ritual?"

He confidently replied, "I learnt from the local trackers; their culture carried on from their ancestors. It's their social gathering just like we're doing now! But our way is with a drink."

"*Isit*?"

Stephan looked deep in thought. He withdrew his hand from mine. He stood up, paused then with a serious face, said, "Look, there's something important I need to tell you, but I'm not sure how."

The beating of my heart matched the frantic rhythm of the drums. I held my breath in anticipation of what was to come. With folded arms, he looked pensively down at me. "When we first met, I didn't think it would get this far—"

I cut in, "Before you go any further, I need to be honest with you." This had to be said. "My breakup with Franco was awful—" I paused as I felt my eyes starting to fill with tears. I took a deep breath, swallowed hard and continued, "This man I thought I loved, turned out to be an arsehole."

"You don't have to do this."

"It's okay." I cleared my throat. "I can't trust men anymore. He only cared about himself."

"Good riddance."

"Then I met you. But you blow hot and cold all the time. You confuse me," I blurted it out.

There was an awkward silence.

He sat down and turned to face me. There was sadness in his eyes. He looked lost. "We both made mistakes. We both came into this relationship a bit broken," Stephan said.

For the first time, he bared his soul to me. I had never seen this vulnerable side of Stephan. My back stiffened and I listened attentively. "Chante, I've spent my life not trusting women."

"But why?"

"My mother cheated on my father. Then my father was killed."

I shook my head and remembered. *Sjoe,* Tristan had been telling the truth.

Stephan's words tumbled off his tongue, "I was a teenager when my father was shot right in front of me. My mother's lover shot him. It was a mistake. From that day, I swore I'd always keep a pistol on me for self-protection."

"Oh my God! I'm so sorry," I exclaimed and felt his pain.

His voice became softer, "I never got to say goodbye to my father. There isn't a day that goes by when I don't think about him."

I moved my hand onto his tensed shoulder. "Shame," I replied which seemed inadequate. I wanted to hold, protect and comfort him. I took his sad face into my shaking hands and tenderly kissed his forehead. I couldn't begin to imagine the awful emotional turmoil he was still experiencing.

Stephan's eyes softened, "I've realised for the first time in my life that I want something more than swimming."

I cocked my head, "Really! You're not going to contest being suspended from the swimming team?"

He shook his head, "Nah! I'm done with swimming. That was my father's dream."

"So what's your passion now?"

He smiled, "You really want to know?"

"*Ja,* of course!"

"Nkuti with you and the animals. And to put an end to rhino poaching. We cannot lose anymore of our endangered species."

I nodded then hugged him tightly. This resonated with me deeply.

He scraped the chair back and stood up. "I need a cold beer. Another *Savannah?*"

"*Ja.*"

I started to see Stephan in a totally different light. This softer Stephan didn't have to prove his machismo with steroids, muscles and money. He was so different from the type of man I'd chosen before. When I thought of Franco, his arrogance, suave demeanour and selfishness, I felt sick and ashamed that I had thought I loved him.

Franco had never cared about me, my safety or leaving me in debt. He turned out to be irresponsible, disrespectful and self-centred. I was a fool to let him manipulate my emotions.

Stephan handed me a large glass of white wine then drank deeply from his frosted beer bottle.

"Chante, it's true. I couldn't commit to any woman. That's till I got involved with you. You're not like any other women I've met."

I'd waited a long time to hear those words. I felt very special. He smiled before wrapping his arm around me and resting his cheek against mine. "I want to forget about everything."

I was in heaven, cocooned against Stephan's body. "All my life I've been afraid of what other people think of me, but I'm done with that. I want to start off on a clean slate."

"Okay, let's make that start tomorrow. I'd like you to understand the bush as I do. You up for leaving at five?"

I crinkled my nose.

"*Eish,* that's seriously early!"

"I'd love to share what I'm doing so that you become a part of it too."

I smiled. "*Ja,* then count me in!"

Chapter Twenty-Two

As Stephan started the engine of the dirty and dilapidated green *Jeep,* it spluttered and roared. He revved it and turned to look me, then slid his eyes over me...from my olive green cap down to my khaki bush shoes.

"Good to see you're wearing the right gear," he winked.

"I learnt from you," I smiled. "Where's your rifle in case we come across poachers? "

"It's in a locker in the back. I prefer to shoot with a camera than a gun, but we may need it – just to scare, not to kill."

Jeez! I hadn't thought about the risks, but Stephan had. He honked the horn and Moses, one of the rangers, jumped onto the back seat. He smelt of the familiar smoke from a *braai.* "Good morning," he greeted us with his wide smile.

"*Gunjanni* Moses?" Stephan asked.

"*Yebo*! Today's good for Miss Chantelle to make her pictures."

I twisted round. "Is it? Moses, please keep your eyes open for some good shots."

"*Yebo*!"

I resisted the urge to recoil from the smell of stale pap on his morning breath. Stephan put his foot down and the *Jeep* roared into action.

After driving for nearly twenty kilometres since leaving *Nkuti* on a very bumpy, dusty road, the dense bush gave way to a scrubby landscape. Seconds later the first rays of the sun cast long shadows. It was only 5.30 am but already so hot I had to roll down the window to keep cool.

Stephan parked under a big shady Marula tree and switched off the engine. "This is a good spot to park," he remarked. I turned to look around and saw Moses nod his approval. Only the sound of doves cooing broke the silence. Butterflies of excitement fluttered in my stomach. I could possibly capture African wildlife at its most raw and natural state.

"Finally I get to use my new video camera. I've waited ages for this opportunity."

"Cool! Let's get on with it then. Here, let me carry that," he said picking up my camera bag.

"Remember if you see a snake, lion, elephant or whatever, freeze. Don't move!"

"This isn't the first time I've been out in the sticks you know," I said with a touch of asperity.

"*Ja*, I know, but you've not been into the roughest parts where we're going today."

Despite the fact I was wearing a hat, my head was burning from the heat of the sun. I walked close behind Stephan and Moses, who were both carrying rucksacks on their backs. Stephan led the way through a clearing into open grassland. I was thirsty, hot and sweaty so I was relieved when we stopped in the shade of a tree. I perched on a nearby rock while Stephan unzipped a rucksack and pulled out three bottles of water. He handed one to Moses and me before he sat down.

"You okay to carry on?"

"*Ja,*" I nodded. I wasn't going to miss out on any photo or video opportunity today. Moses looked up into the tree at the same time glugging down his water.

"What've you seen?" Stephan stood up.

"Just a lourie."

A startled grey bird gave out a drawn-out, 'go-away' cry. I softly touched Stephan's arm. "I always wondered why louries had the name 'go-away' bird."

"It's their alarm call. They only use it when they're threatened by other animals or humans."

"*Yikes*! Does that mean there could be a rhino or elephant close by?" I automatically moved closer to him and immediately felt less tense.

"Could be."

Moses added, "Even we could be the threat!"

I felt my back stiffen. "Now what?"

"Let's find another spot."

Stephan took my hand and led me back to the *Jeep*. He followed a smoother track to gain speed and snapped into top gear. We drove deeper into the bush.

I was jolted forward as Stephan slammed on brakes. A large branch blocked the track. "Looks like the elephants are back," Stephan announced.

"*Yebo!*" Moses jumped out, examined the branch and hauled it out of the way. He wasted no time jumping back into the vehicle. Shaking his head, he remarked, "Looks like a bull did that."

"Was it? How do you know it was a male?"

Moses gave me a wide grin. "None of the leaves were eaten. Elephants only pull down trees for food."

"But when a dude is turned down by the female, he's got to get rid of his mega-high testosterone somehow. Male elephants pull down trees!" Stephan interrupted.

Moses roared with laughter saying, "*Eish*! Imagine if we males did that when our women refuse us!"

"There wouldn't be many trees left in Africa would there?" I said. They both convulsed with laughter. I blushed.

Stephan and Moses scanned the area for wildlife while I set up my new video camera. "This camera's epic. The view's as clear as daylight," I enthused as I panned from left to right.

"Guys, what's that?" I zoomed into a black object. Stephan stretched over me to look down into the viewfinder.

"A rhino. Stay still," he whispered. "It'll charge anything that moves."

Veins in his neck pulsated. Moses silently searched with his binoculars. "*Yebo*, it's about a hundred metres away," he whispered.

"Oh my God! It's got a huge horn."

My stomach somersaulted with excitement as I zoomed in to frame my shot and then took a series of stills. I quickly switched over to 'video' mode and pressed the record button.

"Rhinos look further away than they actually are," Stephan lowered his voice.

"Sir! Poachers!"

"Where?"

He pointed his long index finger towards a large tree about sixty metres away, "Behind the Marula."

Stephan squinted through his binoculars. "*Ja*," he confirmed triumphantly as he ripped the rifle off his shoulder, crouched down and aimed towards the tree.

"Chantelle," he cautioned. "Get down now."

I knelt down fumbling with my camera. My hands trembled as I focused on these human predators. I was determined to get a shot of the poacher.

"Nowadays you're allowed to shoot to kill," said Moses.

"*Ja*, I know but we must catch him. A dead poacher is of no use. You can't interrogate him."

"But he'll be armed."

I couldn't breathe.

"Can you see any others? They never work alone. There's probably another one waiting in a getaway vehicle on the main road."

"Where?" I whispered.

"I reckon that way," Moses gestured towards a dirt track which led to the main road.

"Moses are you ready? Let's go and catch the bastards. I'll approach from behind. You watch my back."

"Okay."

He held his rifle ready for quick action.

"Chantelle, stay here and when it's safe, climb into the *Jeep*," Stephan ordered pulling out the ignition key from his pocket. "Here, take these. Lock the doors and lie down flat on the back seat. Then call the cops."

My stomach was churning, but I couldn't tell whether it was from fear, excitement or concern for Stephan and Moses. They both crept through the grass towards the poacher. He looked to be in his early thirties and was wearing military camouflage trousers and matching shirt. He was crouched down, only twenty metres from the black rhino, where he slowly took careful aim at the rhino with his hunting rifle.

I sensed he was about to shoot when Moses fired a warning shot into the air. This spooked the rhino and made it turn away. The poacher had lost his chance for a straight kill as the rhino charged into the bush. Stephan and Moses crept towards the poacher. I heard Moses shout, "Catch him! Catch him!"

The poacher sprinted towards the dirt road, but Stephan and Moses were gaining on him. Grabbing my camera, I ran back to the *Jeep* and jumped in. I zoomed in to see a dirty, old, black *Toyota Hilux* with a bull-bar in front and a rack on the roof.

This surely was the poachers' getaway vehicle. I took several quick shots of the registration plate. I didn't want to miss any details which could help capture these poachers.

My heart was pounding hard and my shaking hands were sweating as I grabbed my cellphone and punched in 10111. A calm male voice answered immediately, "Police, ambulance —?"

"Police," I cut in.

"What's your name and address —?"

"Chantelle Swanepoel. There's an armed rhino poacher in a black *Toyota Hilux*. We need the SAP. We're about twenty kilometres south of the *Nkuti Wildlife Sanctuary*."

"Right. Stay put. Do NOT approach the poacher. The flying squad will find you on their satellite."

"The number plate's GT167864D. A black *Toyota Hilux* with a big rack on top. It's on a dirt road just off the main road. Hurry. My friend and his ranger have given chase."

"Please ma'am, just stay right where you are. Do not approach the poacher. Our highway patrol will catch the *Toyota Hilux*. Well done ma'am, for getting the registration number."

I started the *Jeep* and drove off in the direction of the chase. When I arrived, I felt a massive wave of relief flow through me. Stephan had rugby-tackled the poacher from behind and flattened him to the ground. Moses had wrenched the poacher's gun from him and was aiming it at his head. Stephan yanked the poacher's hand behind his back.

"Handcuffs," Stephan panted.

Moses pulled out a large plastic cable tie from his back pocket and roughly cuffed the poacher's hands together.

"Move bastard and I'll shoot you dead," Moses hissed.

"*Uku kusuka* Soweto!"

The poacher shook his head, "*Cha.*"

These were the first words he'd said.

"*Uke nehlazo nomndeni wakho.*" (You've brought shame on your family) Moses told him.

"Too tight, *baas*," moaned the poacher.

Stephan stood up and planted his boot firmly on the back of the prostrate poacher and yelled, "*Ethule!*"(Quiet)

Stephan removed his foot. The poacher remained still. He called to me. "You okay?"

Stephan was breathless and I could sense the adrenalin rush. I nodded whilst gesturing towards the dirt road. "I saw a black *Toyota Hilux* up the dirt road, but it's gone now."

"Did you call the cops?" He squinted towards the main road. I passed Stephan a bottle of water.

"*Ja*, they're on their way. I've given them the registration number so they're on the hunt for the vehicle as well."

He glugged down the water, "Well done Chante."

"I also managed to take some photos."

The poacher moved. Moses yelled, "Get down!" and hit the poacher with his rifle butt.

"You're not going to put that poacher in the *Jeep*?" I asked.

"No! There's evidence here. We can't move him."

"I want you out of harm's way. Go over there in the shade where I can keep an eye on you. I'm going to help Moses guard that bastard till the cops get here."

I passed him another bottle, "This is for Moses."

Chapter Twenty-Three

"They're here!" Stephan stood up, brushed his jeans and walked over to meet a blue and white police van as it pulled up.

Two armed police officers jumped out the back and pulled down their navy caps. They were wearing the South African Police uniform, dark blue trousers, pale blue short-sleeved cotton shirts and black army-style boots. Once the dust from the police van had settled, I opened up the window and took more gulps from my water bottle. The heat had become intense with midday approaching. I was tempted to join them. I did not want to miss out on anything and I was keen to take some photos. However, from where I was, I could hear the conversation.

Stephan walked over to the police van, stretched out his bleeding hand to greet the driver, a stocky, dark skinned policeman. "*Yebo*, chief. Stephan Erasmus."

After stretching his undersized shirt over his pot belly and stuffing it into his dark blue trousers, he gave Stephan a firm handshake, "*Ehe!* Mr Erasmus! So this is where you've been hiding," he grinned.

"*Ja, s*aving rhinos and catching poachers!" He gestured to Moses standing over the captured poacher.

"Aha."

He pulled out a tattered A4 notebook and pen and left it on the dashboard.

"He's all yours," Stephan led the way.

The chief officer checked his pistol was in its holster before ordering his two officers to re-cuff the poacher with grubby metal police handcuffs. Moses and the officers conversed in Zulu. Moses gave his accurate account of the events. High-pitched wails from the poacher filled the air when the chief tried to get information out of him. He refused to give anything away. In frustration, the officer grabbed the poacher and threw him roughly onto the back of the caged van .He jotted down a few notes after questioning Stephan and Moses. It then looked like he was asking them to follow him to the police station to make a formal charge.

* * *

The police station was nearly an hour's drive away. When we entered the building, my stomach turned with nausea. I was confronted with the stench of sweat, stale cigarettes and urine. Stephan, Moses and I sat side by side on a hard, metal bench. Phones were constantly ringing.

Prisoners yelled from the cells down the corridor. Heavy steel doors echoed as they were banged to shut them. The grubby, grey walls were stained. I lifted my feet off the floor when I saw several cockroaches scurrying along the filthy concrete floor. Moses was too engrossed to notice the goings-on as he played a game on his cellphone.

Mixed feelings of depression, fear and confinement were overwhelming. I had to get out of there for some fresh air.

"Chante, you okay?" Stephan gently held my hand.

"Do I need to be here?"

"I'd rather you weren't. But the cops insisted because you're also a witness. They need a statement from you. Just wish I hadn't taken you with me and you wouldn't have been involved."

I sighed, "Don't blame yourself. It was me who insisted. Besides, none of us expected to come across a bloody poacher and thank God we were there. You and Moses saved the rhino."

"Bastards, they would've nailed the rhino!" he spat out with a clenched jaw.

His comforting arm drew me into him and in a lowered voice he said, "Go and sit in the *Jeep* with the doors locked and I'll text you when they call us in."

I smiled at him and nodded. Before leaving, I checked my Twitter account. "I don't believe it! We're trending on Twitter!"

"You're joking! How?" Stephan raised his voice.

Moses looked up from his phone.

Stephan moved nearer to peer at my cellphone screen and repeated the tweet: *"Stephan Erasmus, Moses Mbeke and Chantelle Swanepoel in rhino poacher chase."*

"And here I was thinking the *paps* had forgotten all about me. Obviously not," he muttered, biting his dry lip.

"*Ag,*" Moses eyes widened.

Stephan whipped his cellphone from his pocket and tried to sign into his Twitter account and muttered, "I've forgotten my bloody password. Just shows how often I use this Twitter shit."

He shoved his phone back into his pocket, "Next tweet will be: 'hashtag Stephan Erasmus held at police station.'"

I hissed, "The paparazzi are desperate for drama."

He stood up, folded his arms and looked down at me, "I don't like dragging your name into all this. I could kick myself for taking you."

"Listen! Stop blaming yourself. I asked to join you." I swiftly scrolled down my Twitter feed, searching for other related tweets.

"*Eish*! This news gets out fast! They don't miss a bloody thing."

"How did they get to know so quickly?"

Moses grunted, "I bet it's someone here. A cop. Probably has a loan to pay off."

Stephan nodded, "Probably!"

"Mr Erasmus, Mr Mbeke and Miss Swanepoel," called a slim, moustached officer, as he stood looking down at a form he was holding.

Stephan turned to me and whispered, "Wait and I'll see if you really need to be here."

I mouthed, "Thanks."

With hands stuffed into his trouser pockets, he walked up to the scratched metal reception counter followed closely by Moses, "Afternoon Chief."

"Mr Erasmus. Where's Miss Swanepoel?" He peered over his thick-lensed spectacles. Stephan frowned, "She wasn't involved in the incident—"

He tapped his pen on the counter. "It's written in this report that a Miss Chantelle Swanepoel reported the incident. This means she has to be interviewed."

A cold shiver crept up my back when I heard the policeman's words. I knew I had to get it over and done with. I stood and walked up to the counter, "I'm here officer."

He took off his glasses, "Miss Swanepoel?"

"*Ja*."

He grabbed the file and pointed to a side entrance. "Let's go. Through there."

Moses' dark pupils were fully dilated with fear. I glanced at Stephan and he reassuringly placed his strong hand over mine and led the way. We followed the officer down a dimly-lit corridor.

"Wait here!" he gestured to a row of stained wooden benches.

We waited for what seemed like an hour. Several suspicious-looking individuals occupied the bench. One scruffily-dressed man sat holding his head in his hands. A drunken woman kept spitting on the floor and an old man picked his nose. Two prison warders dragged a handcuffed prisoner down the corridor. Were we about to be arrested?

I felt like a criminal, yet all I had done was report a crime. I was beginning to wish I hadn't called the police. But I had no other choice. The poaching had to stop. I wondered where the poacher was, sincerely hoping he would not join us on the bench.

Suddenly a door opened noisily and a tall, stern-faced armed officer stomped out. He bellowed, "Miss Swanepoel!"

"*Ja*," I replied.

His snake-like eyes glared at me as he ordered, "Come with me."

Stephan stood up.

"Not you."

Stephan squeezed my hand before I let go. The officer slammed the metal door shut behind me. I was alone with two scary-looking police officers in a smelly, small room.

* * *

"Let's get the hell out of here!" Stephan led the way to the exit.

"Thank God the bastard's been charged now! That's the last we'll see of him!"

Moses looked up from his cellphone asking, "But is it?"

"What will happen to him now?" I frowned.

"Stephan pulled me close, "You saved the day. Thanks to your clever video footage of the whole thing. Now the bastard and his gang are going down and they'll use the poacher to get to the big boys."

Moses added, "He'll probably get 12 months or a fine. Not enough."

"A fine?" I frowned.

"*Yebo!* The jails are bursting at the seams."

"He'll be back poaching again?"

I shook my head in desperation.

* * *

The sun was fading fast as we stepped out of the police station. What a relief to breathe fresh air. leaving the stench from the station behind us. I pressed my temples with my thumbs in an attempt to relieve my pounding head. My mouth was dry, sticky and I needed a drink. Stephan was rubbing his jaw and Moses trailed behind whilst checking his cellphone.

I squinted and looked over from the glare of TV cameras.

"Mr Erasmus!" shouted a tall, smartly-dressed woman holding a microphone. "SA news! Could you tell us what happened out there today? Did you apprehend a rhino poacher?"

Stephan immediately looked away, yanked his baseball cap right down and nervously gripped my hand. The reporter followed us with her cameraman, shoving the microphone in Stephan's direction. "Stephan, explain what happened. Is this your new mission, to catch rhino poachers?"

Stephan was silent, his jaw clenched and his body stiffened. We were making our way to the car park where our vehicle was. The reporter and her cameraman sneaked around and blocked our path. The glare of the camera blinded us.

I butted in, "Mr Erasmus is a hero. Both him and Moses Mbeke risked their lives today to save a rhino. They chased, disarmed and apprehended a poacher and kept him tied up until the police arrived."

"Was anyone harmed?"

"No!"

"Has the poacher been arrested?"

"*Ja*, he's in police custody now and has been charged. Now bugger off!" I blurted.

The reporter's voice continued to heckle us all the way to the *Jeep*.

"Stephan, will you be joining 'Save the Rhino Organisation now?"

Moses had shot ahead and was perched against the *Jeep*. He opened the door for me.

"Cheers Moses," Stephan nodded as he gave me a hand up into the *Land Rover*, before bolting around to the driver's side.

I urged him. "Quick, let's get out of here."

Stephan roared the engine into life, letting off steam. The tyres screeched. I

gripped hold of the car seat as we exited onto the main road, where he floored it.

"*Eish!* Thanks Chante for saving me from the bloody *paps* back there!" he patted my knee. I turned to smile at him, "I'm so proud of you for saving that rhino. You and Moses did a great job."

I had not seen Stephan smile all day until now.

"I wouldn't have had it any other way."

Looking through the rear-view mirror, he added, "We did well Moses. Good man."

Moses smiled widely, "*Ja,* those poachers are bad."

Cool water soothed my dry, raw throat as I sipped from a water bottle.

"It's been a long day. *Ag,* I hope everything's okay at the sanctuary. I can't wait to be back there."

Moses added, "I called and everything's under control."

I swung round to face Moses, "Thanks, Moses...You okay?"

"*Yebo*."

"Cool," Stephan muttered.

* * *

Cocooned in my arms, I softly stroked Stephan's forehead listening to the radio.

This is the South African Radio and my name is Opus Mbeke. I'm your host till midnight on this warm Friday night. Folks, Facebook or Twitter me on SAR .Opus with your music requests.

I'm going to start tonight with the new track called 'There Will Be Time' by Mumford and Sons. When I first heard this I was instantly hooked. It's from their new album called, 'Johannesburg'. It's gone straight to No. 1 with a distinct influence from the South African music and Baaba Maal's presence. The new track mixes well with Mumford and Sons."

Stephan immediately sat up and pressed the remote to increase the volume.

"This song's epic. Listen to the words. I love it."

As the song ended Stephan turned off the radio and looked into my eyes.

His voice softened, "I want you to listen to me. I want to truly tell you something. I want you to know the reason I love you is because you're the only one who has taught me how to really love and appreciate life."

Chapter Twenty-Four

I smoothed down my fitted emerald green dress before taking one last look in the mirror. The reflection that smiled back at me was a confident, fearless woman. I no longer needed to be a size zero to feel good about myself.

I was free from trying to live up to Franco's expectations. Free from worrying what others thought of me. Free from comparing myself to other women. It never got me anything but sadness, misery and helplessness. Only when I allowed myself to feel authentic love, feelings and emotions for myself did I follow my own dreams. Here at *Nkuti* where I belonged with Stephan and nature, photographing wildlife in their natural state.

Devotion to following my meaningful dreams and passion here at *Nkuti Wildlife Sanctuary,* had freed me from the senseless obsession with my weight, diets and my physical appearance. Seeing my life falling apart, gave me a new perspective on life. I realised I had changed. I was no longer the underdog.

Stephan called from behind the bedroom door, "Babe, are you ready? It starts at eight and we don't want to be late! If you win tonight, you want to be there to collect your prize."

I called," What's the time now?"

"Six. We need to find parking when we get there. The Sandton Conference Centre never has enough parking spaces."

"Coming now," I called. Just then my cellphone alerted me to an incoming text message. I read: *Good luck for tonight darl. I'm just so proud of you to see you're finally being yourself. See you at the awards. K x*

With added confidence I grabbed my clutch bag and scurried out the bedroom. Stephan looked dapper with his freshly cropped hair. He sported dark trousers, no tie and a white cotton shirt, open at the collar. Stepping back he looked right at me. "Wow! You shine like a diamond!"

I winked and glowed, "Thanks. I actually feel like one!"

* * *

The charismatic, cheerful and confident compere TK, announced, "And the winner of this year's African National Geographic Wildlife photographer is...Chantelle Swanepoel!"

A warm glow washed over me as my name echoed loudly round the auditorium. I bounced up from my chair, straightened my dress and quickly walked to the stage as the audience clapped loudly.

Blasting out the speakers, *Enigma's* vocals droned the chorus *of Return To Innocence*. Goose bumps rippled through me. Whenever I heard this song, I believed it was a sign from above.

He beckoned me to come up, "Ladies and gentleman, here she is — our local treasure — Chantelle Swanepoel!"

A *deja vu* feeling gave me confidence as I crossed the stage to the microphone. I turned to TK now standing slightly to one side. "Well thank you TK. Wow! I'm thrilled and humbled to accept this award. I do have a wild South African heart you know."

I paused and glanced over at the table where I had been sitting. I could not mistake Tristan. Wearing his shocking-pink bow tie, he was cheering with a glass raised above his head. Just behind Tristan, was Stephan's mother and without a doubt, Tristan must have been thinking to himself, *I'm not going to let that 'poison dwarf' ruin my evening*. Beside him, Kirsty and Anton were wolf-whistling. Stephan's mother and his stepfather looked elegant. With their heads held high, they clapped their hands.

Mavis was beaming proudly and with no inhibitions whatsoever, she was dancing in African-style celebration. Freya was standing proudly next to my parents. My mother was smiling and cheering, she was happy for me I could tell, but my father sat sullenly with his arms crossed. But where was Stephan?

I raised my hand in a gesture of thanks and the audience was silenced. "My love for wildlife started when I was a teenager. I lost my way in the *National Game Park* and found refuge by climbing the nearest tree. Whilst stuck up there for what seemed like hours I used this bird's-eye view to study the wild animals and their behaviour in their most natural state. They breathed like us; they ate like us and even had emotions like us. I was no longer scared. I wished I had a camera to capture those moments. The camera never lies. From then on I knew my passion would be wildlife photography."

I paused briefly before continuing, "Why wildlife, you may be asking. I realised by watching the animals in their own habitat that they do not care what other animals think of them. They're all eye-catching in their own way. The combination of different species of animals makes a stunning contrast. Why are we humans not more like these animals? We certainly can learn so much from our observation of wildlife."

Taking a deep breath and pausing a few seconds, I concluded, "National Geographic thank you for giving me this opportunity to put wildlife on the map and for enabling me to highlight the scourge of rhino poaching which is presently rife in South Africa."

There was a loud applause, whistling and an affectionate back slap from the compere. A shadow moving in the wings of the stage caught my eye. A handsome man emerged. Stephan walked up to me.

What was he doing? My mouth went dry as he sank on one knee in front of me. From his pocket he pulled out a ring and longingly gazed up at me, "Chantelle Swanepoel, you've won my heart and I've won my Olympic Gold medal … *you*. Please, will you be mine?"

I blushed as my heart raced. Was this really happening? I was overwhelmed with joy. All my life I had dreamed of hearing those words. I was in love with him. Tears ran down my cheeks.

The audience bellowed, "Say yes! Say yes! Say yes!"

I moved the microphone closer to my mouth, cleared my throat and without any hesitation I replied, "Yes, I love you, Stephan."

Stephan slowly slid a diamond ring onto my finger. He wrapped me in his arms and lifted me up as the crowd applauded.

It had only been nine months ago that I had nervously stumbled onto this same stage, embarrassed by having to choose a prize date. How quickly life can change, I thought. A chance prize date could turn into the biggest gift of all.

I had never experienced such inner contentment, joy and love as I did that night. I had not only been named the winning photographer of the *National Geographic Wildlife Competition*, but more importantly, I had won Stephan's heart. Without my first prize I would never have reached the end prize. I was in ecstasy. After all I'd won life's most precious prize. Love.

GLOSSARY

Ag, Oh
Aircon, Air-conditioner
Airtime, Top-up on mobile
Babbelas, Hangover
Bakkie, Pick-up/ Truck
Biltong, Dried seasoned meat
Bliksem, Thunderbolt/ Blast
Braai, Barbecue
Bro', Brother
Boet, Brother
Carjacking, stealing vehicles at gunpoint
Cellphone, Mobile phone
Circle, Roundabout
Cozzie, Bathing costume
Cubby hole, Glove compartment
Dagga, Marijuana
Darl', Darling
Ehe, So
Eina, Ouch
Eish, Gee
Gunjanni, How are you
Gynae, Gynaecologist
Hadeda, Large bird
Hottie, Sexually atttactive
Hun, Honey
Ja, Yes
Jislaaik, Gracious
Joburg, Johannesburg
Klop, Hit
Larney, Elegant/ expensive
Lekker, Great
Loskop, Fool
Lourie, Touraco/ bird
Marula, South African, once a source of nutrition
Nah, No
Obs, Obstetrics
Okes, People

Pap, Porridge
Paps, Paparazzi,
Phwoar, An admiring sound
Rand, SA currency
Robot, Traffic lights
Romcom, Romantic comedy
Rondavel, mud hut with a thatched roof
Rooibos. SA brand of tea
SA, South Africa
Sissy, Little sister
Sjoe, Wow
Skinnering, Gossip mongering
Sozzled, Drunk
Spliff, Joint
Stoep, Verandah
Stompies, Cigarette butts
Sundowners, Alcoholic drinks taken at sunset
Tackies, Trainers
Tsotsi, No good, vagrant
 Veld, Bush
Yebo. Yes
Zulu, African tribe
Zol, home-made cigarette